SETH C. ADAMS

THE RIFT

This is a **FLAME TREE PRESS** book

FLAME TREE PRESS
6 Melbray Mews, London, SW6 3NS, UK
flametreepress.com

US sales, distribution and warehouse:
Simon & Schuster
simonandschuster.biz

UK distribution and warehouse:
Hachette UK Distribution
hukdcustomerservice@hachette.co.uk

Publisher's Note: This is a work of fiction. Names, characters, places, and
incidents are a product of the author's imagination. Locales and public names
are sometimes used for atmospheric purposes. Any resemblance to actual
people, living or dead, or to businesses, companies, events, institutions, or
locales is completely coincidental.

Thanks to the Flame Tree Press team.

The cover is created by Flame Tree Studio
with thanks to Shutterstock.com.
The font families used are Avenir and Bembo.

Flame Tree Press is an imprint of Flame Tree Publishing Ltd
flametreepublishing.com

A copy of the CIP data for this book is available from the British Library
and the Library of Congress.

1 3 5 7 9 8 6 4 2

PB ISBN: 978-1-78758-878-3
ebook ISBN: 978-1-78758-880-6

Printed and bound in Great Britain by Clays Ltd, Elcograf S.p.A.

SETH C. ADAMS

THE RIFT

For anyone – and everyone – who's ever lost someone.
You're not alone.

CHAPTER ONE

1.

The rift first appeared on the eve of the Anniversary of Death. Three-hundred and sixty-four days and counting, that's how Joe Jimenez thought of it: an anniversary. The death was his son's. Picked up on the way to school by a nondescript black van in the morning, the boy was dumped dead in a desert ditch the same evening.

Joe had woken up just the same as he had each morning since: dazed, lethargic, slightly nauseous and with a headache, as if waking up with one bastard of a hangover. He stumbled to the bathroom and started the shower with hard yanks and turns of the knobs and the showerhead. After pulling off his clothes roughly as if they irritated his skin, he stepped under the spray and adjusted the water as hot as he could bear it.

His naked body flushed red, he stepped out when finished and wiped a circle in the steamed-over mirror so he could see himself. Through the vapors rising and whirling in the tiled and marbled room, it seemed like he looked through a portal to some other realm, where a shade of himself stared back.

He dressed – as he often did – in the very same clothes he'd slept in, fumbling the garments on clumsily like a child clothing himself for the first time. Then he moved down the hall and to the kitchen, where he pulled out whatever cold leftovers he found first in the fridge. He fell into a chair at the table, and mechanically shoveled and swallowed the tasteless food.

The phone's message counter pulsed its green light with messages he'd stopped listening to long ago. The last one he *had* listened to was from his wife the day after she'd moved out, six months past. She'd let him know she'd arrived at her new place just fine, and if he ever wanted to talk, she was just a phone call away.

Distantly, on that day and others, Joe had thought about making that call. He'd hover over the phone like a man considering a map, trying to determine a route, setting a course. But eventually he always turned away, his wife's voice an echo in his mind fading with every step he took from the phone.

Showered, dressed, and fed, Joe walked to the front door, crammed his feet into his shoes, and went out and walked with no particular destination, and for no specific length of time. Just getting out and moving seemed very important, very necessary.

The silence of his house was overbearing. With his wife and son gone, the place didn't seem like a home where a family had once been, but something cold and sterile, like an empty mausoleum. If he stayed too long inside, the silence was replaced by creaks and groans from the white walls and wooden floors. So even knowing he was alone, it seemed as if he wasn't, and whatever was there with him was something he didn't want to see, didn't even want to acknowledge.

Outside, the sun seemed too bright, the sky too vast. He squinted as if under a doctor's harsh, white examination light. Whatever direction he faced, though, there it was, that bright vulgar star shining down. But it was either the sun over him, or the empty house around him, and for Joe the decision was easy.

Rural, at the foothills of the San Bernardino mountains, the properties of his neighborhood were spaced comfortably apart from each other for privacy and seclusion, but close enough that one still had a sense of community. Couples and families walked dogs on curving trails that radiated out from the neighborhoods and over gently rising hills; huffing, sweat-stained joggers nodded in greeting as they hurried by; and cars idly passed as if the drivers enjoyed the chance for a peaceful, leisurely cruise before entering the more frantic bustle of the freeways on their commute to work. Sometimes a fog spilled down the mountains in finger-like tendrils, settling and gathering, and everything — the houses, the families and their dogs, the joggers, the passing cars — entered and exited these clouds sporadically, and Joe was reminded of his twin self, glimpsed through the steam in the bathroom mirror.

He'd been the one who had insisted on letting Evan walk to school alone.

The boy was twelve, he'd told Clara, and the school was only a mile away. They could see it out the second-story bedroom window — the buildings and the basketball courts and the baseball diamond and bleachers and the painted white lines of the parking lots — all splayed out there down the hill. This was San Berdoo, not Compton or Long Beach. The buses took the same route Evan would be walking. Parents driving other kids to school would pass by him at regular intervals.

There was nothing to worry about, Joe had said.

And Clara — leaning there against the kitchen counter, just about where he'd listen to her recorded voice one last time months later, looking as pretty as could be in a summer print dress — had given in, trusting him. As she always had.

Only there was most definitely something to worry about: a black van patrolling the streets all that morning, and the driver behind the wheel of the van, peering out from the tinted windows.

2.

The van, abandoned in the same ditch as Joe's son, had been reported stolen two years ago from across the country, in some distant state Joe had never been in, and now never wanted to be. During their search of the vehicle, the police found jars of a homemade Internet recipe chloroform bundled in plush towels in the spare tire compartment in the rear of the van, under a removable strip of upholstery like a trapdoor. A lug wrench and crowbar lay in the passenger side floor space, likewise bundled.

The driver was never found, apparently having hitched a ride back out on the highway, or turning out into the white Mojave for one long walk. Only the van and Evan's dead body were evidence the driver had ever existed at all.

Joe kept a photo of Evan on his nightstand. He looked at it every night before bed. It wasn't a framed photo, but the faded black-and-white image the newspapers had used to sell his son's murder to the public. He kept it folded neatly, like a love letter, within easy reach. When he looked at it, he gripped the newsprint photo tightly, like a reader with a good book. There was something there that he was supposed to see, something he didn't want to forget. But he was afraid he already had.

He tried asking Clara about it in the days and weeks before she'd left, holding the photo up to her face. She'd push by him, find a room, slam a door, and lock herself away.

Joe didn't really see much of anything either, if he was honest with himself. Whether in the photo of his son or out there in the wider world. Sometimes he stood on the porch and looked out over it all and there was just a stretch of earth with mountains in one direction, desert in another, and nothing in between but a vast emptiness that couldn't be filled.

3.

On the June Sunday that he first saw the rift, Joe had walked longer and farther than he ever had before. By the time he returned home his calves were burning, his breath was short, and he was wet and sticky with a sheen of sweat.

He paused on the porch to gather himself. With pincer motions he plucked his perspiration-soaked sweats and T-shirt away from his skin where they clung in itchy places. Kneeling, he turned on the garden hose and took a long swig of cool water. It was noon and warm and he'd set out in the morning when the chill mist off the mountains had still blanketed the air. If he'd had a distance and heart rate monitor like many joggers wore, he wouldn't have been surprised if he'd covered ten miles or more.

He fished the keys out of his jeans pocket, opened the door and went inside.

After his walks, when he was tired and spent, the vacuum-like vacancy of the house was more bearable than usual. Physical exhaustion coupled with emotional created a numbness like a wall, a barrier.

In the dining room, Joe spilled his keys and wallet on the table. Six chairs surrounded the dining table where once three people had sat nightly for meals. Memories of smiles, faded like old photographs, came to him. Ghosts of laughter echoed in his ears. The far end was where Evan used to sit, and Joe avoided that area, giving it a wide berth like one would a hole in the ground.

In the kitchen, the phone's message indicator light blinked away with a new message. The memory of his family hounding him, the exertion of the long walk dulling his thoughts, Joe reached out and pressed the button without thinking, then moved for the fridge and a beer. A click and beep and his wife's voice, distant and ethereal, came up through the static, as if she spoke to him from behind some dimensional veil.

"Hello, Joseph." That wasn't a good start. She only ever called him Joseph when she was angry or determined. Often those two things came in tandem. "I'm driving to Phoenix for a few days to see my parents. They're not crazy about dogs, as you know, so I'm going to swing by with Rusty in about an hour or so. If you're not there, I'll let myself in."

Joe found himself talking to the phone before the message was even done.

"No, no, no," he said through gritted teeth.

He picked up the receiver and punched in the numbers with hard little jabs. As he held the phone to his ear, he crossed the kitchen from corner to corner with something like a death row inmate's frantic panic on the Big Day, pacing the length of his cell.

"God damn it, Clara, answer."

But she didn't, and fifteen minutes later she was there, smiling dog in tow.

4.

When he heard Clara pull up in the driveway, Joe met her at the door.

Rusty was their son's yellow Labrador. The dog – without invitation – dashed into the house with a Morse code clatter of nails on tile. Tufts of his shedding summer coat trailed him, drifting down across the floor and furniture.

For a time after Evan's murder, it was all he and Clara could do to remember to feed the dog. Then, when Clara had somehow discovered the will to continue on with life and returned to work, Joe had found himself not just forgetting the dog's meals, but resenting the furry fuck.

The boy and the dog had been best friends. Closer than friends really. More like brothers. One human, one canine: one very hairy and with a tendency toward crotch sniffing, but brothers nonetheless.

With Evan gone it hadn't seemed right for the dog to still be around. To Joe, it had seemed an affront, an insult. God or fate or the universe, or whatever ran things, may as well have just slapped him across the face and hocked a big juicy one right in his eye.

Back when Joe and Clara had still been in the same house – before World War III as he'd come to think of it – Joe had brought up giving Rusty away on more than one occasion.

Each time, Clara had given him a hard glare that said she'd sooner give *him* away and moved quickly to another room, as if being in Joe's mere presence were intolerable.

Now, while Rusty made his hundredth or so circuit about the house, Clara remained on the porch. Joe held the door open, but stayed on his side, the threshold a barrier between them.

"Well," he said. "Thanks for giving me a heads-up."

His wife shuffled from foot to foot, a bulky bag of dog food cradled in her arms, not as if she were embarrassed or apologetic, but as if she were in a hurry and anxious to get going. Apparently not too much of a hurry, however, that she couldn't spare a long-suffering look with her round, brown eyes.

Joe remembered a time when those eyes looked on him with love and good humor, smiling brighter than the red lips that had kissed him warmly.

"It's the least you could do, Joseph. I watch him, I feed him, I take care of the vet stuff."

"No, the least I could do would be to drop him off at the pound. Anything more qualifies me for sainthood."

"Don't start, please," she said, passing the sack of food over to him then backing away. "Feed him twice a day. Two cups in the morning and evening. I'll be back late in the week."

"Clara."

She was halfway down the walkway. Turning to look at him briefly, she shrugged, then moved her gaze to her watch to show him how little time she had. "What, Joseph? I've got to get going if I want to make good time."

"Are we ever going to...you know...talk?" God, looking at her after so long, so much came flooding back. Memories of touches and sensations so nearly overwhelming, his mind wasn't enough to contain them and a tingle spread across his body like an electric charge. "We've still got things to figure out."

"I've tried talking."

He remembered the invitation to do just that, left unanswered on his machine for months now. Wanting to say something, wanting her to stay, he didn't know how to start and so kept his mouth shut.

Clara considered Joe for a moment, arms crossed. Some force between them seemed to push one from the other. She shrugged, crooked her head in a way that made her short black curls bob cutely.

"I don't know," she added. "Maybe."

Then she turned to the driveway and moved out of sight. The sound of her car door opening and closing was abrupt in the quiet of the foothills. Joe watched his wife's Pontiac roll out of the driveway into the street, stared after her as she shifted into drive and pulled away.

5.

"You know I hate you," Joe said.

He was in the dining room, the Labrador in the kitchen. Gazing up at him with his long tongue hanging out like a strip of unrolled carpet, the dog received this proclamation with a wide, stupid grin. Joe moved past the dog quickly, found a plastic bowl in a cupboard, filled it in the sink, and put the water down on the tiled floor. Crossing the kitchen again back to the dining room, Joe gave the dog another cursory glance and pointed a finger for emphasis.

"Don't push your luck. The shelter's only a phone call away."

Warning delivered, Joe went to the living room, kicked off his shoes, plopped on the sofa, and switched on the television. He turned the volume up higher than necessary, so that with the surround sound speakers the noise seemed to bounce off the walls with a tinny rumble.

The stations winked by with a metronome's hypnotic rhythm. The monotone voices of news anchors relayed stories that weren't news but commercials for the political parties and CEOs that owned them. The hard, scantily clad bodies of hunks and starlets in so-called reality shows failed to offer anything real at all. Infomercials for unnecessary products that only the extremely fat, couch-ridden American populace could ever need flashed by. All of these and more filled the house with a background white noise that numbed Joe as he imagined a sensory deprivation chamber would, drowning out the world. Under such an auditory assault – watch this, buy that, vote this way, believe that way – the walls and rooms of the house were mere stage props, cardboard backdrops.

High on the wall above the brick fireplace, the clock ticked away the minutes, then an hour, and slowly another.

At some point Rusty stepped cautiously into the room. Yellow coat and creeping paws entered Joe's periphery, like an anxious actor stepping onstage. He tracked the dog's progress with eyes only, remaining slumped in the contours of the couch, finger idly tapping the remote.

Rusty slinked along the edges of the couch, head down, shoulders hunched. The dog settled on the floor beside Joe's dangling legs. A forepaw nestled against his toes.

Surprising himself, Joe said nothing.

For a time, man and dog remained that way without stirring. As if the slightest motion could set off a chain of events the outcome of which neither of them was prepared for.

When the clock ticked seven, the television stuttered and flickered, and Joe opened his eyes. Realizing he'd dozed off when he saw the time, he swiveled about, gathered his bearings. Wolf Blitzer on CNN stretched horizontal from interference, his face and shoulders elongating to disturbing proportions, and the picture winked out. The lights flickered also, the bulbs of the chandelier above the dining table blinking on and off, casting swaying shadows on the walls.

Joe stood, rousing Rusty, and looked out the back sliding glass door. He saw no storm clouds in the purple-blue of the evening sky.

Rusty whined and retreated to the hallway.

"Shut up," Joe said without force. "Just a power surge or something."

With evening deepening, fearing being caught in the dark without a light, Joe moved to the kitchen. At the cupboard beneath the sink he knelt, opened the doors, and reached in for the Eveready flashlight there. Turning, he faced the sliding glass door. Through it he could see the one-acre backyard, landscaped with cobbled walkways, patio, and perimeter gardens, where for so many years his son had clumsily crawled, uncertainly walked, and then vigorously ran. The water in the pool glimmered white with the reflected moon. A soft mountain breeze whispering down the foothills made the grand oak's branches sway in a dance.

And the spindle-shaped rift sat in the middle of it all, bright and steady and tall.

It seemed a tear in the very air itself. It hovered a foot or more off the ground, tapered at both ends, slightly thicker in the middle, reaching its peak maybe a foot higher than Joe's head. It rotated slowly on an axis, clockwise. Like the shimmering effect of heat waves off pavement, the distortion effect delineated it against the world beyond – the yard, the pool, the pine fence.

"What the hell...." Joe whispered.

He moved forward on spaghetti legs.

He paused at the sliding door, his hand gripping the latch. In his mind he pulled the door open, and it was like removing the top off a vacuum-sealed container. The whoosh of the suction would yank him forward into that spinning light. Aflame, face melting, he'd have only a moment to regret the stupidest decision of his life. Oblivion would follow.

Until that moment, standing at the glass door, looking out into the deepening shadows of his backyard, Joe would have thought oblivion a welcome prospect. He'd been living in just such a state – feeling little, wanting less, a phantom of a man in an Earth-sized limbo – for nearly a year. A final leap into true nothingness shouldn't have alarmed him.

But seeing that opening in the space of his yard, free-floating and spinning like a strange top, he had the exact opposite reaction. It wasn't nothingness before him. It was most definitely *something*.

Joe slid the door open. Closing his eyes, he stilled himself, and stepped outside.

Rusty whined, then followed.

6.

They circled the rift for a time together – man and dog – while Joe considered his options. He kept a good distance, looking at it this way and that, like a fighter measuring his opponent.

That the hole in the air before him could be dangerous was at the forefront of his mind. Radiation was the first thought that came to him, but he'd never heard of radiation that could be repelled by a glass door, and now that he'd opened it there was no going back. The damage, if any, was already done. If he woke up in the morning with a second head growing out of his ass, at least he'd have a new career in the freak show of the carnival circuit.

As a high school science teacher – at least formerly, whether a job still waited for him Joe had no idea, and he didn't give a shit – he checked off the most obvious possibilities that came to him. Ball lightning? No. That moved in arcs and streaks. It didn't just hover in place, spinning like a dangling ornament. An aurora of some kind, maybe, the tail end of some solar flare? Nope. Once again, those moved in waves across the sky. They didn't just rotate on an axis in a stationary position.

Next, he thought of computer-generated visuals of black holes in science documentaries, aloft in space and sucking in great cosmic debris. Or wormholes, spitting out planet-sized chunks at some distant location light years away.

This, Joe felt, was closer to the truth.

The rift *went* somewhere.

And with that thought his course was set.

When Joe realized the rift *went* somewhere, he knew he had to throw something into it. He couldn't say no to this impulse. It was like trying *not* to look at a car crash.

As if on autopilot, he scanned the lawn for stones. From the flowerbeds along the perimeter, the garden rocks seemed to flash a message to him, stark and white in the blackening night. Joe went to them, knelt, scooped up a handful.

Walking back toward the rift, he was stopped by Rusty. The Labrador parked on his haunches between Joe and the rift, looking up at him. The dog's lips quivered. His tail was tucked away between his legs. A high whine escaped the dog's throat and the quivering spread through the rest of him.

Though this one had gotten on his bad side by outliving his son, Joe had spent a lifetime with dogs. Growing up, moving out for college, getting married, having Evan; in all the stages of his life there'd been dogs. He knew fear and warning in the canine posture when he saw it. He should have known to trust it.

But he didn't fear the rift before him, not then. At least what he felt wasn't solely fear. It was like swimming out into the Pacific from the beaches of Redondo and Hermosa when he was a kid, his parents on the shoreline calling out for him not to go too far. Or vacationing with Clara and their son, as they'd scaled an old watchtower at the Grand Canyon and stared down into the great chasm.

It was wonder *and* fear, rolled into a hot little ball in his gut.

"Stand aside, butt licker," he said, moving around the dog, closer to the rift.

As he got closer still, he felt a charge in the air like static electricity. Prickly fingers seemed to walk up his arms, scale his spine. Another step, and another, until Joe was little more than a foot from the anomaly.

From his left palm he selected a stone, oblong and smooth. With an expansive breath and an underhand toss, he sent it arcing through the space between him and the rift. With a rasping sound of wind-blown autumn leaves scratching the ground in little cartwheels, the stone disappeared in the white-yellow light of the thing.

Then there was an absolute silence.

Joe looked about himself to make sure everything was still there. The earth beneath his feet. The still, oil-black water in the pool. The tall pine fence surrounding them.

The rift pulsed three times, steady and evenly. In his mind Joe saw a lighthouse, blinking the way for wave-tossed ships on foggy waters. With the third pulse the thicker middle of the rift stretched wider still. It seemed like a throat, swelling, ready to purge.

And then something fell out with a thud.

Joe stepped forward, lowered himself to his knees. The freshly watered lawn, drizzled misty by the automated sprinklers, felt cool and wet through his jeans.

Under the bright full moon, what was on the lawn before him was clear. A rock, roughly the size of the one he'd tossed in. But this one wasn't round, or white.

A shade blacker than any volcanic obsidian he'd ever seen, jagged and angular, the stone spit out by the rift looked almost like a badly formed archaic spear point. Something Neanderthals used against the beasts of their time.

Joe reached out to touch it.

And saw the smoke rising from it. The blades of grass charring and falling apart in crisp and flaky ashes. The spear-point rock sunk into the soil of his yard as if in quicksand. Inches it descended, then deeper until out of sight, the earth about the new hole tumbling in little avalanches, following it down.

Staring into this fist-sized shaft, the canopy of space above him, a veil of shadows around him, Joe learned the first rule of the rift:

For everything that went in, something came out.

And what came out was *wrong*.

CHAPTER TWO

1.

World War III didn't start with an invasion of Muslim radicals or the launching of nuclear warheads by trigger-happy, oil-drunk superpowers. At least not for Joe.

For Joe, World War III commenced when Clara decided to go back to work, he asked with vitriolic venom in his tone if she'd forgotten their son so quickly, and she slapped him full across the face. The clap of her palm on his cheek was thunderous. The sound of it echoed in the house and hung in the air between them.

Though a lean, small woman, Clara was fit and strong from years as a dance instructor – fueled stronger by the pain inflicted by his words – and the slap stung. But what hurt worse than the hot throb of his reddened face was the sting in Joe's heart, when he saw the trembling anger building up in her, directed at him.

She stormed away without saying a word and was gone the next morning. A trail of clothes fallen in her haste to get out – a sock here, a scarf there – greeted him when he woke. Leading down the hall and to the front door, they tracked his wife's last route in their home.

The silence after her departure seemed to fill the house like a living thing. The absence of noise wasn't a comfort. Rather, it was like a threatening presence with eyes that watched, and a menacing mind that formulated plans, always waiting around the corner just out of sight.

The silence that Sunday night when – after some thirty minutes or so of hovering there in his backyard, alight and spinning – the rift winked out, was similar.

In the shadows creeping beyond the small island of light cast by the porch lamp, the heavy black evening seemed to carry within it things Joe couldn't see, but which saw him. The sense of wonder he'd felt earlier – of being in the presence of a mystery worth knowing, worth experiencing – was still there. But now, with the rift gone, in retrospect Joe felt an ominous streak to it as well.

He collapsed heavily into one of the patio chairs. Stared out into the empty yard. Rusty settled and curled at his feet.

They sat there for another hour, waiting for the rip in the air to reappear. At some point he lowered an arm, found the Labrador's head with his hand, and started stroking. Joe knew he was comforting himself as much as the dog.

The dog rose, leaned into the strokes.

They found a rhythm together – petting human, petted dog – and Joe's quick heartbeat seemed a part of it, and so too the breath of the wind off the high mountains, and the dappled waters before him.

2.

Sleep was slow in coming. When it did arrive, it was in fits and starts. There were brief dreams of holes in the sky, holes in the earth. Joe peered into them and saw gears turning. Squinting, leaning closer, he glimpsed things in the darkness with glowing eyes, pulling levers, working the gears.

Each time he startled awake, sat up, looked about the bedroom. On the king bed next to him was a dog instead of his wife, and Joe remembered everything that had happened the day before. Then he closed his eyes and tried for sleep again, and the process was repeated.

In the morning he got up, pushed the Labrador off the mattress, and trip-walked to the bathroom. He showered, the water scalding hot, then stepped out, found his mirror through the steam. He stared long and hard at the haggard face looking back.

Jeans and T-shirt yanked on, Joe went to the kitchen. There he tore open the fifty-pound bag of dog food Clara had dropped off, scooped two cups of the brown chunks into a bowl, and set it down beside the water for Rusty. Once the dog was busy chomping away, Joe settled at the dining room table.

He stared out into the backyard. Where the rift had been last night, there was nothing. Just a yard and a pool and the emptiness about them.

He glanced at the clock in the living room, saw that at about this time one year ago to the day his son had been walking to school. A van would have been pulling up alongside Evan, the driver leaning over, smiling genially. A lug wrench and crowbar in the passenger seat waited patiently.

Although he hadn't read it for a year, the morning paper was still delivered. Joe went out onto the porch, bent down, grabbed the bundled *LA Times*, turned, and strode back to the table. He removed the protective bag, stretched the rubber band off, and flipped through the paper to the local section.

Scanning every page, he searched for something about the rift. Maybe rifts similar to his had popped up all over the county, like aftershocks from a central quake. Perhaps it had indeed been some sort of aurora or ball lightning, filaments of the phenomenon peppered over miles. In the newspaper were adulterous politicians, coke-addled celebrities in rehab, and a new terrorist threat, but nothing Joe could even remotely tie to the zipper-like rift.

Clara called a little before nine. He picked the receiver up in the middle of her message, not wanting to appear too eager. As if he hadn't been waiting all yesterday and this morning to hear her voice again, after having not heard it for so long.

"How's Rusty doing?" she asked after the requisite hellos.

"He's alive," Joe said. Even as the words were coming out, he regretted them. But the day he told her he'd spent the prior evening petting the furry bastard, and falling asleep only with the comfort of the mutt on the mattress beside him, was the day he gave his balls away to charity. "I canceled the euthanasia."

"Har har, really funny, Joseph."

His full name as affirmation that he'd gone too far, Joe muttered words he'd never imagined himself saying. These he didn't regret, though they caught him off guard.

"I'm sorry. That was cruel. Rusty's fine."

Clara seemed as stunned as he, and there was a soft clatter and shuffle on her end as if she'd almost dropped the phone. He heard her breathing carefully in and out before replying.

"Thank you. I appreciate you watching him."

A minute or two passed as they exchanged words about inconsequential things. She told him the drive had been long but smooth. He asked how her parents were doing. She asked if he'd returned to work yet. Though awkward and a little forced, these were things spouses asked each other and it was almost normal.

"Well, Joe, I better get going."

He said okay, and was about to hang up when something occurred to him.

"Hey, Clara, one more thing. It's a six- or seven-hour drive from here to Phoenix, right? You would've arrived early evening."

"Yeah. Why?"

"Did you notice anything...strange during the drive?"

"What do you mean?"

Her tone was confused but also mildly bored, or preoccupied, as if she was ready to hang up. Whatever sense of normalcy, of maybe at least approaching the way things had once been, was dissipating on her end. If she'd even felt what he had at all.

"I don't know," he said. "Nothing in the sky? No storms or lights or anything...weird?"

A long drive through the desert highways would have given Clara a spectacular view of the skies around the time the rift had appeared.

"What's weird about a storm, Joe?" She paused as if for an answer, then spoke again before he could. "Wait, if you start talking about UFOs or something, telling me you've been probed, I think I'm coming back early for Rusty."

"Har har, really funny, Clara."

"I learned from the best," she said, and in her voice he thought he heard a smile. In the best of times, humor had been their language, as powerful as their love, as satiating as their lovemaking. There was that sense again for Joe of approaching a line, nearing a threshold, with something tantalizing on the other side.

"Forget I said anything," he said, and though he meant it in a lighthearted, nonchalant manner, it still served to bring things to an end. They said their goodbyes, and with the click of the receiver returned to the cradle, an ending was what it seemed.

3.

In the garage, Joe searched for the tape measure. Through mazes of boxes and totem-like stacks he made his way to the workbench he and Evan had used together, pulled open a drawer of the worktable, found it. As he crossed the concrete floor again to the door leading to the foyer, he looked back.

For the briefest of moments he could actually see himself there, with his son, straddling the bench, measuring and cutting and fitting things together. Something crafted for Mother's Day, or a school project, or just for the hell of it. Father and son, creating together. Then it was gone and he turned out the lights and closed the door on the things that were lost.

In the backyard he fed out the tape measure into the hole in the ground.

Rusty first sniffed about the hole as Joe worked, then, apparently not caring for what his sense of smell registered, slunk away and settled under the giant oak at the far end of the yard.

At twenty-five feet the measuring tape stopped, yet Joe could still wiggle and dip it and felt no bottom to the shaft-like hole. About as wide around as a golf course's cup, it made him think of core samples taken by geological surveys, the drills of great machines puncturing the earth and probing deep.

"Shit," he whispered, standing, rolling the measuring tape back up and looking around. His eyes fell on the garden hose curled up at the side of the house. He walked to it, twisted it free of the water spout, and after looping it like a lasso in the crook of his forearm, carried it over to the hole.

The hose was fifty feet if he remembered correctly. He and Clara had landscaped both the front and back yards themselves. The physical work, creating something together – as he'd done with his son at the workbench in the garage – had brought them closer than Joe would have imagined possible. Clara, shiny with sweat in a sleeveless shirt and jeans, gleaming under the morning summer sun, was one of the most erotic images he'd ever seen. No men's magazine, with touched-up glossy images of breast-enhanced twenty-something starlets, could even come close to matching his wife's beauty and allure there in the grass and dirt.

Joe began to feed the hose into the hole, wiggling it when he felt obstructions, pushing it further and further into the thin shaft. In his mind he thought of Morlocks and dwarves and demons, subterranean things living in the depths of the Earth. He imagined diagrams of geological strata, and the hose going further and further past the layers of ages. Deeper and deeper the hose went, until Joe held one end flush against the ground at the rim of the hole, and still he felt no bottom to it.

Muttering a string of curses, Joe stood and wound the hose again.

With the looped hose returned to the side of the house, Joe walked once more back to the hole, squatted, peered down into it. Stretching out prostrate, chin touching the grass, closer, he squinted, stared harder.

The light of the morning sun shone only a foot or so down the shaft before the shadows swallowed the interior in darkness. Then he may as well have been staring into a starless stretch of space, some desolate realm even God had long abandoned.

Getting to his feet again, brushing off grass and dirt from his shirt and jeans, Joe looked east and west. Though his home was on a rise and those of his neighbors a bit lower down the hill, he found it hard to believe no one else had seen the rift in his yard. The fencing was tall, over seven feet high, but even if the tear itself wasn't seen, the light it gave off was bright in the evening and should have caught the attention of anyone peering out a window. Say a wife doing the dishes, or a kid gazing out a bedroom window with binoculars or a telescope.

No one had been by, though, asking about the strange glow in his backyard.

Joe also knew it was possible that, like himself, his neighbors weren't the rubbernecking types. That whatever went on with the families and in the houses about them held no interest for them.

Joe remembered a couple years ago he and Clara had learned from a neighbor that further down the street an old veteran had shot himself. So busy with their own lives, neither of them had seen the ambulance or police arrive or depart, hadn't even heard the gunshot that had taken off the top of the old man's skull.

But if the rift returned, tonight or some other, could he count on the disinterest of others to keep people away? Did he *want* to keep others away? Or was this something that should be reported?

These questions and others for the time being unanswered, Joe waved for Rusty to follow and together they went inside. He slid the glass door shut behind them, a weak barrier against the mystery that had revealed itself to him.

4.

Bereavement leave, vacation hours, and sick time long ago depleted, Joe had never returned to work, hadn't returned his colleagues' messages, didn't know if he even had a job waiting for him, and didn't give a shit.

Or so he'd thought.

After parking in the faculty lot at the rear of the high school for the first time in a year, Joe got out of the car slowly. The squat gray stone buildings before him seemed like a fort, he an invader. Archers aiming through arrow slits sighting him, or pots of boiling oil waiting for him to pass under, would greet him with a well-deserved death.

Not wanting to leave the dog alone in the house so soon after the appearance of the rift, Joe had brought the Labrador along. In the rear seat of the Ford Explorer, Rusty glanced from the school outside to

Joe, his head cocked to one side and a big grin on his face. *Am I coming along?* the dog seemed to be asking, and Joe shook his head, extended his middle finger in the great American salute.

"You're staying here," he said, and pushed the corresponding buttons for all four windows until they were a quarter of the way down, admitting the cool mountain air for the dog.

He walked across the parking lot with his head low and his shoulders hunched, trying to will himself invisible. The lot was nearly full. The vehicles provided a welcome blockade behind which Joe could duck, soldier-like on a battlefield, in an attempt to avoid detection until he got to where he was going.

Joe stepped from the parking lot up the curb onto the campus proper and paused tentatively, as if he'd just crossed a boundary. He looked up at the familiar contours of the buildings, and the step-like structures of the quad planters and benches that had always made him think of Aztec pyramids hidden deep in thick jungles. He gave a shit, he realized, as he scanned the length of the flagpole and the California white field and bear and the red-white-and-blue snapping in the wind. The landscaped, cobbled paths inlaid in the rich-soiled perimeter of the various halls, the cafeteria and the auditorium, shaded by the widespread branches of firs and spruce, were strangely serene, like forest trails. He'd walked these paths countless times in the past decade, knew the feel and grade of the earth beneath his feet. Treading them was like striding up his walkway, home again after a long trip.

A small cluster of squat, brick bunker-like structures Joe and much of the faculty had described as being in the *Cheapskate Nouveau* style, the Science Department seemed a cast-off from the main campus. Like a weird relative – an uncle, a distant cousin – that no one wanted around on holiday get-togethers, the placement of the Science classes and laboratories at the rear of the campus had always seemed to say something to Joe, about the priorities of schools, the priorities of parents, and those of society in general.

The third classroom down was his destination.

Dr. Milton Cooper was one of his old colleagues in the Science Department, a friend (or used to be), and a former officer stationed on the now defunct Norton Air Force Base. Maybe letting his idle fondness for Discovery and History Channel programming concerning Area 51, paranormal phenomena, and end-times prophecies – sometimes, amazingly, converging themes on the same program – get the best of him, Joe thought that if anyone would know anything about strange happenings in the area, Milton would be the one.

Milton was at lunch, as Joe had hoped he would be. The door was propped open for students who wanted to take advantage of an unofficial study hall, but today it was just Milton. Hunched over a foot-long sandwich, Milton didn't see Joe in the doorway, and so Joe knocked hard and loud, startling the taller man.

"Holy crap, you bastard!" the balding biologist yelped, a smear of mustard coating his just-so measured and shaved goatee. "So you *are* alive!"

Milton Cooper rose to his full height of six and a half feet, towering over Joe and most of humanity, and walked over with giraffe-like strides. So high up the man stretched, his lab coat, sized just for him, seemed not so much a coat as a toga on an Olympus god come down to visit the mortal realm. The man's long, insectile arms wrapped about Joe and squeezed powerfully. Even if his head had popped off like a rocket launching with a spray of blood, Joe didn't think he could have stopped the burst of laughter that escaped him.

"Have you been to see the Big Man?" Milton asked, releasing Joe. "Are you finally coming back to us?"

The Big Man was actually a big woman, Pamela Caruthers, the administrator of the school. Large, round, with forearms like tree trunks and an on-again-off-again peach fuzz mustache, the teachers called her the Big Man when at a safe distance. And even then only in low whispers and with furtive looks over their shoulders, as if afraid of being overheard by the mountainous woman and dragged away, kicking and screaming, to some underground chamber never to see the light of day again.

"No," Joe said, surprised to feel a sliver of disappointment at the pronouncement, and ashamed to see that disappointment mirrored and magnified in his tall friend's frown. "I actually came to see you. I wanted to get your opinion about something."

Milton's frown grew longer, drooped lower. "I heard about Clara," he said. "I'm very sorry. The two of you always seemed so happy. But if you're looking for relationship advice, I'm even sorrier. You know I'm the wrong guy for that job."

The one bout of romance that Joe knew of concerning Milton Cooper had involved Delores Somers of the History Department. As short as Milton was tall, as clumsy as he was strangely graceful, and as introverted as he was sociable, Delores Somers had surprisingly courted *him*. The four-week affair had ended in disaster, though, when Milton, reaching to help her out of a car, aimed poorly and grabbed a breast instead of a hand. Delores let out a screech that would have frightened a howler monkey according to witnesses, and both of them ended up in a tangle in the still-wet sidewalk gutter of the restaurant where they'd had reservations.

"No," Joe said. "Given everything that's happened, I have to say I still think I've got you beat in that department."

Milton slugged him in what was meant as a brotherly blow to the shoulder, but delivered by the taller man's slab-like fist, it sent Joe reeling. This was followed by a half-assed apology with a smirk spread wide across Milton's face, while Joe massaged the site of the punch. His friend and colleague motioned to a seat pulled up beside his desk, Joe took it, and Milton folded himself like an accordion into the cushioned swivel chair.

"So, what can I do for you?"

Joe had considered many ways in which to approach this on the drive over. In his mind he tried directness, a more circumspect route, and humor. Each time in his imaginary conversations, however, when he got to the part about the hole in the air of his backyard, Milton laughed uproariously, told him to lay off the booze, and stumbled, guffawing, out of the room.

Thinking again of the white light of the rift, and the black smoking rock burning through the Earth, weighing all other options, Joe settled on circumspection. If he was going to be laughed out of the room, he wanted as much warning as possible, probing and testing the mood of the conversation with caution.

"In your time at Norton did you ever see anything...strange?"

Milton's response was immediate. "If you're talking about aliens, I'll have to kill you."

Joe searched the man's implacable face. Not a wrinkle or twitch hinted at a joke. Then, just as he felt the anxiety in him building, his friend's roar of laughter blew forth like a gale-force wind. Something – maybe a fleck of sandwich – struck Joe on the cheek.

"I had you going!" Milton said, leaning over and backhanding Joe on his still-sore shoulder. "You should have seen your face!"

Milton did a good approximation, eyes wide, mouth hanging agape. As an added detail – call it improv or creative license – he held his hands up and out in surrender, and shook with mock fear. "Oh! The men in black are coming to get me! I think I just peed myself!"

Joe couldn't help himself, and smiled again.

When Milton had control of himself, he apologized, picked up his sandwich once more and took a great bite, followed it with a swig of something in a Thermos and, finally discovering the mustard in his beard, wiped himself with a napkin. After balling up his trash and basketball-throwing it into a wastebasket in a corner, he turned his attention back to Joe and motioned him to continue with a little roll of his hand. "You really saw something."

Joe nodded.

"What was it?"

"I'm not really sure. I was wondering if you had any way to find out about test flights in the area. Or anything astronomical going on that I wasn't aware of."

"I have a few people I could call. Care to elaborate, so I know what I'm asking about?"

Not knowing what it was he'd seen himself, Joe pondered this. Whatever details he shared, once spoken, couldn't be taken back. He still wasn't sure if the rift was something he wanted to let other people in on.

The feeling of being a kid stumbling onto something magical lingered, and part of him wanted to keep it to himself. Vagueness seemed the best course. For all he knew the rift had been a fluke, some cross-wiring of nature that he'd never see again.

"Just lights," Joe said, giving a dismissive wave. "Near the San Bernardino mountains."

Milton's jovial mood turned solemn quickly. "I know when I'm being bullshitted, Joe. There's more that you're not telling me. You wouldn't have driven down here otherwise."

Joe stood, leaned forward to hug his friend again. Him standing and Milton seated were about the same height, face to face, and Joe turned to break the eye contact.

"Just let me know if you find out anything," he said, starting for the door.

"That would require you answering your phone, Joe."

Joe offered his friend the one-fingered salute much as he had with Rusty back at the car. Then he turned to face Milton again.

"I'll answer the phone. Just promise me none of your heavy breather erotic stuff."

"Oh, talk dirty to me, you rascal."

Joe was outside the classroom when Milton called him back, a ring of urgency in his tone. Joe swiveled back to the doorway.

"Now that I think of it," Milton said, "there was this one time at Norton I worked on retro-engineering this saucer-shaped craft...."

Miming the turning of the crank on a jack-in-the-box, Joe raised his middle finger again. Then he gave an elaborate bow and backed out of the class.

"You're a funny guy, Milton. You should take your act on the road."

"There was also this time-travel experiment we tried once, involving calibrating supercomputers with the Zodiac star alignments...."

Joe walked away, shaking his head. Once more he took in the campus around him.

"And I almost forgot the time we cloned Jesus from DNA found on the Shroud of Turin...."

With Milton's voice fading behind him, and the school's familiar layout around him, there was no doubt at all for Joe. He did give a shit, and when he was back in the Ford and pulling away onto the boulevard, there was a tug on him. From somewhere inside, from the heart, it felt like a tether and it led back to his old life and the things that had once mattered.

And he ached when he realized he wanted such things to matter again.

5.

The rift appeared again promptly at seven o'clock that night.

Prior to its appearance, the television picture on the Sony big screen – this time Anderson Cooper instead of Wolf Blitzer at the center, providing narration for the day's atrocities – filled with static bars, skipped up and down, stretched, and winked out. The lights of the lamps and the chandelier bulbs blinked and stuttered as they had before.

As if on cue, the rift spread vertically in the backyard, between where the patio ended and the swimming pool began, and widened like curtains drawn open. This time, seated on one of the patio table chairs, waiting for it, Joe saw the thing actually form, and it was as if an incision had been made in the sky itself. Quick and neat as if by an invisible surgeon's skilled hand.

Rusty barked from where he sat on the patio and Joe hushed him.

The rift stretched tall and bulged at the middle. There was no sound accompanying the formation of the thing. With the spin about its axis, he half expected to feel a breeze, as if by a turbine's propellers, but the same as last time, there was nothing.

Joe rolled the stone in his hands from palm to palm, like a die ready to be cast.

He considered the hole in the yard below the rift. He wondered if on the other side of the world a black stone had burnt through and kept on going in freefall across eternity.

When he stood, his knees popped as if in protest. Taking a step forward, Joe heard the Labrador whine and a scrabble of nails on patio concrete as the dog backed further away. With an underhand toss Joe lobbed the garden stone into the rift.

There was a hiss as it entered the light. Seconds passed, and then the three pulses blinked. A black stone fell out, thumped onto the yard, and smoking, fell *through* the yard. The second shaft stood almost exactly beside the first; they seemed a pair of dark eyes staring up into the black night.

The prior night's experiment reproduced, Joe proceeded with what he'd really been waiting for. He pulled the slip of paper out of his pocket, unfolded it, and reread what he'd scribbled on it earlier in the afternoon.

Balling it up, the crinkle of the paper loud in the silence, he then tossed it with the same underhand motion he had given the stone, into the rift. A hiss as it entered. A few moments passed. Three pulses of the rift's light brightened.

And then something came out.

On Joe's sheet of notebook paper he'd written HELLO in a big child-like scrawl.

On the leathery skin-like scroll that emerged from the rift – Joe rolled it carefully open with the toes of his boots – were harsh, sharp characters in a powdery black substance like charcoal. Joe thought of ochre drawings in ancient caves. Primitive depictions of bison and hunters on rock walls where early man had sat out storms by firelight.

As he stood there watching – whether by a breeze he didn't feel or some other means – the leathery scroll snapped back into a tubular roll, tottered at the edge of the newly formed second hole in the yard, and fell in. Joe dropped to his knees to try to track its descent, but it was gone.

But those characters, reminding him a bit of hieroglyphics, stayed with him, clear in his mind, and when he found out later what they read Joe learned the second rule of the rift:

When it spoke it was with promises and earnestness, but these were lies, and the things it said beneath the surface – its true voice – were temptation and corruption. And if you listened, the lies became sweeter, the deceit deeper, until the roots of the rift wormed low, latching tight, holding fast.

CHAPTER THREE

1.

Joe didn't go to his son's funeral.

Clara, sitting beside him on the sofa, had told him that in times of great tragedy, the only way through the pain was with family and friends at your side, and the strength of their love. She told him this while holding a leather-bound Bible in her lap, as if reminding him of the beliefs he'd once held. He'd slapped the book out of her hands, watched it tumble off the sofa and to their feet. He enjoyed the way it landed splayed open as if for the world to read its solicitous lies.

She'd gone to the cemetery without him, he'd stayed home, and from that day on until Clara walked out, they'd slept in different rooms. The walls between them seemed of a substance greater than wood and plaster. They walked wide around each other whenever possible.

But with the rift opening initially on the eve of the anniversary of his son's death, then making a repeat appearance on the dark day itself, Joe saw a pattern. Knowing full well that it may not actually be there – this pattern, this sense of order just beneath the surface, of direction and a *director* – but was rather wish fulfillment of a lost man, a lost soul, he nonetheless felt compelled to visit Evan's plot for the first time.

Afraid to go alone, Joe loaded the dog into the Explorer, and they drove to the cemetery in silence. The traffic on the streets around them made him tense. That others should go about their day, going to work, running errands, as Joe drove to see his dead son seemed an affront.

In the parking lot of the cemetery, Joe got out of the car and merely stood for a time. Rusty trotted to the edge of the grass, and looked back at him impatiently.

Finally, Joe started walking, remembering the path to the plot he and Clara had chosen together in near silence.

There amongst the marble busts and plaques and the angelic statuary; amid wide-armed sycamores and solemn elms; upon a blanket of crisp, freshly cut grass; he knelt and read the inscription his wife had decided on. Just a name — Evan Francis Jimenez — and the hyphenated dates inadequately framing the boy's short life.

On that day a year ago, with the Bible in her lap, Clara had told Joe simplicity was the key. Not because their son wasn't deserving of anything more, but merely for the fact that no words, no monument, could do him justice. All that mattered was the love in their hearts and the memories they had of him. Joe had thought this bullshit, told her as much before knocking the Bible out of her grasp.

Now, one year later, here he was, kneeling at the spot where his son was buried.

Joe removed the small pocket notepad from his rear jeans pocket. Flipped it open to where the clipped pen marked his place.

Last night he'd delivered two more messages, balled up, fist-sized, unto the rift. And twice more he'd received responses.

Keeping the garden stone experiments in mind, Joe had come up with an hypothesis of sorts. The scientist in him sought patterns, derived meaning from hard data. Each time he'd tossed a stone into the rift, something like it in certain respects, different in others, had been returned to him. With his first note Monday evening – reading HELLO in his purposely large scrawl – the pattern had apparently continued. He'd received a message back, albeit written with a tool other than a pen, and on something not quite the paper he'd sent in.

What if what came out of the rift wasn't merely similar in structure – a stone for a stone, paper for paper – but in *meaning* also? Joe had delivered a greeting, and maybe he'd received one back.

So after reading the first rift-note scrawled on its strange leather scroll, and watching it fall into the newly formed hole in the yard, Joe had raced into the house and found the notepad now in his hands. Recopying the weird hieroglyphic-like symbols he'd seen onto the notepad to the best of his ability, he'd then written the word HELLO above them. Five characters each: five letters of the English alphabet, and five of the other.

His two follow-up notes came next, and thrown into the rift he received two back.

Written with the same charcoal-black grainy substance and in the same sharp-angled hieroglyphic characters. This time Joe was ready with pen and paper, toeing the skin-scrolls open and copying the symbols down, along with his original messages over them.

Before the rift winked out for the second night, he had a primer.

Settling on the grass of his son's plot, Joe looked at the small notepad, mulled over the results of his experiment. Feeling like a kid with his comic-book ad private detective's kit before him, he scanned the amateur cryptography. He again had the sense that he was bearing witness to a power far beyond his comprehension.

Scribbled on the pages before him, both in English and – if he was right – the other language, the language of the rift, was the following:

Hello.

My name is Joseph. Who are you?

What is the rift?

If the thing appeared again tonight – and something in the very core of Joe's being told him it would – he would begin a new stage of his experimentation with it. The time for mere translations was over. He was ready for full-blown communication.

A dialogue.

Inlaid on the cool grass beneath him, his son's marble plaque gleamed with streaks of the reflected sun. Joe put his hands to the stone and traced its contours with gentle brushes and strokes of his fingertips. The smoothness of the stone was interrupted by whorls and hairline cracks and imperfections, and these geometric details, stared at close up, had a passing resemblance to the characters of that other language.

The language of the rift.

Joe strived for interpretation. Tears dropped and flowed as if naturally to the chiseled letters, pooling there and filling the spaces.

For a moment Joe could almost hear his boy. His hearty laughter, his voice that seemed like a constant smile given form. So close, and yet so far. As if they could see each other across a chasm.

It was like there was a…rift between them.

The dog, forgotten behind him, walked closer, settled on his haunches, leaned closer still. Bodies pressed together, Joe felt the rhythm of the dog's heart, the breath of life in and out, and he put one arm around the Labrador, squeezing hard, crying harder.

Man and dog comforted each other, on a course together down a road of mystery.

2.

Milton Cooper called at noon with the results of his inquiries concerning strange lights along the San Bernardino mountains. In the middle of setting up his equipment for what he'd come to think of as Project Weird Shit, Joe set aside the digital camcorder, skirted around the tripod it would eventually sit upon, and went to pick up the phone. He answered when he saw his friend's number on the caller ID.

"Hey, Milton. What'd you find out?"

"You mean aside from the three hundred and five anal probes and cattle mutilations reported?"

"I'm guessing that's your way of saying you found nothing."

As he spoke, the receiver held precariously between shoulder and jaw, Joe moved back to the video camera. He placed it onto the tripod, made some adjustments to the height and angle, then looked through the viewfinder. The center of his backyard, framed in the camera, made him think of those Discovery Channel documentaries he enjoyed so much. Where families attempted to catch ghosts or UFOs on film, but rather than showing the images to questionably more legitimate media – say CNN or MSNBC – they found themselves on programming where spooky music and dramatic lighting sold their stories better to home audiences.

"Sorry, buddy," his friend said. "Nothing at all. No test flights. No dropped flares. No weather balloons. Nothing."

"Except the anal probes," Joe said, unable to stop the bitterness from entering his voice. He knew Milton was doing him a favor. His old colleague had no obligations to him, especially seeing how Joe had abandoned students and co-workers alike.

"Three hundred and five of them," Milton said. "And the cattle mutilations."

They bantered a little longer. Talked about campus politics. But Joe's heart wasn't in it, and he soon found himself closing the conversation with a bullshit excuse about errands he had to run. With the click of the receiver back into the cradle, he felt as if he'd been physically pushed back to square one.

And square one was the polite way of saying he didn't know what the fuck was going on, or what he was getting himself into.

3.

Camera and tripod ready, notepad primer on the dining table before him, Joe tapped a nameless tune and stared out the back door into the yard. If the rift followed the schedule of its first two appearances, Joe still had hours to wait. Only early afternoon, he didn't know what to do with himself.

Errands, as he'd lied to Milton about, seemed a waste of time in the wake of something so momentous as the rift. Grocery shopping, pushing a cart down aisles and loading it with eggs and milk and other crap, was ridiculous. Driving to the post office to mail the bills, absurd.

Had Moses, after receiving the Commandments on Sinai, gone back down the mountain and commenced with mowing the lawn? Once he'd delivered the Sermon on the Mount, did Jesus then go back to Jerusalem for a haircut?

Everything was irrelevant before the magnitude of the rift and what it represented. Everything except his son. That was always there, and, he suspected, always would be. Then with that realization there was another. He stood, walked to pick up the telephone again, and settled back in the chair.

He dialed the number from memory, and when Clara's father answered Joe nearly lost his nerve. The man's tone was as commanding as he'd remembered.

"Hello, Will," Joe said, shrinking inside and hoping it didn't show in his voice. He felt small – *was* small – under the scrutiny of his wife's father. Will Shepherd was a bear of a man, a retired cop, and even in the best of times he'd only just accepted Joe, if not wholly embracing him as a son-in-law. "I was hoping I could speak with Clara."

"I don't think I need to tell you how disappointed I am, Joe."

The gravity and solemnity were heavy in the other man's voice. The passage of a year with no communication from Joe's end had probably done little to improve Will's opinion of him.

"If it's remotely as disappointed as I am in myself, sir, I think I have a good idea."

He hadn't planned on saying anything like that, and yet the words just came out. Worse, Joe realized, was that he spoke the truth. What he'd done to himself, to his family, his friends, and most despicable of all, to the memory of his son over the past year was very low, very cowardly.

The honesty with which he spoke must have been clear in Joe's voice, because his father-in-law said nothing else. Joe could imagine the scene on the other end. The big man handing the phone over to his daughter. Stepping aside, away from Joe's voice, away from Joe.

"Hello, Joseph."

His wife's voice. The music of it.

Joe swallowed, trying to find his own voice as the next words, which he *had* planned, struggled to come out. "Clara. I should have called yesterday."

The dark anniversary. When a boy, so beautiful, so full of life, had been plucked like a weed from this fallen world.

She said nothing, but he thought he heard a sniff and a soft intake of breath.

"I loved him so much," Joe said, hearing his voice break, trying mightily to reinforce it. "I didn't know what to do after he was gone."

There were no maybes about it now. On the other end of the line, hundreds of miles away, his wife was crying. He so badly wanted to hold her. Perhaps even more so, he wanted her to hold *him*. She'd always been the stronger one.

"I failed, not being there for you. I should have let you cry if you needed it. I should have cried with you, because I sure as hell needed it."

A couple times she tried to say something. He paused for her to do so, but apparently the effort was too great. The words broke in her throat with little choking sounds.

"It's okay. You don't need to say anything. I'm not sure I deserve to hear you say anything. I just needed to tell you these things, Clara."

"Okay..." was all she could get out, and that was fine because Joe knew what he deserved was far worse.

"Thank you for listening," he said, gave her another moment or two to respond, and when she didn't, he said goodbye, turned off the phone, and gently returned it to the cradle. Turning, Joe saw the dog curled beneath the dining table, head on paws, looking up at him.

"What now, Rusty?" he said. He realized he hadn't called the dog anything insulting, wondered if that signified something. "What do we do until seven?"

Rusty rolled onto his side, exposing his furry belly as if in invitation, and so Joe lowered himself to the floor, scooted in carefully under the edge of the table, and started rubbing the dog. The big dumb dog grin returned, and Joe rubbed harder.

"This is as good as anything, I guess."

And with the silence of the house around him, it was. It truly was.

4.

The joys of giving a dog a belly rub rediscovered, the peaceable experience lasted a good thirty minutes before Joe felt the urge to get up again and *do* something. Knowing the effort would be fruitless, he nonetheless went upstairs, down the hall to his office, booted up the computer, and opened up his Internet browser. Connecting to YouTube, he typed in his search criteria and began a marathon strange-lights-caught-on-camera video-viewing session.

Many were obvious hoaxes where the filmmakers and 'actors' apparently couldn't even read off cue cards convincingly. With unsteady camerawork and poor lighting, pointing fingers and copious use of vulgarity directed the viewer to unidentified lights, blinking, flashing, and moving in forested areas or along distant mountain ranges. Only, with careful, detail-oriented viewing, some of them were embarrassingly *very* identifiable.

Joe saw hubcaps, Frisbees, and pie plates aplenty named as UFOs, some seemingly tossed into the air from afar to give the momentary illusion of flight, while others were coasted down lengths of visible string between trees or poles for a smoother effect. A select few of the videos were more sophisticated, probably involving remote-controlled vehicles affixed with lights and launched from backyards or parking lots. But none were convincing, and more importantly, not what Joe was looking for. He refined his search criteria from 'strange lights' to include 'strange lights and weather phenomena' and was rewarded with closer matches.

The list of videos loaded onscreen was long, and numbered clickable icons showed several pages for Joe to view. A frame of each video and an accompanying title tag allowed him to quickly navigate the results, bypassing those – like ball lightning and aurora borealis flares – that he'd already considered and dismissed. Those that passed the hurdles of looking nothing like the rift and not being something he'd already thought of were interesting but, ultimately, still *wrong*.

Haloes of the sun, sometimes refracted by moisture in the air at such angles to produce impressive arcs, displayed brilliant curves of light at the rims that had a passing resemblance to the thing that had zippered open in Joe's backyard. But the similarity was only glancing, and haloes neither spun on an axis nor pulsed.

Noctilucent clouds were atmospherically high formations that appeared at dusk, and like haloes, refracted sunlight. The shimmering effect was eerie and startling, and the illumination was of a factor similar in color to the rift. Again, though, the likeness ended there, and the contours and geometry were all wrong.

Other, even rarer phenomena also teased Joe with vague similarities. But after two hours of viewing dozens of videos, he saw nothing even close enough in form and manner to the rift to make him sit back and think, *Maybe, just maybe that's what I saw.*

The corner window nearest the computer desk looked out from atop the rise to the rest of the neighborhood and city below. A grayish haze of smog hung over the further reaches, but up here where he sat the air was clearer. Joe could actually see where the fuzzy border of the pollution ended and the pure sky started. It seemed to him two worlds touching, yet separated.

He found himself again wondering why none of the neighbors had seen the rift. Perception and intent seemed a part of the answer, as up here he saw both spans of the sky: the filth and the clarity. The old veteran killing himself down the street and he and Clara knowing nothing of it until later, preoccupied with their own lives, also suggested a piece of the puzzle.

Perception and intent.

Did one have to *want* to see the rift in order to see it?

And like the two parts of the sky – the gray miasma of smog and the blue-white expanse – could a person who saw the rift also see *both sides*?

As a science teacher, Joe had taught an introduction to astronomy as part of his Physical Science course. His telescope was stored in its case in the bedroom closet. He hurried to the bedroom, slid the closet door open too harshly, pulled the long case down from the top shelf.

Setting it on the mattress, Joe flipped open the latches, threw the lid up. The tripod was similar to the one used for the digital video camera downstairs. He pulled it out and set it aside. Then he pulled out the scope tube and held it aloft before his eyes, like a treasure.

It looked about long enough to safely insert through the rift, with him safely on *this* side, and just as with the idea of throwing something into the rip in the world that first night had been impossible to ignore, so was this one. And Joe knew that tonight, should it appear again, not only would he record the rift on video, and pass notes through it with his primer to translate, but he would see what was on the other side.

He would *see*.

5.

From the backyard patio chair, Joe watched the rift cut itself into being promptly at seven o'clock in the evening. A light and fluttery feeling entered his chest and his palms became sweaty. He wiped them and gripped his pants legs tight.

To his left and slightly behind him the sliding glass door was open, and the camcorder, perched on the tripod just inside the threshold, filmed away. The green light of its RECORD button glowed like a bright eye in the night.

Joe held another page from the notebook, again filled with his overlarge scribbled handwriting, tight in his right hand, like a talisman. The meter-long telescope tube was in his left hand. When Joe stood and approached the slowly spinning rip in the air, he raised the scope instinctively like a weapon. Catching himself, not wanting to piss off whatever may have been on the other side, he forced himself to hold it in a looser, non-threatening manner at his side.

Close to the rift, the charge in the air again coursed through him.

First, he folded the notebook page carefully. Balling it up this time seemed inappropriate. With fuller communications hopefully about to begin, a certain etiquette felt right. Page folded to an eighth its original size, Joe sent it sailing into the rift with a little flick of his wrist.

The hiss of it entering the rip. The three pulses of light. The return message, on that leathery skin-like material rolled up in a scroll, deposited onto the yard.

Quickly, Joe raised the telescope eye level and pushed half the length through the spindle-shaped rift. He waited briefly for something to happen. Maybe a powerful, flesh-melting charge to travel the length of the scope and liquefy him into a puddle. Or some horrendous *thing* on the other end snatching the telescope and pulling him into the rift with it. But nothing happened. Just him holding one half of the telescope on this side, in his backyard, and the other half...somewhere else.

Joe craned and stretched, still holding the telescope aloft awkwardly, to peer around the rift. He saw only the pool, bright blue in the evening, and the yard stretching away to the fence, on the other side. Joe stepped forward, closed his left eye, and looked through the eyepiece with the other.

He saw many things in his first glimpse of what was on the far side of the rift. The color and lighting were different, somehow...*off*. His eye strained to adjust.

There was an expanse of red that he took to be a sky. High up there, great things soared in large numbers. Below that a vast stretching dark topography of angles and bulges, its features violent and inhospitable. Across this ebon landscape shapes skittered hectically.

And closer to the telescope, blurred and amorphous from being too near the magnification of the lenses, a moving shape with legs and arms and a head, all oddly proportioned, that looked back once and then strode away out of Joe's frame of sight. But it had eyes, that much he could discern, and it was *large*, much larger than any man.

Breathing hard, heart thumping harder, Joe backed away, not liking those eyes, and pulled the length of the scope with him. It slipped out of the hole in the air with another frictional hiss somehow obscene this time around.

The third rule of the rift was the harshest of them all:

When you looked through to the other side and *saw*, something looked back and saw *you*, clean through to the soul, and marked you.

CHAPTER FOUR

1.

Wednesday morning crept up on Joe like a thief.

After watching the rift zipper up and wink out, he went back into the house – the newly deposited skin-scroll held carefully at his side with a pair of kitchen tongs – retrieved the digital video camera from its tripod perch, and retired to the living room. Camera hooked up to his flat-screen television, remote in hand, he watched what had been recorded. Dumbstruck, he rewound it and played the footage again.

Skin-scroll unrolled on the footrest before him, consulting the primer notebook beside him, Joe translated the message from the rift. Recalling how the first scroll had seemed to roll itself up and tumble into the hole in the yard, remembering how the holes themselves had been formed by the burning black rocks, he was reluctant to touch the leathery scrolls and used the kitchen tongs to handle the new one, and the television and DVD player remotes to weigh it down. Translation complete, he read it, went back to the beginning, and scanned it a second time.

The hours passed like minutes, and when next he looked up, Wednesday morning, the fourth day of the rift, had arrived. Rusty, looking on quietly and still in a corner, seemed like a taxidermist's glassy-eyed creation and not a real dog. Joe only remembered the dog was there when he happened to look briefly away from the screen or scroll.

The video recording unnerved him and pissed him off in equal measure. What it showed was…nothing. No spinning rift. No pulsations as it vomited forth the new scroll. No images of him approaching it, sticking the telescope through, leaning forward and peering in.

Instead, a blank, black screen stared back at him, with only the occasional hiccup or twitch of pixilation at the corners. According to the time stamps of the camera's viewfinder and the television screen, Joe had recorded nearly an hour of nothing.

His first inclination was that he'd done something extraordinarily stupid, like leaving the lens cap on, forgetting to press RECORD, or not realizing the camera's memory stick was full. He'd checked all those, though, and the lens was unobstructed, the RECORDED date and time displayed true on the screen, and when connected to his computer the memory stick showed ninety-percent storage space free.

Perspective and intent.

Joe remembered thinking those things, ascribing those qualities to the rift. That maybe the rift was seen only if it *wanted* to be, and only by those it wanted to see it.

Then there was the hide-like scroll, and, if his translation was correct, what was written on it. His note this time had been detailed, explanatory in his desires, rather than mere listed questions. The response from the rift had been likewise.

Joe looked again at the copy of the note he'd made before tossing the original through. The message he'd sent into the rift last night read:

To whoever is on the other side. I have figured out your translation primer. Now that I have a rudimentary understanding of your language, please answer my initial questions. Who are you? What is the rift? And why have you chosen me?

And the response from the rift, from that other place of the dark red sky and the things that flew across it, and the great black landmass like a geologic cancer:

Your son is here. All are here. The way between is open. Come.

2.

He checked his translation with the notebook primer several times. Knowing only some of the characters of the rift's written language, and assuming a direct letter-to-letter relationship, Joe knew the work was spotty. There were gaps in the sequence of his translation, like empty spaces in a game of Hangman. But the translation kept coming up the same.

Your son is here. All are here. The way between is open. Come.

For a brief time his heart soared upon completing the conversion of the hieroglyphic rift-language into English. There was a pleasant flutter from inside him as Joe realized the significance of what he was reading. In his mind, when the rift next opened, he would run and leap straight through it, land on the other side, and there Evan would be, and Joe would scoop the boy up in his arms and they'd dance away together into eternity.

Then Joe thought of what he'd seen when he'd peered through the telescope. The way the things there scuttled quickly away. The large forms crossing the blood-red sky. How the immense humanoid shape had strode fast out of sight, as if it hadn't expected Joe to look through and didn't want to be seen.

He recalled that first night, standing at the sliding glass door, staring out at the hole in the sky, wondering if some radiation was emitted from the rift. Having not found any new limbs sprouted from his body, Joe thought he was okay on that count. But what if there were other dangers associated with the rift?

Perhaps the rift itself was natural. Despite the things he'd seen – the black rocks, the skin-scrolls, the creatures there on the other side – the rift itself could be just a natural phenomenon. Some earthly or astronomical occurrence like ball lightning or auroras, just as he'd initially supposed.

Even so, that didn't settle matters. The waves of a storm-tossed ocean were natural too, though they could still harbor things underneath. Even if the rift itself was both natural *and* safe, maybe whatever inhabited that desiccated land on the other side *wasn't*. Like sharks beneath calm waters that could still rip and rend and pull things under, maybe it was what was *over there* that was malicious, and not the rift itself.

There was also the greatest possibility of all. One no father could ignore. That the message of the rift was real and true.

Your son is here.

For even if there was one chance in a million that it was true, then like the compulsion to throw the first stone into the rift, and then to stick the scope through so he could see, Joe had no choice. If his son was there in that other place, he had to find out, and if the boy was, then what came next was frightening but immutable.

Joe would be going in after him.

3.

At his office desk with a pen and blank sheet of paper, Joe started a list.

Making the decision to step through some dimensional portal, if necessary, wasn't an easy one. There were issues of logistics, like how to traverse the harsh landscape he'd glimpsed on the other side. He would need hardy hiking gear made specifically for tough terrain. This gear – maybe rope and pitons and clasps for climbing – would need to be packed and carried.

Survivability was another concern. If what he'd thought he'd seen was actually over there – the winged things in the crimson sky, the scuttling things, the giant that had strode away from the lens of the scope – Joe would need protection. Weapons. Not a gun guy, he'd have to buy one (or more) and familiarize himself with the firearm. And if things got up close and personal, perhaps knives or a hatchet would be in order too.

Finally, even if he was able to cross the land and fend off the things there, he'd need to find his way around and then back. He had no idea *where* his son was over there, or if the boy was really over there at all. Assuming things like compass directions even existed in that other land, he'd have to establish a route, mark it, and be able to follow it back for the return journey.

But before any of that took place, there was one very pressing question that needed answering. Joe had thrown stones and paper into the rift. These were inanimate objects, though.

What he was thinking of was a whole new ball game.

Would something living from *here* live over *there*?

Rusty was sprawled on the carpet near the fireplace, and looked up at Joe just then as if hearing his thoughts. The dog cocked his head quizzically and issued a low whine.

"It's a question that needs to be answered," Joe said, looking back at the Labrador. "Think of the contributions to science."

Gathering his list, wallet and keys, Joe clipped Rusty's leash on and together they went shopping.

★   ★   ★

As if aware that he'd been excluded as a potential test subject for rift traveling to other dimensions, Rusty followed at Joe's side, looking up at the gerbils and goldfish and parakeets they passed in the aisles of the local PetSmart with a solemn, stoic expression. With his round eyes and drooping dog lips, he seemed to be beaming sympathetic fare-thee-wells to the mammalian, aquatic, and avian prisoners in their respective cells.

Though determined to send a living thing through a rip in the universe, Joe nonetheless found it difficult to make a selection from the species on display. Never a radical animal rights activist, not a member of PETA, no doubt a lifelong dog owner because the canine showed some degree of emotions and intelligence at least somewhat similar to humans and thus identifiable, Joe suddenly found features in other creatures he'd never noticed before.

The way fish cheeks sucked in and puffed out with each breath appeared inquisitive, and made him think of wise old men shooting the breeze on rickety front porches. The songs and twittering of birds in cages as they fluttered from one perch to another seemed deep with meaning, as if full-fledged conversations were taking place in a language he couldn't understand. Gerbils and hamsters scampered and frolicked in hay-like bedding and through wheels and tubes with a playfulness akin to children in a park.

Imagining himself sending these creatures through the rift, Joe thought of nightmarish pictures of melted flesh puddles with stray fish scales, bird feathers, and gerbil whiskers poking out of the mess. He passed by the displays without selecting any of the critters, cursing and pulling Rusty along with him.

Frustrated that he had no test subjects, but pleased that he wasn't about to become the next Hitler of the animal kingdom, Joe moved down the aisles toward the front of the store and the red exit sign, empty-handed. Before he made it to the turnstiles leading out, however, large garish writing in orange marker on a whiteboard sign caught his eye, and he made a sharp militaristic march-turn in that direction.

CRICKETS! the sign's massive scrawl pronounced boldly, visible to all save the blind. The fixture the sign stuck up, periscope-like, from was octagonal and wide, and atop it dozens of small plastic vials held hundreds of the leg-rubbing, antennae-wiggling insects. Previously a background white noise while he'd been striding up and down the lanes of the store, this close up the chirping of the crickets seemed to Joe's ears as loud as a stadium crowd cheering or jeering loved or hated sports teams.

"Jackpot," Joe said, and the dog gave a swish of his tail as if in approval.

4.

It was just after noon when they got back home. Joe opened the driver's-side door, unclasped Rusty's leash, gathered up his insectile rift test pilots, and made for the front of the house. Inside, he set his hopping merchandise on the dining table, then returned outside, the confused dog following beside him.

Joe reached through the window of the Explorer and hit the garage door opener control hanging from the visor, then entered the garage from the front rather than through the foyer. The large bay door rattled upward with a motorized hum, and dust actually shook loose from the aluminum siding, like sand spilling from an ancient pharaoh's uncovered tomb. The daylight flooded into the interior of the garage, chasing the shadows away, illuminating every corner.

The workbench to his left where he used to sit with Evan was empty and bare. As at the dinner table, the boy's absence was almost palpable. But that was where Joe had to go for what he had to do, and so he entered slowly, nearly creeping.

Once there he lowered himself inch by inch like a rider testing a skittish mount, cautiously settling onto the workbench. A familiar groan and creak issued breath-like from the bench's frame as it took his weight.

When it occurred to Joe to send living test subjects into the rift prior to going through himself, the practical scientist in him immediately thought *how*. First with the garden stones and then with the notes, it seemed that some sort of exchange took place whenever something entered the rift. He thought of frontier trade barterers for some reason, giving this for that, some unspoken value allotted to things. If that was the case – that something over there claimed what entered and sent another item in return – then Joe would need a method to forcibly bring back his test subjects, thus negating the trade.

In science fiction films, NASA teams or their futuristic equivalents sent in automated probes to explore such phenomena as the rift. With remote-controlled gadgetry, unmanned vehicles bedecked with cameras, robotic arms, and other high-tech wizardry explored the entity, be it a black hole, a star gate, or a doomsday asteroid on a cataclysmic collision course with Earth. Bruce Willis or Arnold Schwarzenegger, armed with laser cannons or space nukes, would then leap dramatically into the camera's frame and save the day by unnecessarily blowing something up.

Since he was neither a NASA-funded scientist nor a Hollywood hero, Joe's resources were far more limited. With boards of wood laid out on the table before him, saw, carving blades and chisels at the ready like a doctor's implements on a surgical tray, Joe got to work on his very un-Hollywood, non-NASA-like alternative to advanced vehicular probes.

He was initially startled and then calmed by the work. His hands moved the pine boards over and through the saw's whirring blades with an expertise he would have thought lost, unused for over a year. The low vibrations passing through the table's frame and the high whine of the saw made a steady rhythm that sent pleasant tingles down the length of his body, as if he were lounging, listening contentedly to good music. The sawdust wafted a piney clean scent in the air that made Joe breathe deep and slow, relishing the woodsy fragrance.

As he had in the past, he worked by sight and insight; measuring with tape or protractor was unnecessary. Drills and screws and rivets flashed in and out of his fingers with a magician's sleight of hand surety. Bits and parts assembled before him into a larger creation brought with them bits and parts of the past, and Joe again saw Evan there beside him on the bench, looking up at him, listening to his directions with a boy's intent, worshipful gaze.

When he was done, the thing before him resembled a miniature wagon or a wheeled coffin, he couldn't decide which. The body was rectangular and deep, like a truck bed. A hinged lid with latches currently yawned open as if ready to bite. There was a pivoted shaft on one end of the body with a handle at the tip. The four wheels rolled silently and smoothly when Joe tested the contraption with a push across the length of the table. A foot long, six inches wide, and three deep, the little wagon or mobile coffin would hold the half dozen cricket vials and their occupants with room to spare. In that spare room in the bed of the wagon Joe would place the camcorder. A round hole cut in one end would allow it to film with the lid latched shut, so it wouldn't topple out.

The first attempt to record the rift had been a failure, but Joe wasn't ready to give up.

Maybe there was something about the rift itself that rejected attempts at recording it, as certain space-age materials, in an attempt to create invisibility effects, bent light. Perhaps once through the rift itself the video camera would function properly.

Joe stood, lifted the mini wagon from the worktable, and took it into the house. He left the garage's big bay door open, liking the way the sunlight filled the space, how it chased away the shadows but left the memories, bright and clear.

5.

Just as nationalistic tensions and the invasions of Poland and China by Germany and Japan, respectively, had been the forewarnings to World War II, Joe and Clara's World War III had started long before the slap that had stung his face and heart.

Clara, after moving from heart-stricken, life-draining grief – the kind that sucked the soul dry and left behind a brittle husk – to the old sorrow that never goes away, and shouldn't, but strengthens us with the knowledge of the brevity and preciousness of life, wanted to give their son's stuff away. Previously, the boy's room had remained untouched, his playthings and furniture just as Evan had left them on his final morning in this world. It had been for both mother and father a resistance to the cruelty of their son's death. If they didn't touch the boy's room – didn't straighten his bed covers or rearrange his desk or pick up his cast-off pajamas – Clara and Joe could pretend that their son was just late. He'd come home, throw his backpack down in the foyer as he always did despite his mom's regular chastisement, grab a soda from the fridge, race out back with Rusty trailing him, and laugh and run and wrestle in the grass with his dog, under the sun, as boys and dogs were meant to do.

Joe refused his wife's request and Evan's room was left unmolested, still and sterile, like a museum exhibit behind a glass partition.

But the days passed, and they buried their son (or Clara did, Joe staying home). Then weeks passed, and under the weight of hurt and pain and self-pity, they buried their marriage. Finally, after months had passed, Clara seemed to awaken from her stupor and pressed again to give their son's possessions away – to the Goodwill, the Salvation Army, it didn't matter – sitting down on the sofa next to Joe with her Bible in hand, and the first shots were fired.

Now, a year and two days since his son's death, Joe stood in the doorway of the boy's room. He saw how things were still untouched: the clothing on the floor, the rumpled bed cover and sheets, the papers and books on the desk. Today, it didn't seem a testament to his son, a denial of the injustice of the boy's murder, but the bitter self-induced lies of a tired, sad man. The film of dust over everything seemed to highlight this fact, blotting the light and the vibrancy with which Evan's presence had imbued the room, the house, and the world.

Rusty, golden in coat and spirit, entered the room ahead of Joe. The dog sniffed here and there as if testing the space for something and not finding it, pressed on.

Emboldened by the dog's courage, Joe followed. Crossing the threshold was like striding a fissure atop a great peak, a vast chasm below. He had a brief sense of losing his balance, losing a foothold, and then he was over the line and in the room.

Approaching the closet, Joe chose his path across the room with care. With slow and deliberate steps, he avoided touching anything. The closet door slid open smoothly on its track.

There was a brief moment when he thought the rift would be there, open in the small space amid hanging Marvel Comics T-shirts and faded jeans. This time he wouldn't need the telescope to see through the whirling vortex to the other side. It would be like a window and he would see his son, maybe, or those other things that skittered, or the ill-proportioned giant with the cold eyes, stomping across the black landscape. But only the clothes were there, dangling from the closet rod. Stirred into lazy motion by the sliding door, the garments did a little wavy dance and went still again.

The item he'd come for lay on the floor beneath his son's clothes.

Joe knelt and picked up his son's fishing rod, holding it, feeling it, remembering warm days standing knee deep in the Kern River, or with the ocean breeze blowing in misty sprays along Pacific piers. His son beside him, practicing the motions, reeling in invisible catches before Joe put the actual rod in his small hands to let the boy cast the line.

Joe had thrown his own rod away months ago. Without his son there had been no use for it. He'd broken the thing in half over his knee, buried it deep in the trash, piled other things atop it.

Holding Evan's rod tall at his side – a soldier with his battle standard – Joe retraced his steps out of the room, disturbing nothing else. Down the hall, down the stairs, it was a battlefield he crossed, scarred and pitted by the loss of faith and hope, old friends fallen in this life, the longest war there is.

In the dining room, his purchases from PetSmart on the table, the crafted wooden storage box alongside them, and now the long fishing rod laid out beside it all, Joe considered the collection. Rusty in the kitchen, lying near his water dish, likewise considered him. Hands on hips, Joe considered the dog right back.

"Commencing Project Weird Shit, phase two," he said to the dog, to himself, and to no one in particular. The words seemed to weigh in the air of the quiet house for a time and then dissipate, leaving only the work that was ahead of him.

6.

As on the previous three nights, the rift appeared at seven o'clock. It split open with the smoothness of elevator doors, as if some interdimensional bellhop had just reached Joe's level, greeting him and inviting him aboard the cab. The eerie white-blue light of it cast shimmering patterns across the pool water and the glass of the back door.

Seated at the patio table, Joe loaded the cricket vials into the wheeled coffin-box sitting atop his lap. Fishing rod clenched at an angle between his knees, he then affixed the small wooden box by tying off the end of the fishing line about the lid's hinges. Dangling it before him like the world's strangest lure, he cranked the reel handle to test the weight. Once his chirping subjects were inside, he nestled the digital video camera in among them, again doing another stress test by feeding the line out and reeling it back in.

The camera-and-cricket-loaded box couldn't have weighed more than five pounds, less than a nice-sized actual fish. Unless something seized the box there on the other side and pulled hard, the line would hold. He turned the camera on, set it to RECORD, and fit the lens into its view hole. Strips of duct tape in strategic locations held it firmly in place.

As ready as he would ever be, Joe stood and approached the rift.

Joe reeled the coffin-box out to about three feet of line, stretched the fishing rod out and fed his chirping lure into the spinning sky-rip before him. The spindle of light hissed snake-like as it accepted the box, fishing line, and topmost inches of the rod.

Moments passed. The rift maintained its steady blue-white glow. There were no pulsations as before, when the garden rocks and the notebook paper had been tossed in.

When he'd poked the telescope in and looked through, nothing like the telescope had popped out. He'd been holding on to it from this side, as he was now holding the fishing rod, and the line of the rod held the box, and the box the crickets. Could this chain of connection inhibit the rift's properties?

He slowly played out more line.

Joe thought of the giant man-thing that strode that other black volcanic landscape. The high-flying shapes in the scarlet sky. The things that skittered beetle-like across the jagged topography. He waited for them or something like them to seize the line and pull him through.

The line fed out. He could feel the weight of the box over there, and the taut bending of the rod's frame as its burden was lowered. He thought of cranes lowering freight at harbors.

There was a slight jolt of impact as the coffin-box met resistance on the other side. The sensation was somehow…*muted*…as a pounding just barely felt through insulated walls. Joe ceased feeding the line, bobbed the whole of the rod up and down a bit to feel the drag of the box and the tug of the fishing wire as the slack was made taut, and lifted the load again. Then he set it back down, affirming the presence of a surface on the other side of the rift.

Forearms nearly at eye level as he held the rod, Joe glanced at his watch.

When two minutes had passed, Joe figured the crickets had been over there long enough. If the insects couldn't breathe on the other side, or were mashed under the pressure of greater gravity, or were frozen or burned to a crisp, it would have happened by now.

He started reeling the line in. The feel of the wire taking the weight, lifting the box, traveled through the length of the rod to his hands. The box met the tip of the rod.

Joe backed up, bringing the rod out of the rift with him.

It looked like a splinter being pulled out of the very sky. There was the box now, a corner coming through, a strange crowning, an enigmatic birth. A full third of it through, and that serpent's hiss of the rift as things went in and out of it, that scraping friction. The glimmer of the camera's lens peeking through the cutout hole.

A brief chorus of chirrups from beneath the latched lid, and Joe thought, *They're alive! They're alive!* Excitement built as he realized it had worked, his experiment was a success, what went in could come back out, alive, and he smiled and laughed a short chortle of triumph.

So that when something *did* grab the box, and pulled, he was caught off guard and lurched forward with the violent tug. He stumbled frighteningly close to the rift before letting go of the rod and the box tied to it, so he could pinwheel his arms and regain his balance.

The rod was slurped up into the rift as if by hungry lips.

The tear in the air before him flashed brighter three times.

First, something stick-like came through, but knotted and knobby and jointed unlike any stick or branch Joe had ever seen. And the surface of the stick-that-wasn't-a-stick glistened, like worms under the sun. Then it moved, flexing and undulating and bending at its knobby joints, the head of it softly tapping the ground before it, like feelers. It found the hole in the yard, where the skin-scroll had snapped back to its tubular form and fallen in, and the moving flesh-stick followed it down. Worming its way obscenely into the hole, inch by inch, foot by foot, it was swallowed into the earth.

Second, a bone-white box spilled from the rift. Looking at it, watching it totter on one corner then coming to rest on a side like a large cast die, seeing the smoothness of the thing, Joe thought maybe it wasn't merely bone-white, but actually *made* of bone. As he stared at it, the bone-box jumped with an internal pressure, like popcorn kernels popping, and Joe shouted in surprise. Something was *in* the bone-box.

It jumped again. A third time.

It shattered, the bones forming the structure clattering like a child's building blocks toppled, and what was inside came out.

They may have once been crickets, innocently chirping with their violin-legs. Here, on Earth, they could have been such creatures.

From the rift, though, there was no such thing.

Large as puppies, obsidian-shelled, mottled like age-spotted skin where glimpses of flesh showed beneath the shell, with legs both under them and *atop* them protruding periscope-like, and eyes round and wide and milk-white, they were something else entirely. A dozen of them, somehow impossibly packed in that bone-box, and now free, marched across the lawn in every direction, climbed the fence, dived into the pool, and two darted past Joe standing in the yard and Rusty growling under the patio table, straight through the wide-open sliding glass door.

Monsters in his yard, monsters in his house, Joe did the only sensible thing at a time like that: he turned, grabbed his dog, and ran screaming like a little girl.

CHAPTER FIVE

1.

All the tools needed to successfully eradicate interdimensional demon crickets from one's home could be found at the local outdoor swap meet.

The San Bernardino swap meet was a converted drive-in theater. Vendors set up their tented or tarp-topped lots where parking spaces and speaker boxes had once been. The vast white screens standing high could have been enormous flags of surrender – unused in this age of digital theater, digital films, digital everything – towering over all else, announcing their defeat to the encroaching march of progress. Their shadows created an eclipse effect where they landed, giving temporary reprieve from the baking summer sun.

Joe walked the pathways of the outdoor market bleary-eyed and slump-shouldered. Rusty, leashed beside him, likewise walked with heavy, paw-dragging strides.

They'd spent the night in a Motel 6, Joe sitting upright in bed staring at the room's single window, waiting for gargantuan rift-crickets to leap through. Hopping atop the bed, their bladed legs would saw his face to ribbons and slavering, clacking mandibles would greedily lap up the mess. Reverting to childhood fears of the dark, he'd held the covers of the cheap bed up to his chin, as if the worn and frayed material would provide an impenetrable barrier should the mutated insects find him and attack.

In the morning, sleep-deprived and irritable, Joe had taken a lukewarm shower in the motel room's claustrophobically small bathroom. Pelted by abrasive mineralized hard water for a spell, he then exited the shower stall more ill-tempered than when he'd entered. Fueling himself with a pot of the motel's free coffee, he parked himself in a lumpy chair in the lobby, newspaper in hand, trying to think. Rusty at his side earned Joe stares from the desk clerk, but the stare from the rift-giant when he'd looked through the telescope was far worse, so too the large beady black eyes of the rift-crickets, and Joe ignored the pimpled employee without concern.

It was in the paper that he'd seen the advertisement for the swap meet, and he recalled how walking through them had once been a semi-regular outing for his family. Clara was always pleased when stumbling across some earthy vase or pot to liven their home with for only a dollar; while Joe and Evan would search eagle-eyed for comic book bins where pulpy treasures awaited discovery. The hustle and bustle and harking and barking of prices negotiated, and a snack bar or two somewhere at the fringes with greasy hot dogs wafting their juicy scents in the open air, gave such places a certain pastoral, frontier-like vibe.

And, as was always the case in such a venue, there was a vendor like the one Joe currently stood in front of. The meaty proprietor, ball cap pulled low, lounged in a lawn chair and chopped Joe a salute. Joe waved back and started browsing.

He eyed the items on the tabletops and splayed-out blankets on the ground before him. Weighed his options. Pictured himself with each in turn.

Machetes, hatchets, baseball bats, pitchforks, clawed hand rakes, shovels, hammers, sledgehammers, chains, knives, hacksaws, fireplace pokers, and every other imaginable instrument used for stabbing, cutting, slicing, bashing, smashing, gouging, ripping, and pulverizing were laid out for perusal. A smorgasbord of death and dismemberment – or yard work and home repair, if you were into that sort of thing – surrounded Joe, and he looked this way and that, hefted the wares, tested their weight and the feel of them in his hands. He felt like Rambo, readying to take out half of some communist regime's population single-handedly.

Despite the monster infestation of his home, and the terror such creatures had awoken in him, Joe kept coming back to the words of the last rift-letter: *Your son is here. All are here. The way between is open. Come.*

He had to go back.

Joe thought of insects here in our world. Their exoskeletons and carapaces lent them a proportional protection against impacts, falls, and assorted assaults that made them resilient and tank-like. What had come out of the rift last night, multi-legged and glassy-shelled, might share such qualities.

From atop a blue-sheeted folding table Joe selected a sledgehammer, holding it at the haft, liking the feel of the mass of it in his hands. He also grabbed two smaller but still impressive ball-peen hammers, the iron ball sides of their heads looking to him like hard little fists.

In a bucket at one leg of the table Joe saw odds and ends, and a leather work belt bundled in the mess, like a serpent in some Indian snake charmer's wicker basket. He bent, picked it up. Loops along the length of the leather belt looked about right to accommodate the smaller hammers, and he leaned the sledgehammer against the table, made sure the ball peens did indeed fit. Satisfied, Joe gathered his selections, approached the beefy guy in the lounge chair. When the guy told Joe his total, his thick, curly beard moved like a living bush, and Joe thought of the moving, undulating stick.

He paid and hurried away, Rusty padding along beside him. Back at the Explorer, Joe loaded his purchases. The Labrador hopped in after them and Joe shut the rear door. Behind the wheel, he met the dog's eyes in the rearview mirror.

"You ready for this, mutt?" he asked, but received no response. "Neither am I."

2.

Parking along the sidewalk rather than in the driveway – as if just a few extra yards of distance from the house would protect him against what was inside – Joe left the engine idling and stared out at his home. The brick and stucco walls, the gabled roof, the rustic trim and overhanging eaves should have been warm and inviting, blending with the natural setting around it as the Spanish Ranch style was intended to. Instead, with his family gone and monsters skittering unseen about the place, the house, with its wide panel windows, seemed a forlorn face staring back at him in solemn warning. Daylight didn't lighten this mood as one would think, but rather heightened the suggestion of threat.

Joe got out of the car, rolled down the windows for the Labrador as he'd done back at the school. Should things go south fast, he half surprisingly found he didn't want Rusty in the path of danger. He opened the rear door, told the dog to stay, scooped up the leather work belt. Strapping it on, he slipped the ball peens into it like a Mexican bandit's six-guns. Next, he hefted the sledgehammer, backed up, and shut the door.

Rusty scooted close to the window, wedged his head through the gap. Gave a little whine to show his discontent. Joe leaned over, pecked the dog a kiss atop his furry head and backed away.

"You stay here. I'll be back soon."

Knowing this very well could be a lie, Joe turned away from the dog's wide, accusatory eyes. At the sidewalk in front of his house he looked up and down the street. None of the neighbors were out yet, or were already gone, which wasn't unexpected for a Thursday morning. Kids would already be shuttled away to summer school or ball games. No summer break for the working class, most everyone else would be at their jobs or on their way to them.

The street seemed abandoned. He thought of ghost towns in the Arizona desert, where he'd vacationed so often. Joe realized just how alone he was should things go bad in there.

Crossing the front lawn, he could feel the lush grass beneath the soles of his shoes, and he thought of the holes in the backyard, and in his mind the entire property was atop a great hole. Soon, the earth would give way and swallow it all, like the rift swallowed smaller objects, and he'd tumble down forever.

Then he was at the porch. Joe stood on it, and the front door was like an opponent in a duel. He rested the butt of the sledgehammer on the concrete, fished in his jeans for the keys, and pulled them out with a wind-chime jangle. Working through them with suddenly damp fingers, Joe found the house key, jabbed it at the doorknob. His hand now shaking, he missed three times before getting the key in, unlocking the door, and swinging it open.

The door's hinges, usually silent, gave a slight creak like a cemetery gate in a horror movie. Joe raised his mighty hammer like Thor and entered the house.

Though it was daytime and the dining room lights he'd left on last night were still glowing, the interior of the house seemed too dim. The walls appeared gray rather than white. The beige carpet he and Clara had chosen together not beige, but mud-brown. The furniture of the living room – dressers, bookshelves, coffee and end tables – looked dull and muted, as if they rejected light itself.

In the foyer Joe listened intently. He willed every muscle and joint of his body stone still. A phantom in his own home, he held his breath as long as possible, only letting it out in tiny exhalations softer than whispers.

From deeper inside he heard nothing. No thumps of jostled furniture or creaks of floorboards disturbed by softly treading trespassers, lurking, creeping.

He saw the hole in the living room floor first. Ruptured upward and out, it seemed like a small crater, about a foot in diameter. Carpet fibers and wood chips and stone lay about the rim of the puckered opening in an outer circle. Raising the sledgehammer, Joe approached the hole.

With each deliberate step he could see more of the interior of the fissure. Layered atop each other he saw the wood floor panels, the stone foundation beneath, and below that the broken earth, clods and rocks and little pieces of root pushed up and away as if something had burrowed out.

Standing at the rim, Joe started to lean over to peer directly down through the hole. Instead, his attention turned to something in his periphery, some off-color form he knew shouldn't be there against the backdrop of the white walls.

At the mouth of the downstairs hallway, where the stairs swept up and around to the second story and the length of the hall moved away to the downstairs bath and guest room, was another hole. In the lower portion of the wall, right above the baseboard, it was rightly placed for mice to gain access to the house.

If mice were a foot thick at the body.

After the second hole at the baseboard of the hallway, Joe quickly spotted the others, spread throughout the floor and walls and ceiling of the house so that the whole structure seemed porous, like a giant sponge. Moving now more surely from the living room to the dining room, hastened by the strange assault to his home, he saw them everywhere.

There was one high in the corner of the dining room's vaulted ceiling, bits of splintered wood and strings of insulation hanging out, the center of the hole dark, the interior unseen. Another under the dining table, where he and his wife and their son had sat for years for meals, stirred a sense of violation in Joe, as if something sacred had been desecrated. One leg of the oak table had slid into the hole and the table dipped, slanted at an angle, heightening this sense of wrongness. In the kitchen, tiles were cracked and strewn where yet another rupture from beneath had occurred.

Others dotted the first story, a dozen or more immediately visible now that he was looking for them. Joe thought of a rotten apple, spoiled, with worms and insects squirming through it, *eating* it. This wasn't a house anymore. It was an infestation.

That was when he heard them.

The susurration of serrated, rubbing violin-legs. The friction-whisper of carapaces dragging. And the click-clack of scissoring mandibles.

Vague at first, the sound grew louder as whatever moved within the structure of the house came closer. From all directions the noise came; the floor, the walls, the ceiling. He tried to watch all the ragged openings at once, turning on his heel this way and that in a clumsy pirouette.

The sandpaper scratching grew louder. Becoming a steady roar, the low rumble echoed through the house. The floor beneath Joe vibrated as if a low-scale quake were passing through the earth.

The first creature poked out of a hole low in the wall near the fireplace. Joe, still spinning in his queer dance, happened to turn in that direction and saw the thing peeking out like a Whack-a-Mole arcade game target. So close, it was even more hideous than the clear but quick glimpse of the things he'd had last night.

Black legs, multi-jointed, rose and fell, testing the rim of the hole the thing crept from. Carapace, smooth and round, rasped against the edge of the punctured gap in the wall as it pushed forth and out. The mottled cancer-flesh of the head was pale and sickly, and the eyes, milk-white as if blind, but *seeing*, saw Joe. These orbs nestled in a face with a mouth and lips that quivered as if in anticipation, the mandibles cutting the air before them like yard clippers, opening and closing, opening and closing, made for rending, wanting to rip.

If he were going to run, Joe knew now was the time. He thought about it, seriously considered it in the space of a few seconds. He could bring the police – hell, the army – back with him and maybe a reporter or two, and the whole city, the country, shit, the world, could know about what was in his house, the rift in his backyard, and yes, his son on the other side of it. With such resources at his disposal a part of him said if there was any hope that Evan was somewhere over there, that's how he'd find the boy.

Then the effects of decades of Hollywood films and conspiracy theories took hold. And rather than setting out to save his boy, Joe imagined the intelligence agencies of America quarantining his home, planting some glass biodome over it, installing probes and sensors about the site of the rift to study and analyze it. His son would become nothing more than a footnote, probably not even that, probably forgotten. Joe would be intimidated into signing nondisclosure agreements and be relocated like someone in federal protection, but his protection wouldn't be the real reason. It would be the powered elite, the oil barons and military-industrial executives, and what they could exploit there on the other side of the rift, that would be the true focus.

His son would be lost to him a second time.

Joe couldn't allow that to happen.

He didn't run. Sledgehammer held high over his shoulder, like a batter stepping up to home plate, Joe strode to the thing coming out of the hole near the fireplace. His hands clenched the haft tighter, his body turned, coiling for the backswing.

And with a bestial scream, he swung.

The crunch of the rift creature's carapace was brutal. A sound like brittle sticks breaking underfoot. He pulled the sledgehammer back from the yellowish smear it left behind – multiple jointed legs still twitching, bodiless – and more of the things came forth, crowning out of the holes.

He ran and swung, swung and ran, from room to room, hole to hole. Sometimes he missed, adding new craters to the walls. Mostly, though, his blows struck home. Spatters of gore and chunks of alien mottled meat burst forth. Dripping down the walls in viscous dribbles, splattered out in Rorschach patterns radiating from the rents in the floor. His home seemed to be bleeding or suppurating.

Still they came, skittering, tapping arrhythmic beats with their multi-directional legs. In a waterfall spill of clicking-clacking-tapping, more of them tumbled down the stairs. Joe swung side to side in croquet swipes, knocking them away, and with the head of the sledgehammer aimed down, he pounded and squished, kicked and leapt, jumped and landed. Circling him, climbing over their fallen, mandibles rending, tearing, *eating* their dead and dying, they surrounded him, pressing forward despite his attacks.

Nowhere to go, clacking jaws snagging his boots, his jeans cuffs, pulling at him, eager for him, Joe felt the battle rage leaving him. Fear replaced it, and he thought of all that was lost: his wife, his son, all of it.

Jabbing touches as flicking legs tested his denim-clad shins, started to scale him.

Something from above him dropped, landed on his shoulder, caressed his cheek briefly with a cold, hard feeler, lost its purchase, toppled off.

"Oh Christ I'm not ready…" he muttered, cried, felt for the ball peens at the loops in the leather belt, grabbed for them. He fell to his knees, swung wildly with each arm, connecting with some blows, missing with others.

His right sleeve was grasped. The tear of the fabric was loud in Joe's ears. The hem of his shirt was caught and yanked, pulling him down.

Failing once more, as he'd failed at everything since that dark day his son died, Joe gave himself over to the black-shelled rift-spawn. He allowed them to pull him down without further resistance, toppled down atop them, felt them moving beneath him, wiggling free, moving over him.

He waited for the first bite, wondered bleakly how much pain having strips of himself ripped free would cause. Would shock take him, or would he leave this life in agony?

Enveloped by the things, their legs touching him with wicked tickles, mocking prods, he shouldn't have heard anything else. The clatter of their hard bodies, the hum of their demented violin tune, was a wave-like roar, all-encompassing.

But he did hear something else. Vague at first, as a sound heard through thick walls. Then closer, and louder.

A demonic growl. The wet-spittle slapping of hellhound jowls. A familiar click-clack of nails on tile accompanying the monstrous snarl.

Amazingly, the poking and prodding stopped. The mass of the countless bodies scampered crab-like off him. Little wet pinpoints dotted the length of him in several places, tiny pinpricks of pain, but Joe flexed his hands, curled his toes in his boots, felt all his extremities intact.

He pushed himself up to his knees so he could see what was happening. Across the dining room and into the living room where the front door stood open still, backlit by a sunlight most bright and dazzling, stood the dog. Rusty leapt into the fray, snapping and pouncing, jaws clapping shut and shaking, shaking and tossing. Further into the house the dog came, a beast unleashed, and the rift creatures drew back before the canine wrath. The hellhound advanced.

The dog stopped beside Joe, snapping and yapping still, clearing a circle around them. A hand on Rusty's collar, Joe stood on shaky legs. He took the great hammer up once more.

Man and dog together, they fought. For the home that had once been, for the memory of it and for what it could be again, they swung and bit and pounded and threw. The black creatures dwindled in number, dying or retreating, but dwindling just the same. A few returned to their holes, most made for the open doors, the front and rear both, abandoning their attack.

Until there was only Joe and his son's dog, now his. He knew that now. Where once he'd spurned the Labrador, now in the aftermath of battle they were brothers, bonded through blood and the source of blood, the heart.

3.

Riding all the highs and lows of his three-plus decades of life – the awkward teenage years and the first cherry-flavored kiss; the intellectual freedom of college and all the future seeming a vast plain of hope and opportunity; meeting his wife for the first time on the lightly lapped shore of a shining lake; the birth of his son in a tide of blood and sweat and tears; the death of his father soon after in similar fashion; the loss of his son and the near dissolution of his marriage; and so many other countless events, large and small alike, some really no more than fleeting moments in the totality of his existence – Joe had arrived at one, and only one, immutable truth:

Dogs that saved people from hellish monster crickets deserved pot roast for dinner.

Together, Joe and Rusty made multiple circuits about the house, upstairs and down, searching every nook and cranny. He armed with his hammers, the dog with teeth and jaws, they entered every room boldly, empowered by their earlier victory. Joe leaned close and peered into every hole they found, prodded the interiors with the haft of the sledgehammer.

Nothing leapt out at them.

Except for the two of them, the house was empty.

In his mind, Joe kept a running tally of the crater-like holes throughout the house. Ticking each one off with a nod of the head or a pointing finger, coming back down to the living room where it had all started, he counted twenty-five of the burrowed punctures in the floor, walls, and ceiling.

Joe crossed the living room to the foyer and entered the garage. The midday sun washed over the threshold, over him, and brought vibrancy back to the dullness of the house that he'd felt when first walking in. Along the wall where the workbench sat were metal shelves loaded with buckets of paint and plaster, and the brushes and spackling tools to accompany them. Joe set the sledgehammer down but left the leather belt on. He picked up a bucket in one hand, implements in the other, and went back inside. A return trip for the aluminum ladder propped in a corner and he was set to go.

In the kitchen he set his work tools down, knowing full well the day ahead of him, and also knowing the dog beside him was far more important than patching holes. So, there in the middle of the kitchen floor Joe knelt, waved Rusty over, and hugged the dog hard and tight. With a tremulous voice he thanked the Labrador, mouthing the words close to the mutt's floppy ears so the dog wouldn't miss them, and squeezed him again. Rusty accepted this all with a confused but bemused grin, the tip of his tongue hanging out one side as if to say, *Yeah, what's the big deal?*

Releasing the dog, he dug the Crock-Pot out of a low cupboard, pulled the roast from the refrigerator, got it all going, and with the scent of it filling the air he mixed the plaster, that thick smell joining the other, and patched holes in the walls, holes in the ceiling. The dog watching him all the while, Joe realized with each hole of the house patched, like bandages covering wounds, he was also patching himself, tending to the wounds of his soul inflicted over the past year.

He worked well into the afternoon, arms sore, legs hot and rubbery, a dew of sweat clinging to him, tickled by the cool draft of the air conditioner against his skin when he removed his shirt. He stood and opened the doors and windows of the ground floor at one point, replacing the processed wind of the air conditioner with the softer but purer summer breeze outside. At length, Joe realized he was smiling with the work of reclaiming his house, and when he finished the last patch, dried plaster flaking his knuckles, making them seem aged and battle-worn, he felt like a fighter, having gone twelve long hard rounds and coming out the winner, the champion.

When the kitchen timer dinged, Joe's stomach growled with anticipation. He went to the kitchen, prepared two plates, and sat on the floor with his dog, that furry grinning warrior, the real champion.

*   *   *

Later, Joe looked out the sliding glass door to the backyard, saw the fallen pieces of the bone-box – what looked like phalanges, carpals, and metacarpals scattered like Legos – still lying out there in the grass. He also saw what was poking out from among them, half buried.

Returning to the kitchen, he retrieved from a drawer the tongs he'd used previously to carry the skin-scrolls. Back at the rear sliding door, he pulled it open, went outside.

The sky was the deep arctic blue of approaching dusk. Only a few short hours from now, if it kept to its routine, the rift would appear once more. This gave him some time to consider what was at his feet among the remains of the bone-box. Using the tongs to push aside the bones, Joe uncovered the thing beneath them.

It looked like a VHS tape. White like the bones strewn about it rather than the standard black plastic casing of a VHS cassette, and the spooled film visible through the small frontal window fleshy and organic like stretched tendon, it was still recognizable for what it was: a video tape from the rift.

Joe had sent through his digital camera, a device that recorded images. He'd received something similar back.

Though they were nearly obsolete in the age of DVD and Blu-Ray discs, Joe remembered VCRs and VHS cassettes well. The cassettes had a space on the top and front for labels; pre-produced if a studio film, blank for scribbled titles of the owner's choosing, say if recording a favorite show. Where these labels should have been on a standard earthly VHS cassette were instead those harsh slashes and marks of the rift-language.

Joe carried the white-cased, tendon-taped cassette carefully with the tongs back into the house and set it on the dining table. His notebook primer was on the sofa across the room. He went over, grabbed it, and returning to the cassette on the table, he flipped open to the appropriate pages, used his translated messages to decipher the writing on the rift-tape. The markings on the wide top and slimmer front of the cassette read the same.

WATCH.

At the entertainment center in the living room, buried amongst the stereo system and the big-screen television and the DVD/Blu-Ray player, collecting dust like some ancient artifact, Joe found the VCR and pulled it out to the front. A decade ago the machines were still somewhat common, though even then falling rapidly in popularity. He and Clara had used a VHS camcorder – the grandfather of the digital one he'd used to attempt to film the rift – to record Evan's early years. Just as Joe hadn't touched his son's room in the past year, neither had he the presence of mind to discard the old machine.

Now, he was glad he hadn't.

He checked the three-pronged audio-video cord and thicker coaxial cable at the back of the VCR, made sure it was still hooked up to the television. Finding the large remote in a cabinet of the entertainment center, he checked it for batteries, pushed the POWER button. The VCR blinked on with a green neon readout, displaying the current time and date, apparently the internal clock functioning even after so much time and disuse. Joe turned the television on also, switched to the proper channel for the VCR input.

Then he stepped back.

He stood between the VCR and the rift-cassette on the dining room table. Looking from one to the other, weighing things in his mind. Did he really want to do this? So far, his dealings with the rift hadn't produced anything good.

He had some rudimentary understanding of what the rift did, but not why it did so. He'd communicated with something on the other side, but didn't know the intention of that other. He'd caught a glimpse of what was over there, but knew nothing of that place.

Burning rocks, moving skin-scrolls, undulating sticks, and giant crickets didn't exactly foster confidence in what was happening. Though something had told Joe his son was *over there*, so far what was over there wasn't very appealing. Each and every thing that had come from there to here had been somehow *corrupted*, but even that wasn't the right word. It was more as if the things *here* were mocked by some heinous caricatured mirror image over *there*.

Why should the suggestion that his son was there be any different?

But this realization required that Joe admit his son was dead and gone. That the episode in the van in the desert was a finality.

He moved to the bone-shelled, tendon-taped rift-cassette atop the dining table and picked it up with the tongs. He crossed back to the living room and stood in front of the entertainment center. The steady green glow of the VCR's power light beckoned like an airport runway marshal waving his glow sticks, guiding a pilot down. With the tongs Joe coasted the strange cassette into the VCR feeder, and though technologies from different places, different realms, they accepted each other and the rift-VHS tape was sucked in. The flat-screen television flickered with a blue light, pulsed three times as the rift itself did when taking something into itself, and the video started to play.

The image was snowy with interference. Crackling static bars rolled up the screen. Behind the snow and static were shapes moving to and fro. Like silhouettes through curtained windows, the figures were bulbous and ill-defined, yet recognizable. There was the impression of activity, hurried but deliberate. The many shapes then parted, leaving one. Whatever produced this image – rift-director giving direction to some rift-cameraman, perhaps – zoomed in closer to this remaining singular form. Close up, through the jumping static bars and snowy fuzz of interference, the shape of head and shoulders was unmistakable.

And it spoke:

"Daaaaaaaddd...."

Even with distortion feedback similar to a hot microphone, a slight echo as in a corridor, and stuttering, clipping in and out like sound through bad speakers, the voice was clear enough. Joe wasn't imagining it. He wasn't finding a pattern in meaningless dissonance. He heard what he heard.

And, from the cherished memories fresh in his heart and mind, overlaying the ever-familiar face over the insubstantial shape on the screen, he saw what he saw:

His son, over there, calling out to him.

4.

With Rusty at his side again, Joe sat on the back patio, waiting for the rift to arrive. The black expanse above rolled out, and the stars like diamonds on the cosmic jeweler's velvet display blinked their light across the void. The phone rang but he didn't answer it. Legs crossed, hands in his lap, he watched and waited.

When it curtained open in the sky before him, spinning its slow, relaxed spin, he didn't move, kept watching. He didn't approach the rift. He threw nothing into it. Vertical rather than horizontal, the rift had a reptilian eye-like aspect, and it seemed to stare back at Joe with a cold-blooded calculation.

Wondering if sound – a frequency of the electromagnetic spectrum, a disruption and oscillation of space and time, moving and thus *something* – would enter the rift as matter would, Joe spoke loud and clear, in his mind envisioning the words traveling through the air before him, approaching the rift and going through.

"I'm coming, Evan. I'm coming for you, son."

Half an hour later the rift zippered shut, the sudden motion almost petulant like a child closing its mouth against a rejected food, and whether lizard-eye or hungry mouth, watching him or wanting to devour him, Joe didn't care. Whatever the rift was, whatever operated on the other side of it, it wasn't a father, angry and righteously so, seeking a son that had been taken from him. As in his year-long grief the pain fueled him, kept him going, now not with self-pity but with an eye toward justice and vengeance and love, strong and unyielding.

CHAPTER SIX

1.

Fourteen years ago, he met a girl by a lake.

In the interest of full disclosure, Joe didn't so much *meet* her — accidental-like — as he had been *following* her. But he wasn't following her in a creepy stalker I'm-gonna-slip-a-roofie-in-your-drink sort of way, either. He'd been kayaking across the widest stretch of Vale Lake in the high desert, saw her slim and small and bronzed in the sun, several yards away, doing the same and overtaking him. Her slender frame taut with each stroke and misted by the spray of the lake, pulling her kayak faster than his, was both spellbinding and irksome.

His ego threatened, Joe paddled harder, slapping and pulling the oar through the crystal waters. She never looked his way, apparently oblivious of him, and this was a further affront, so Joe pulled even harder, chopping the oar through the current. In his heavy-breathing sweaty fervor he lost his grip on the oar, it fell into the water with a splash and started floating away. Unable to steer, Joe drifted aimlessly, bobbing there in the lapping waters, the shore hundreds of yards away in all directions.

Looking every which way for someone other than the young woman, seeing no one else, the already oppressive late morning sun beating down on him, Joe sighed, faced the dwindling shape of the female kayaker, and called out to her. His shout of *"Hey! Excuse me!"* traveled loud and clear over the otherwise stillness of the lake, and she turned, her short black locks plastered against her face and temples, one hand up like a visor against the sun.

"Yeah?" she'd hollered back. Over the surface of the lake and in the surrounding forest, her voice echoed, almost dreamlike.

"I'm kind of stranded here!" Joe had bellowed, arms held wide to indicate his quickly escaping oar and his drifting kayak and the embarrassment of the whole situation in general. Across the span between them he thought he saw her smile, and then she was turning, the kayak arcing a blue wake, coming back his way.

When she pulled up beside him there was no doubt about it. Her smile worked her whole face, showing the lines of years of laughter, bringing it alive. Joe couldn't help himself and grinned back, indignant but strangely enjoying the circumstances.

"What's so funny?" he'd asked.

She'd only shrugged, not looking at him directly, as she handed over a line and directed him to tie it through the grab loop at the stern.

Anchored to her kayak, ready to be towed ashore, he asked again, "Why are you laughing?" and she shook her head as she redirected her own vessel, nosing it toward shore, and started paddling. Behind her, unwatched, Joe found himself staring at her, noticing the way every line of her seemed sculpted and shone with the dew of the lake spray.

Once ashore, pulling the kayaks up out of the water so they didn't drift back out, Joe thanked her and she said no problem. Her orange life vest and modest one-piece blue bathing suit covered most of her, but what did show was trim and firm and the rest filled the suit with alluring contours. Joe struggled to keep his eyes on her face, and was pretty sure he succeeded.

"I could have drowned," he said when her smile refused to go away, and when she started to laugh — a full-throated, breathy sound, musical and airy — he followed up with, "I could have died, and you're just laughing it up," which made her laugh harder until she was almost crying. And then he said, "Okay, so I'm foolish around beautiful women," and her tears and laughter soon stopped, but the smile remained, and the lapping of the water on the shoreline sounded like a metronome ticking away the moments. They walked back to their cars together, and the trees high and dense about them formed a wall, so the rest of the world was out there, but in here it was just the two of them.

She gave Joe her name and number and they got in their cars, started the engines and pulled out of their spaces. Before driving off she pulled alongside him, much as she had with her kayak on the lake. Giving the cranking gesture to get him to roll down his window, she leaned out of hers and those brown eyes affixed on his.

"I'm glad I was there, Joe, to bring you back before you drifted away," she said, and Joe said something about maybe next time she could wait a little longer and resuscitate him. She laughed that throaty laugh and drove away, giving him a honk of her horn as she turned a corner. Then she was gone.

Those words stayed with Joe over the years, in the back of his mind like lyrics from a favorite song: *I'm glad I was there, Joe, to bring you back before you drifted away.*

2.

Clara got back from Phoenix at ten Friday morning. She'd called the night prior to let Joe know she'd be getting to his place early, but he was staring into the rift in the backyard and hadn't answered the phone.

Then she was there on the porch, and Joe remembered those words she'd spoken that first day by the lake. He thought of the video from the rift, and the silhouette in the foreground calling out to him, and Joe feared maybe he was drifting off again.

"You made good time," he said.

"Yeah. I only made a couple stops. Drove pretty much straight through."

She wore form-fitting jeans and a light white blouse, loose and billowy, the skin beneath just visible through the sheer fabric. The blouse made little whispering sounds as she moved, like secrets muttered in a crowd.

"You want to come in for coffee?" he asked, stepping aside and motioning with one arm into the house.

"Thanks, Joe, but I'll pass. I'm pretty beat, need to crash."

This wasn't exactly an excuse or lie. Joe could see the lines of exhaustion about her eyes. Her hair was mussed as if merely raked back by a comb or her fingers. Even so, Clara was the most beautiful woman he'd ever seen and he wanted to tell her this.

Rusty padded up behind Joe, squeezed in between his left leg and the doorway. The dog didn't immediately rush out to greet her. He paused at the threshold, looked from Joe to Clara, back and forth, indecisive.

Clara frowned. She glanced from the dog to Joe, scowling but not angry.

"What's going on here? You have bacon in your pockets or something?"

Joe shuffled a bit from one foot to the other. He felt like a kid about to tell his parents something embarrassing.

"I was actually hoping Rusty could stay with me a bit longer."

Those brown eyes widened in mock awe, and her brow furrowed inquisitively. "What kind of bachelor shenanigans have you boys been up to?"

Her singsong voice brought lilting notes to each word. Joe remembered breathy whispers in his ears on cool nights, bundled in damp sheets.

"I was hoping you'd stay too."

Caught off guard, Clara likewise shuffled, looked to the sides, turned, looked behind her as if there was something of interest out there in the street. When she turned back to him there was a stiffness to her posture. Her face, set but not hard, made her seem poised for defense.

"Joseph. This isn't the time."

There was no time like now. How to tell the mother of your dead child that her boy wasn't dead? Or, if dead, that death wasn't what we'd always thought?

He reached out. Put a hand on her arm. Took hold not with aggression, but tenderness and need.

"Come in, Clara. It's just a cup of coffee."

It was oh so much more. He needed her. *She* needed what he'd seen.

She didn't pull away from his touch. He felt her tremble, though. Not in fear but for the things that had been. Joe knew this because he felt it too.

Joe pulled gently, taking a step back.

She took one forward, not looking up, not looking at him, but down, as if perplexed by her feet going before her.

Once across the threshold, they paused together. She looked around at the walls about her. Joe followed her gaze. He thought they waited for the house or the world to shatter. Neither did, and he closed the door behind them, led his wife further inside.

3.

While neither house nor world shattered, as Joe led the way across the living room into the dining room, Clara saw the patched walls and floor and ceiling, the ladder still standing in one corner, and the empty and half-empty buckets of plaster and paint planted on the tarpaulin on the kitchen floor. Hands on hips, she spun slowly, taking it all in, her brow furrowing in a comically cute frown of long sufferance.

"What the hell's going on here, Joseph? I leave for a few months and this is what happens?"

Her tone wasn't so much anger as it was confusion. When she was facing him again, her mouth in a crooked smirk spoke of exasperation, but something like humor also.

"Renovations," Joe said, giving a shrug, his hands buried in his pockets.

"Well, they suck."

He laughed, indicated a chair at the dining table. Clara sat, folded her hands primly on the tabletop, looked about warily. The chair she sat in was the end one Evan had regularly occupied. Framed by the rear sliding glass door to the backyard, Joe could see the two holes in the yard behind his wife. The coffee pot beeped the completion of its brew. Joe turned away, filled two mugs, brought them to the table.

Taking the chair at the other end of the long table, nearest the kitchen, Joe felt they were at a conference, and not a husband and wife sitting together. Yet he knew the situation between Clara and him was tenuous and didn't want to crowd her.

"About the other day," he said after taking a sip, watching her do the same, the two of them peering at each other over the rims of the mugs. "The phone call?"

"Joe...."

The tone was as wary as the look she spared the rooms about them. But it wasn't *Joseph*, that vocalized warning that he'd crossed a line, done something wrong. Taking this as something of a good sign, Joe continued.

"Thank you for listening. I don't deserve your forgiveness. I wasn't the husband I should have been. He was your son, too, but I was too absorbed with my pain to help you with yours. I'm sorry."

Clara said nothing. She nodded, though, kept sipping at her coffee, remained seated. Each of these small things made Joe's heart swell with something like hope. She was *there*, in the house with him, and that was more than he'd ever thought possible. After a time she nodded again to the patched holes in the house, the ladder and the buckets.

"So, what really happened here? Looks like a war zone."

"If you spend the day with me," Joe said, "I'll tell you."

Her squinty gaze seemed penetrating, intelligent and seductive.

"You're not going all Jack Torrance on me, are you?"

"All work and no play makes Joe a dull boy."

"You want to play games with me, Joe?" she asked, her tone like her eyes now, demure and suggestive and coy all at once. "What kind did you have in mind?"

His resolve failed him. This was unexpected, more than he'd hoped, more than he was ready for. As he had the other day when placing the phone call to her parents' place and her father had picked up, Joe felt nervous, uncertain.

Joe stood and moved around the table to the rear glass door. Within inches of his wife, he felt a charge similar to that of the static electric current of the rift. He stared out at the holes in the ground, saw the rift clearly in his mind, and the things that had come from it.

Was this right? Bringing his wife into this? Should a husband willingly put his wife in harm's way? If – knowing what he knew – he was certain that she would *want* to be involved, did that change the equation?

What was right and wrong, Joe found, staring out at the holes in the yard where the black stones had burnt through the earth, marking the place where some portal to another realm, another world, had opened, was not so easily determined. The very existence of the rift changed everything. The lines between what he'd thought he'd known, and what was actually so, had been blurred and were blurring further still.

"Joe? Are you all right?"

The soft brush of soles on carpet approached him from behind. The secretive whisper-rustle of fabric against warm flesh. A light hand on his shoulder, pausing there, uncertain, then grasping, pulling him around.

Her face, looking up at him. The lines and curves of his dreams. The eyes round and dark and deep. The red lips parted, the breath escaped between them and puffed a caress on his. Joe leaned in, and for the first time in over a year kissed his wife long and hard and good.

The taste of her was life and light and all things good in a world gone so bad.

4.

A single kiss and Joe felt energized, refueled. That simple yet powerful contact – mouth to mouth, breath for breath – also brought clarity.

He decided to tell Clara most of what had happened over the past few days. But he would leave out any mention of Evan for the time being until he knew better what the rift was, what was over there, and what he was going to do about it. Just sharing the rift itself, its appearance and properties, with another person was like a burden lifted from Joe, and he felt tension leaving his body.

"It happened last Sunday," he said.

They stood over the two holes in the backyard, the depths of them black like miniscule mine shafts in the earth. Joe wished there was something to hint at their remarkable nature, but with the rift gone they looked like what they were: two holes in the ground.

"There's no bottom to them," he added, after telling her about the appearance of the rift, how he'd first thrown a garden rock into it, and then other things on the following nights. "I measured fifty feet with the hose. Nothing, no end, as if it just keeps going."

Joe couldn't read her reaction. She could have played for big money in Vegas with that poker face, flat and unexpressive.

"When I called, this was what you were talking about? Asking if I'd seen any lights during the drive to Phoenix?"

She made a little gesture toward the holes and the general space where he'd indicated the rift had formed.

Joe nodded. He waved for her to follow, knowing the holes themselves – without what had formed them – weren't very impressive. Fortunately, that wasn't all he had. Surprising him, Clara followed.

Back inside, from a cupboard above the refrigerator, Joe took down a rectangular plastic Tupperware container. He set it down on the dining room table and pried off the lid, the suction sound of its removal unnervingly like a moan to his ears.

He recalled how the first skin-scroll had rolled itself up and dove down the hole in the yard. In its plastic-walled prison, this second one sat still, as inanimate objects were supposed to.

Joe asked Clara to get the kitchen tongs. She looked at him with not quite apprehension but maybe delayed comprehension, blinked, then went to the drawers, found the tongs and brought them to him.

As Joe plucked the leathery scroll from the Tupperware container, he could feel her behind him, looking over his shoulder and into the plastic dish. Her minty breath puffed against him like a breeze, sending familiar tingles down the length of his body.

With the tongs and the spoon from his coffee mug on the table, Joe rolled the skin-scroll open.

"After tossing the rocks through, I wrote a note and threw that in too. This is what came back."

A hide-like material, not something that any standard office supply store would sell, the skin-scroll was a little more impressive than the holes in the yard. Clara actually made an inquisitive hum sound and pointed at the harsh, black-ochre script.

"What is that? Hieroglyphs?"

He still couldn't read her. Whether she believed his story or thought he needed to be institutionalized, he couldn't tell. But she was still there, hadn't made a mad dash for the front door.

"Do you know what it says?"

"It's not Egyptian," he said. "I looked it up."

This wasn't a lie, but it didn't answer her question either. Here was where he walked a line, wanting – *needing* – his wife on his side, and yet not ready to tell her everything. About what was over there on the other side of the rift, and what it meant for their son.

"I also tried to record the thing."

"The rift?"

The way she said that – the rift – was as if she were testing the words, speaking them for the first time. Weighing the syllables, deriving meaning from the sounds.

Joe nodded.

"You said 'tried'. What happened?"

Joe set the tongs and spoon on opposing corners of the skin-scroll, weighing it down on the table. He crossed to the living room, stopped before the entertainment center. He opened a cabinet there, blocking as much of the interior with his body as possible. Inside was another Tupperware container. Inside that plastic box was the bone-white, tendon-taped rift-VHS cassette. He couldn't show her that – not yet. She'd want to watch it. He'd play it for her if she asked him to. She'd see what was there to see, and then there was no telling what would happen.

Reaching around the plastic container holding the rift-cassette, Joe found the memory stick of the digital camera. He closed the cabinet door and turned back to Clara.

"This is what happened," he said, holding the small storage device up like a specimen between thumb and forefinger. "I recorded it for an hour."

Joe motioned for Clara to follow again and he led her upstairs. The hallway at the top was longer to Joe's eyes than it had ever been before. His office at the end of it seemed the finish line at the far side of an obstacle course.

In his office he told her to take the chair in front of the computer. When she was seated, he leaned over, inserted the memory stick into the flash drive, woke the computer and monitor up with a couple keystrokes. The dated, time-stamped recording of nothing blinked to life on screen; only the digital readout of the seconds and minutes ticking away at the bottom of the frame validated that they were actually *watching* a recording.

"The rift was right there in front of me. And yet the camera didn't record anything."

Here Joe was relying on her former trust of him before the dreaded day a year ago. The husband he had been, the faithful partner. Showing someone a blank recording and asking them to believe it depicted interference from a rip in the universe was asking for more than a leap of faith. It could also suggest delusion, rather than an actual experience.

Yet his wife's reaction was still unreadable, almost nonexistent.

"Say something," he said. "Do you believe me?"

Clara stared at the running time stamp on the computer monitor for a few moments longer. Then she turned away and walked to the leather sofa at the other side of the room, and sat down slowly. Joe stopped the playback, ejected the memory stick, dared to follow her and sat down at the other end of the sofa. Close, but leaving a space between them.

"Milton called me while I was at my parents," she said. She looked right at him, boldly, displaying no concern for his reaction to this revelation. "He told me you spoke to him, too, about seeing something strange. You asked him if he could look into things for you. See if there were test flights in the area, or whatever."

She paused, gave him an opening to respond.

Joe said nothing, waited for her to continue.

"That scroll is certainly strange. I don't think you'd just up and fabricate something like that. I don't disbelieve you, Joe. I think you saw something. I think something happened, I just don't know what."

At the mention of him fabricating the skin-scroll – even stated in the negative, that she *didn't* think he'd do something like that – Joe bristled. He ground his teeth for a moment, felt the whole of him tense. It lasted only a moment, though, as Clara was still there in the room with him, and her mere presence after having been gone so long was greater than his brief frustration.

"I'll stay tonight," she said. "But I know you well enough to know you're not telling me everything."

Her gaze was steadfast, uncompromising. She saw through him. He wilted beneath such scrutiny, bowed his head.

"If I see this thing tonight – this rift as you call it – you're going to tell me everything."

It wasn't a request. She wasn't brokering a deal with him. She was telling him how things would be, dictating the rules.

Joe nodded. He found the will to raise his head again and return her hard stare. "When you see it, I'll tell you everything."

Inside, in the place where right and wrong are always known, that reliable compass set and sure, Joe asked the God he'd once believed in to forgive him beforehand should that acquiescence to his wife, the woman he loved, prove his undoing.

5.

They passed a good portion of the day packing Evan's room. Knowing what he did about the rift, what the strange VHS tape suggested was on the other side, Joe had thought it would be a difficult thing to do. But he wanted Clara to stay, and when she suggested the two of them do this – as she had many months ago – Joe found the old anger and outrage gone.

The reasons for this were twofold, he thought. One was practicality: if his son was over there on the other side of the rift, he would be a year older, not the same boy as when he'd left this world. Superman posters and Spider-Man bedcovers probably went out of style for young teenagers. Reason number two was a bit more ethereal, harder to put into words: if Joe got his son back, he wanted to start things over. Not literally rewinding the clock, reeling back the years. That was impossible. But with his son's old things gone, and the shrine-like sense of sacredness they'd had on Joe likewise departed, maybe the three of them could mark a new beginning for their family.

As he and Clara worked – folding clothes, stacking books, labeling boxes – Joe saw his wife's gaze repeatedly roll toward the corner where Evan's bed was. It had been pulled away from the wall it had previously been set flush against, and the space it had occupied revealed a freshly plastered, patched, painted hole there at the lower corner.

When Joe was chasing down the rift crickets yesterday, sledgehammer in hand, this had been one of the final burrowed holes he'd discovered. The violation of this space had seemed to work both Joe and Rusty into a further frenzy than they'd already been, and the monstrously sized rift-insect they'd found here, clicking and clacking away under Evan's bed, had been furiously brutalized by hammer and canine jaws alike. Perhaps that in itself – bringing the fury of battle to his son's room – had in a way worked to break the spell his son's old belongings had over him.

"So," Clara said, nodding toward the patched hole in the wall, "at least tell me about the renovations."

She sat cross-legged on the floor behind a wide box, a damp rag in one hand wiping down various things – picture frames, Hot Wheels cars, action figures, and other artifacts of the lives of boys – and the other hand taking the wiped-down items and placing them into the carton.

Having heretofore left out the most disturbing aspects of the rift – what he knew the skin-scrolls read, the way the first had seemed to move of its own accord, his glimpse through the telescope of the creatures that roamed the black land on the other side, and yes, the giant ill-formed crickets that had Swiss-cheesed their home – Joe didn't know how to begin. Now, with the matter directly before him, he knew he had to tell her. He couldn't lie about what had made the holes in the house and ask her to stay for the rift's nightly appearance. She had a right to know, even if only by vague suggestion, that she could be in danger.

But he could carefully choose the details he shared.

"On the fourth night," Joe began slowly, "something came out of the rift."

Earlier, he'd suggested to her his theory of the rift's property of exchanging things. Rocks for rocks, notes for notes. He'd stopped there, though, and hadn't told her about the crickets from PetSmart. Now he realized with something approaching excitement that he had evidence other than the holes in the yard, the hieroglyphic leather parchment, and a recording of nothing.

Joe hadn't wheeled the garbage bins out for trash day.

He stood, waved once more for Clara to follow him, and led the way downstairs, out the back door, across the patio and to the side alley. Rusty trotted before them to the lopsided mountain of filled trash bags leaning against the wall there, lifted a leg and urinated on them

"This is what came out," Joe said, indicating the stacked bags. The gleam off the plastic sacks was dull and muted.

Distantly from inside the house the phone rang; a soft sound, hushed and forlorn.

Clara looked at him, and he nodded toward the fat black bags. Moving forward with slow, shuffled steps, she bent, grabbed the topmost garbage bag by the knotted drawstrings, and slung it to the ground at her feet. The bulging sack made a wet smack as it slapped the concrete. On her knees she undid the knots, unwound the cord, and pulled wide the opening.

The stench was strong and immediate. Joe could almost see the stench wafting out. The way Clara stumbled back, one hand pinching her nose closed, the other cupped over her mouth, made it clear she'd gotten a face full too.

Braving the reek, though throwing him a glance that said he'd pay for not warning her, Clara stepped forward again and looked down into the open trash bag. Joe walked up beside her.

Shards of black carapace, lengths of shattered serrated leg, broken points of clawed mandible, and a congealed puddle of yellowish slop like old vomit – all in a thick rounded mound – peeked out from the folds of the bag.

Clara turned away, stumbled toward the brick wall, and with a hand against it to brace herself, leaned over and threw up. Wiping herself clean with a sleeve of her blouse, she faced Joe again.

"What the hell…" she muttered.

And all Joe could think of as he smiled at her sympathetically was that he was glad he'd done this *after* he'd kissed her.

6.

At ten minutes to seven they sat together at the patio table. Their son's dog settled beneath it at their feet, his moonlit canine eyes fixed on the space where the rift would soon be. The blood-red dusk ushered in a greater darkness, unfolded across the heavenly expanse with a deliberate grace.

"What are you going to send through it this time, Joe?" Clara asked.

Seated on the other side of the glass-topped table, Joe glanced her way. The cream color of her face was pale in the evening and she seemed like a specter there, floating before him.

"Nothing this time. Tonight I just want you to see it."

"You know what the note says, don't you?"

The slow blinking of her eyes was like little portals opening and closing. Brief windowed glimpses of another place. *Not unlike the rift itself*, Joe thought.

He looked away from her, back to where the rift would zipper open in a few minutes. He nodded, said a soft 'yes' that was hardly a whisper.

"What did it say?"

Surprising himself, Joe told her.

Your son is here. All are here. The way between is open. Come.

The words repeated in his head as he spoke them to her, again and again like an audio track on a playback loop, so that he had to consciously force himself to stop thinking them. His wife's reaction was quick and fierce.

Across the span of the patio table her hand slapped down, gripped his forearm. Her nails latched on to him like claws, digging little crescents into his flesh. Joe tensed but didn't pull away.

"What?" she said.

That single word was a demand, a threat, and a curse all at once. Such force of will commanded him to look back at her despite the venom in her tone. The subtext of accusation hurt, and he felt like an injured animal cornered, the stalker-hunter bearing down.

"Clara...."

His pathetic weakness was clear in the way that word trailed off. Her pale oval of a face was no mere specter now, floating there hauntingly. It was twisted and contorted in something approaching hatred.

Then Joe felt the fizzle of the charge in the air.

The curtained *widening* of the partitioned sky before them.

The white-blue light of it glimmering off the pool's dappled surface. Spinning oh so slowly, like a toy ballerina on a geared music box. The motion of it darkly graceful and hypnotic.

"My God," Clara muttered, the rage in her gone now, replaced by the wonder Joe had felt each night over the past week. She stood, uncertain on shaky legs, crossed the patio toward the rift. One slim arm, one small hand, held out to the thing as if in supplication. "My God."

Joe was up and between her and the rift with an Olympian athlete's speed.

Her hands in powerful little fists struck him on the chest. She tried to move past him, around him, but Joe was there at each twist and turn, blocking her.

"Is he over there, Joseph?" she cried. The child-like wonder had disappeared. Now there was only maternal grief, old wounds ripped open anew, raw and aching. *"Is my son over there?"*

Joe heard another voice, other than his own and his wife's, calling out. His attention was on Clara, though, her face warped by pain as she leaned into him, beat on him, collapsed against him as her efforts failed, as the grief exhausted her.

"I don't know, Clara. I don't know!"

He tried to put his arms around her but she slapped them away. Flailing anew, she tried once more, ducking beneath his arms and darting toward the rift. He caught her, barely, his fingers clenched into her blouse tearing the fabric, the ripping of the threads loud in the night.

Far away came the pounding of fists on the front door. Footsteps thudding as the fists went unanswered, storming to the gate of the alley, past that barricade and coming toward them fast.

Rusty was there now, too, barking shrilly, adding to the confusion of things.

Spinning so that his wife was away from the rift again, his back to it, a wall between her and the tear in the air, Joe saw the man emerging from the alley. Milton Cooper, tall and long-limbed and gangly, striding toward them, arms wide as if asking, *What's all the ruckus about?*

He started to ask something like this, said he'd called earlier and no one answered so he came over and heard the yelling. The sentence was halfway out of his mouth when he saw the rift behind Joe and Clara. He stopped, mouth agape, pointing.

"What the fuck is that, Joe? Is that it? Is that what you came to me about?"

Joe nodded to his friend over his wife's still-struggling form. He indicated her with his eyes, and Milton, taking the cue, hurried over, tried to put his hands on her in comfort.

Clara thrashed once more. Rusty, in the midst of it all, squirmed out of the way. Milton tripped over the dog, stumbled. Joe, with Clara in his arms, moved out of the taller man's path.

From patio to grass there was an inch drop. Enough for someone already off balance to be caught off guard, to go sprawling further.

Joe watched in terror as his friend and colleague, Milton Cooper, dove face-first into the rift. As it had the fishing rod and its strange lure, the rift seemed to slurp him up like a morsel.

There was silence for a few moments. Clara went still in his arms. Their breath misted in plumes into the night air.

The rift pulsed three times.

What came out wasn't a man.

CHAPTER SEVEN

1.

Not a man but man-like, the thing that lumbered out of the rift possessed the basic features of the humanoid form. It swatted at Clara with a lumpish stump of an arm – a thick appendage knotted and knobby like a child's Play-Doh sculpture – and sent her careening across the patio. She hit the table with the small of her back, upturning it, and the glass top shattered into a thousand little daggers that sparkled in the moonlight. The dog ran to her aid and the rift-thing kicked at Rusty with a twisted and malformed limb, angled in strange ways at ill-placed joints. The Labrador yelped, the momentum of the blow sending him tumbling over the edge of the pool and into the water with a splash.

The thing then turned its attention on Joe.

The moment it had stumbled out, lurching toward them, Joe had spun toward the perimeter garden and the tools lined up against the fence. He tried to watch the awkward man-thing and find a weapon at the same time. Saw it strike his wife and then the dog. The large, flat, square spade of the shovel propped against the storage shed seemed just the right size for the monstrosity's head. Joe dashed for the shovel, snatched it up, and strode to meet the rift-freak just as Clara struggled up and the dog found the steps out of the pool.

Confused, Joe paused before the hulking horror.

He couldn't find the thing's face. An empty plane of waxy flesh was all that looked back at him.

With shuffling, clumsy strides it approached, reaching for him, yet the shovel hung in Joe's grip, dangling impotently at his side.

The man-thing was nude. But like its malformed limbs, the rest of it seemed...*runny*...like a wax candle melting. There was an enormous phallus a foot long, stiff and pointing in a permanent erection.

It came closer still, looming over him, and immobilized by fear, Joe watched. The thing's twisted anatomy and faceless head were *wrong*, impossible. Clara's motion caught the man-thing's attention and it adjusted its course, turning away from Joe and shambling again toward her. That's when Joe saw its face, and in sheer horror for his wife, yes, but also for himself, he was able to move again.

With its back to him, Joe saw the thing wasn't faceless at all. Its head was on backward. And the face was upside down.

The mouth was at the center of the forehead. Thin lips opened and closed and strings of glistening drool connected them in a wet web. The nasal passages were centrally located, as on a normal face, but below them were the eyes planted in a broad curvature where a chin should have been. They were colorless and roamed, rolling about in their sockets, as if searching frantically for something to fix upon.

Which they did once the inverted, backward head faced Joe.

It smiled, a wicked, perverted expression on that bizarre countenance, and shuffled more quickly toward Clara. Even from this angle the tip of the great member could be seen, and it pointed at Joe's wife like a large finger.

Joe yelled, raised the shovel high, and charged the man-thing. He swung hard, grunting with the effort.

The iron spade slapped the inverted face broadside with a tremendous clap, stark and surprising like thunder in the night.

The creature lurched, stumbled, but didn't fall.

Clara ran along the wall of the house, out of the way. A strange, strangled huffing screech, high and intermittent like a tea kettle whistling, issued from her throat.

Rusty, wet dripping coat pattering on the patio, darted to her side.

Half swiveled by the impact of the shovel, the waxen rift-man looked at Joe askance. Its upside-down face considered him with a sulky expression as if Joe had hurt the thing's feelings. Then its forehead mouth stretched wide, and it spoke.

Or what passed for speech where it came from.

The sounds were punctuated with consonant and vowel sounds like any earthly language. And the length of the noises varied, so that starting and stopping points could be distinguished, as with any spoken words and phrases.

But that's where the similarities ended.

It was a shrill and abrasive sound. Somewhere between screeching cats fucking in the night and arctic walruses honking. The issuance of the blast was harsh and offensive, like a loud car horn blowing within inches of a pedestrian.

Joe gasped, dropped the shovel, pressed his hands to his ears.

No way in hell did his neighbors not hear this.

It reached for him with thick, greasy sausage fingers. Joe saw the tips of the fingers ended with quivering sucker pads. With hungry anticipation these ten little mouths trembled eagerly.

Still holding his palms to his ears – even so, the creature's honk-screech was audible – Joe tried juking to one side. His flip-flop-clad feet slid on the wet trail and splashes left by Rusty's tumble into – and exit from – the pool. He fell, right ankle and knee smacking the concrete hard.

Standing over him, backward face now hidden from view yet somehow still *seeing* Joe, the rift-man reached down. The sucker pads quivered quicker in expectation. Its large rift-dick bobbed up and down stiffly like a conductor's baton. The thing's screech-honk became less alarming, more eager somehow, losing some of its volume but increasing in frequency. The great member throbbed disgustingly.

Joe knew what was coming.

He rolled away, toward the pool, just as the rift-thing ejaculated.

Where he'd been, the patio fizzled and smoked as if doused with corrosive acid. Large dollops of the thing's ejaculate arced toward Joe as the rift-thing readjusted its aim. Remembering the giant crickets that had dove into the pool a couple nights prior, not really wanting to swim in those waters but with no other choice, Joe rolled off the edge of the patio.

The water was shockingly cold in the early evening. His body went achingly numb for a few torturous seconds as it acclimated to the temperature. Underwater, Joe rolled over, looked up and through the surface. He saw the hulking rift-man, blurred and amorphous through the disturbed, rippled water, and kicked away from the pool wall with a tremendous push just as he saw the thing's cock pump once more.

Beneath the water he heard the dog barking. He heard his wife screaming. At the far end of the pool, Joe kicked to the surface, bench-pressed himself up and out. Water cascaded off him in trickles and splashes. He tumbled onto the patio, then stood carefully on his slippery flip-flops.

Across the blue stretch of the pool the man-thing looked at him with the faceless side of its head. Its organ continued to spill its load into the pool.

What used to be the pool started to boil. Like some thick broth over an oven flame, percolating gurgles issued forth with each bursting bubble. As if some living thing were under the surface, breathing.

Across the pool Joe saw Clara darting forward, reaching for the shovel he'd dropped. Turning from the frothing brew before him, Joe started around the pool, moving as fast as possible with the unreliable purchase of his flip-flops.

"Clara! Don't!"

But she already was. The shovel was in her hands. She hefted it up and over her shoulder. She wielded the length of the shovel sideways like an axe chopping. The sharp-edged spade flashed with its arc, the swoosh of its motion an eager, drawn-out breath.

It sunk deep in the rift-creature's neck. Sprays of oil-black blood spattered the concrete around it. Where the fluid landed, the patio smoked, sending up thin undulating tendrils.

Clara had the presence of mind to step back, avoiding the spray.

The rift-thing's shout shot up an octave or two again, from droning siren-warble back to cat-fucking-walrus-honking pleasure-rage. But its throat was torn. The cry lasted only a few moments, then stopped. The air of its cries blew forth from the tear in the neck, a hideous scratchy sound reminiscent of a hot wind through a hole in a wall.

As the spray of its wound died down, Clara stepped forth and swung-chopped again. The second chop freed the head from the body and it rolled a few feet along the wet concrete. The body leaned to one side, unsteady, gravity taking over, and collapsed with a thud.

The head continued to roll its eyes at them, from Clara to Joe, back and forth, accusatorily, the forehead mouth trembling with hatred.

2.

As a boy, Joe had been fascinated by his father's transistor radio perched on a shelf in the garage. Long rabbit-ear antennae turned experimentally this way and that, signals from across the state would come crackling in on the AM band from the speakers. Vague voices talking or in song rose up from beneath the fizz and hum of static interference. Stretches of silence would at times break the distant voices, so that in the dim light of the garage Joe imagined himself a survivor of the apocalypse, a hermit holed up in a bunker far beneath the earth waiting for the atomic fallout to clear.

The head of the rift-man on the backyard patio sat with eyes open – still roaming – and mouth agape, a low hiss escaping those quivering lips, interrupted then continuing like that old radio searching for a signal.

Clara, standing over it, raised the shovel again. She was shaking, and the shovel shook with her.

Joe held a hand out toward her.

"Don't," he said.

She looked at him, perplexed and angry. Her face contorted, moving from expression to expression – rage, terror, sorrow. She held the shovel high over her head, started to bring it forward in an arc.

Joe stepped boldly in front of Clara. Standing between her and the still-moving rift-head, her intended target, he imagined her swinging anyway and hitting him instead. Still, he held his ground.

"Don't," he repeated. "Can't you hear that? It's trying to talk."

She didn't swing. Instead, she lowered the shovel and leaned on it tiredly like a crutch.

He motioned her closer. Another wave of confusion rolled across her face as she tried to comprehend what he was saying. Joe saw clearly in his mind how she'd flailed against him when he'd told her what the rift-note had read, when the rift had appeared, and she'd charged for it.

She was on the brink. Dangerously staring down a precipice of distress and torment that, once descended, she might never rise from again.

Joe knew this well.

He'd been staring down the same chasm for nearly a week now.

Along with this borderline madness, though, of experiencing the rift and the dark promise it delivered of their son over there on the other side, was the knowledge – only days old but indisputable – that the things the rip in the air insinuated (*Your son is here. All are here. The way between is open. Come.*) were not what they appeared on the surface. Running down the mental list of what he'd already seen – the stones, the scrolls, the walking stick, the crickets – Joe found himself already thinking with rift-logic, gazing down upon the still-living head at his feet and considering it.

Perception and intent. Corrupted forms. An exchange of things. A mockery of what was sent in, returned. Each of these were close to the nature of the tear that even now spun on its axis behind him.

Which meant that the inverted, backward head still moving at his feet was more than just some freakish monster's warped countenance. It had a design, a purpose. Just as his friend, Milton Cooper, was the sum total of a lifetime of experiences, the aggregate assimilation of information by a human mind and the totality of human emotions – fears, hopes, love and loss – the thing at Joe's feet was something similar. What passed for a brain in that misshapen skull processed information and calculated things just as the human brain did, if for different reasons and with dissimilar goals.

It would have seen things over there across the rift. It would know the geography of the place. It could tell Joe of these things, prepare him for what was to come.

It could tell him about his son.

Behind him, the rift winked out. He was aware of it in his periphery: a light dimmed and gone, putting the patio and yard into a gloom challenged only by the weak illumination of the single bulb above the sliding glass door.

"Jooeee...."

His wife's tortured moan carried in the lonesome night like a fading sad song. She stumbled to where the whirling vortex had been, dropped heavily to her knees. Freed of her grip, the shovel balanced precariously for a moment, and then toppled with a thud like a felled tree. Face in her hands, she made terrible mewling noises that chipped away at Joe's resolve.

Taking up the shovel, Joe leaned closer to the hissing, humming head. With a careful scooping motion as if he were shoveling a major pile of dog shit, he maneuvered the head with its inverted face onto the spade. Then he began walking with it to the rear sliding door.

"Clara, come on."

His mind occupied with the possibilities of what information the head might possess, Joe's words held a mild heat and frustration he hadn't intended. But it seemed to have the desired effect. As he reached the door, he turned back to face Clara. Still on her knees, still sobbing, she'd nevertheless shuffled around and was facing him, face red and puffy.

"Joe...where's Evan? Where's my son?"

She made a vague gesture to where the rift had been, now just an empty space on a dark night.

Holding a shovel loaded with a decapitated head, Joe hoped his reply carried the note of optimism he intended. Standing in the backyard where an interdimensional monster had blown its load into his swimming pool, though, Joe wasn't sure if he succeeded.

"That's what we're going to find out."

3.

Before settling on physics as his major in college, Joe had briefly considered anthropology as a career. The rare but exhilarating branch of science that studied both social and natural phenomena – from ancient cultures to biological evolution – it had seemed the perfect area of study to find out both the why *and* how of things. Raised an Orthodox Catholic by his parents – as seemed a staple of life for most Mexican-Americans – then branching out to a more liberal, nondenominational Christianity in his young adulthood, Joe had always held dearly both the divine and the natural. In fact, he saw both as aspects of the same thing, complimentary sides of the same coin.

In his two semesters of anthropology classes Joe studied everything from the Mediterranean civilizations of the ancient Greeks and Romans, to the ever-popular-with-undergrads Egyptian dynasties, to the Mesoamerican cultures of the Aztecs, Olmecs, and Mayans. What he found fascinating early on in his studies, both as a student and a young man thinking of his own life and future, was that every civilization, everywhere, had stories of the heavenly and hellish spheres crossing over into the human realm. All cultures had prophets and clergy and shamans and magicians and incarnate gods and oracles, vehicles and vessels by which the supernatural forces interacted with man.

As he planted the rift-head on a spinning cake platter he had Clara retrieve from the kitchen, Joe wondered if that's what this thing – with its blinking chin-eyes and quivering forehead-mouth – in fact was: some sort of messenger of the gods. Remembering the brief glimpse of the rift-world he'd had when poking the telescope through the vortex – the black, glassy landscape, the skittering multi-legged things, the winged creatures in the blood-red sky, the striding giant – he thought if there were gods over there, then they were of the dark variety.

Picturing Soviet secret police interrogating civilians in dark Siberian gulags, Joe parked himself in a chair at the head of the table, facing the inverted rift-head on the cake platter. If he'd worn a crisp, sharply creased military uniform, now would be the time he'd snap the shirt smooth, brush away nonexistent particulates from the sleeves, and lean in close to his prisoner with a cold smile. He'd promise them that they'd go home to their families safe and sound if they just answered a few questions. Never mind the tray with the shiny surgical implements in the corner of the room.

Clara returned to the kitchen after delivering the cake platter. She stood at the sink, leaned over and peered out the window there. A good stretch of the street in either direction could be seen from that vantage point.

"Anyone coming?" Joe asked.

With the shattering of the patio table and the rift-man's screeches, he still thought it near impossible that no one had heard the commotion. Some twenty minutes had passed, though, according to the clock on the wall above the fireplace, since the opening and closing of the rift, and no one had come charging up the porch, pounding on the door. Emergency sirens sounded distantly in the city, but none approached their neighborhood.

"No," Clara said. "No one."

She crossed the kitchen tile floor with deliberately soft steps. Joe noted the way her arms were crossed protectively over her chest. She parked herself several feet away in the space between the dividing wall that separated the living and dining rooms. A good place with multiple exit routes; the front door, the back door, upstairs if there was no other option.

"Let's get this over with," she said, and Joe nodded.

Facing the head on the platter again, Joe began. "Where does the rift go?"

The upside-down, backward head blinked slowly. The orbs set in the space where the chin should have been stared out at him from a milky white and gray film, as if a dark cloud floated across its vision. Behind that fog was a deep blackness, the eyes themselves as black as the obsidian-like, glassy geography of the land it had come from.

The forehead mouth worked its glistening lips. They yawned open and inside that cavern was a thick yellowish twist of a tongue that flicked side to side, in and out, testing its confines. The voice that came forth – hissing, fading in and out like that old radio signal – was abrasive and painful to listen to.

"Desolation...."

The syllables were drawn out and enunciated, so that Joe heard *Dessss-sooo-laaaayy-ssshhhiiin.* More a hot wind through a length of pipe than actual vocalization.

"What happens over there?" Joe asked, thinking specifically of his son, but of Milton Cooper also.

"Ruination...."

Rooo-iiiin-aaayyy-ssshhhiin.

A desert wind given the powers of speech, blowing over a wide, white wasteland.

The stump of neck that the head rested on ended ragged and uneven, so the head leaned slightly to the right. From beneath the flaps of flesh at the end of the neck, strings of muscle and tendon flopped and curled like maggots. These little ropy tentacles stretched themselves, touching the diameter of the cake platter with tentative inquisitiveness as if they had minds independent of the head.

"Desolation. Ruination," Joe repeated. He recognized the absurdity of the situation. Talking to the head of a creature from another world or dimension or whatever. Yet the past week had primed him for the impossible, and the insinuation that his son was a part of the whole affair solidified the reality of the rift as nothing else could have. "What does that even mean? What's the purpose of the rift?"

The rift-head's misplaced mouth turned up in a derisive smirk.

"No meaning," it said. Each syllable was a dry, frictional sandpapery scrape, an assault to the ears and mind. *"No purpose. Only decay."*

"Decay of what?"

With his arms on the tabletop, Joe clenched and unclenched his hands into fists. He realized he was leaning slightly forward over the table, saw the flopping neck stump tissue unfurled and probing, and he leaned cautiously back.

"Everything."

He noticed he could feel the breath of the thing. Warm and arid and thick, it was as if the head emitted pollutants like a smokestack. The very air it drew in to speak was poisoned and spoiled upon exhalation.

Desolation. Ruination. Decay.

What Joe had seen through the telescope verified these things. The world he'd seen over there was dead or dying. The creatures that moved across its landscapes and skies could be nothing remotely similar to life here on Earth. The very word — *life* — did not and could not apply to the things there, he realized. And wasn't that the greatest mirror image yet from the rift?

He'd seen stone for stone, note for note, insect for insect, machine for machine, passed from here to there and back again. An exchange of properties of one item for the other in wicked funhouse mirror fashion.

If our world was the world of life — with all its pain and loss and disappointments and failures, sure, but the other things too, laughter and love and art and human endeavor — then the rift-world could only be one thing in its totality: the realm of death.

Steeling himself for the answer to his next question, wondering, even as the thought formulated in his brain, if he should ask it, Joe braved the proximity of the twitching, twisting torn neck strands and leaned forward again.

"No bullshit," he said, his tone tight and low and forceful. "Is my son really there?"

The rift-head's smile broadened. Its teeth were yellowed and blackened and ended in wicked little points. The cancerous twisted tongue licked them with eager anticipation.

"Come and find out."

4.

It was decided after a long and heated debate that Joe would cross the rift and Clara would remain behind. There was shouting and cursing and tears from both of them, and once Joe thought they almost came to blows. But he explained all his dealings with the rift over the past week, the things he'd sent in and what had come out, and how the exception had been his strange homemade fishing lure probe with the woodwork wagon. How when there was a chain of contact connecting what went through the rift firmly to *this* side – hand to fishing rod to fishing line to probe – things seemed *anchored*, and no exchange took place between worlds.

She would have to be *his* anchor.

But eyeing the still-moving rift-head on the platter; and remembering the rift crickets and their pulpy remains in the trash bags at the side of the house; and then turning and looking out the back sliding glass door and seeing the brackish brown fluid that had replaced the pool's blue waters; Joe knew he couldn't leave his wife (and his dog) in the house in its current condition. Which meant before they went shopping for his rift-traversing gear, they had some wet work to do.

*   *   *

Joe retrieved two pairs of thick work gloves from the Duramax storage shed set in the far corner of the yard. Standing over the decapitated waxen body of the rift-man, he and Clara pulled the gloves on and took up their tools. Joe had the shovel again and Clara claimed a long pitchfork lined up along the fence. Two forty-gallon trash cans were between them, one already half full with the droopy wet trash bags holding the dead rift-crickets. Looking from each other to the lumpish, malformed man-thing at their feet, husband and wife both gave small, simultaneous nods.

"Let's get to work," Joe said.

Clara sighed heavily.

"I knew there was a reason I left you in the first place," she said.

But there was a flash of a weak smile, and Joe smiled back. She was trying, God bless her, he thought. She was trying.

The body of the rift-man was strangely malleable, flexible not just at the joints, but along the length of the forearms and shins and even the back, where longer lengths of bone structure should have kept it firm and unbendable. But like a plush doll shoved into a full toy box – after some poking and lifting and pushing with the shovel and pitchfork – the entirety of the rift-freak was crammed into the trash can. Staring down at it packed in there – arms folded under legs, legs bent around the torso

– Joe thought of those snake-in-a-can party favors, where pressurized papier-mâché serpents popped out when the lid was snapped open by some unsuspecting schmuck.

Clara knelt, picked up the lid to the can and fitted it down, covering the mangled body. Joe went inside, came back carrying the cake platter, and upended the rift-head into the second trash can atop the bulky sacks holding the pulverized cricket-things. It landed with a muffled thud atop the black plastic; the head's eyes watched them still and the forehead mouth continued to grin.

The wet lips worked as if to say something.

Clara drove the second trash-can lid home, cutting off whatever the thing had been about to say.

"Let's go," she said.

And so they went.

In the Explorer, Joe driving, Clara in the front passenger seat, Rusty in the rear, it was almost like old times. In the cool and quiet evening they could have been a family going out for a movie. If dogs were allowed into theaters, that was, and if not for the two trash cans shoved into the cargo bay of the SUV.

In the rearview mirror Joe could see the rounded tops of the cans. A couple times when the Ford bounced over a bump or dip in the road, they jumped or swayed a little, and their contents bumped their rubber confines with sounds like light rapping on a door. Joe had a horrifying thought of the rear hatch releasing for some reason, rising open, and the trashcans rolling out, the lids popping open, and monstrous cricket parts and a headless body and a bodiless head scuttling away into the night.

Ever present in the back of Joe's mind – despite the SUV's grotesque load and the events of the night so far – was the proximity of his wife. They hadn't slept in the same bed for over half a year. Hadn't been intimate for even longer than that. But now the nearness of her sparked a heightened sensitivity in every square inch of him. His right arm on the center armrest dividing the seats brushed hers occasionally, and like a schoolboy seated close to a beautiful girl in the auditorium benches, Joe's heart leapt and an electric thrum coursed through him.

The northern outer bounds of San Bernardino touched mountainsides with roads that slowly rose and dipped with an almost fluidic rhythm. The miles passed smoothly, the car seemingly buoyed in the dark expanse drifting along a cosmic current.

The quarry opened before them mouth-like, cavernous and wide.

Great machines had excavated the quarry decades ago. Long drills penetrated the earth, powerful explosives blasted impressive scars upon it, and years of weathering had widened the whole of the site into something of a lopsided crater. Half of the vast hole was along a flat plane of the mountain; half crawled up the side vertically. Almost a doorway into the mount's rocky wall.

Joe stood at the rim of the grand hole in the middle of the night; the bottom was lost in a deep swath of blackness. If Joe and Clara hadn't known better — as a young couple they'd had a number of packed lunch dates in this very area — it could have been that the quarry *had* no bottom at all, and was a drop through the Earth, through eternity. A winding metal stairwell led down from the rim where they were parked, and descended into that unfathomable shadow, the railing and meshed walkway first dimming and then disappearing altogether. Cut off quick and sharp as if erased from existence.

Joe opened the hatch of the Explorer and he and Clara eased the two trash cans down from the storage bed. Each sway and jostle of the trash cans produced a wet sloshing from within, like soup in a bowl. Together, they shimmied each receptacle upright to the rim of the quarry, then turned back to the open hatch and grabbed for the other items there.

Clara snatched up the long box of fireplace matches and the flashlight.

Joe picked up the gasoline canister.

The headlights were on but lighting the road in the other direction; the bulky Eveready flashlight's bright, wide beam provided enough light for them to see their work by. Clara set it on the edge of the tailgate, aimed it out and over the quarry. She adjusted it according to Joe's directions, then stood aside.

Joe lifted first one trash-can lid and then the other. He did so with arms extended, leaning back, like a man working with a sensitive material that might explode in his face at any moment. He drenched the bent, folded, contorted body first, the gasoline's pungent fumes heavy, wafting up to his eyes and nose and mouth. This done, he turned to the second trash can. Flipped the lid up and open.

The inverted face of the backward rift-head stared straight up, unblinking, smiling still, as if it hadn't moved at all since the drive from the house. Then it winked at him.

Joe upturned the gasoline canister, spilling the amber fluid into the thing's abominable countenance. It blinked now, the liquid burning the milky eyes, and it coughed and sputtered as the gasoline splashed into its open mouth.

"Do it," Joe said.

Without hesitation Clara stepped forward, struck a match. The flame was strong and bright in the night, a red-orange as dazzling as the sun. She dropped the first match into the waste receptacle holding the pretzel-twisted body. The flames flickered high and snapped and crackled like flags in the wind. She turned next to the can holding the cricket parts and the head, withdrew another match, lit it, dropped it in.

As it whooshed alight and burning, the rift-head gave one more of its shrill screeching-honking cries. Above the quarry, with stone walls all around, the thing's shriek rebounded in every direction.

Joe pushed one can to the edge, heaved it over. Clara did the same with the other. The flaming receptacles rolled and bounced into the yawning black pit. Like volcanic fireballs they lit the walls of the quarry as they descended and the light on the rocky, jagged sides threw up shapes and shadows.

Moving before thinking, guided by heart rather than mind, Joe reached out, found his wife's hand, held it tight. There was a shuffling from behind them as the dog exited the vehicle and padded up beside him. With the remnants of his family at his side for the first time in a year, Joe Jimenez looked out over the great black pit, wondered about the things the darkness held, but also the beam of the flashlight shining into it, strong and steady.

CHAPTER EIGHT

1.

After switching on the filtration system and dumping five gallons of liquid chlorine into the murky pool, Joe stepped aside to watch what happened. Far more chlorination than normal, he was hoping the shock treatment – usually reserved for such situations as algae growth or bacteria – would have some effect on the scum from the rift-freak's bodily fluids. Seeing the brownish gloom of the pool water gradually swirl away to at least a semi-natural tone, Joe was a little more comfortable with leaving Clara behind, alone in the house, as his anchor.

Clara was a few feet away, hunched over the ruins of the patio table, a wastebasket at her side, picking up gummy shards of glass and depositing them into the plastic liner. As he watched, he saw her reach behind with one hand and massage her lower back, where she'd collided with the hard rim of the table.

Joe walked over to her, put a hand on her shoulder. She looked up, tried a smile. Wetness glimmered jewel-like at the corners of her eyes.

Lifting gently but insistent, unrelenting, Joe brought her up to a standing position, spun her slowly around and led her inside. Rusty, curled in a corner of the dining room, watched their two-person procession with content curiosity.

Joe lowered Clara onto the living room sofa. The cushions accepted their burden with a relaxed billowy sigh.

She had a hand on his shoulder and the other on his face. Light fingertip touches brushed his cheek with a dancer's graceful assurance. Clara's eyes held his for a time. Joe smiled down at her, then turned her onto her stomach.

He rolled the hem of her blouse up inch by inch, revealing smooth skin marble-white in the dim light of the house. A blue-purple band of bruising striped her flesh across the lower back.

Joe stroked the bruise with his fingertips, barely making contact. Clara breathed in and out audibly with each touch, the drawn-out moans escaping from between the throw pillow her face was buried in, hitting notes somewhere between pleasure and pain.

They remained like that for a time, Saturday morning crawling along, replacing the deep-purple of the prior evening with a bright blue sky and a fire rising above the horizon in the east. As the sun revealed the Earth beneath its light, laying everything bare, so too did they lay each other bare, tentatively peeling off layers of clothes and dropping them to the floor.

Husband and wife held each other close and warm in the early hours.

2.

Showered and dressed again, seated at the table where a bodiless head had conversed with them the night prior, Joe and Clara spooned up eggs and sausage, mopped up the remains with toast, and chased it all down with tall glasses of orange juice. There hadn't been much conversation since they'd awakened on the couch, their naked bodies touching in a dozen places. Breakfast was eaten in silence, though they shared furtive glances like teenagers, turning away only to look sidelong at each other again when they thought the other wouldn't notice. Under such pleasant uncertainty, the only solution was to ignore the situation and change the subject.

Unfortunately, the change of subject wasn't nearly as pleasant.

"Have you thought about what that place is?" Clara asked as she took up the dishes and glasses and carried them to the sink.

"What place?"

Of course Joe knew what she referred to. But a few seconds' delay could steel the heart and mind, fortifying resolve.

"The other side of the rift," his wife said, sitting down again across from him.

"I think it's pretty clear what it is. It's the place of the dead."

"Because Evan's there."

She said this with her hands beneath her chin, her voice muffled, like a secret cautiously shared.

"Yes," Joe said. "Because Evan's there."

"But he's not the only one over there."

Joe didn't immediately reply.

"There's the other things, Joe. The creatures. Like the thing last night. And the insect things you told me about. If it's just the land of the dead, then what are those things? They sure as hell don't look like anything that ever lived."

Joe pushed the last crumbs of his breakfast around his plate, like an archaeologist hoping to uncover some ancient artifact. Whatever he was looking for wasn't there and he said nothing.

"What if it's lying?" Clara said. He'd thought of this himself before. Hadn't liked it then, didn't like it now. "What if Evan isn't over there?"

Joe looked up from the plate. Stared hard at his wife.

"What if he is, Clara?"

He saw the same firm resolve he felt inside settle on her face. She could never look hard and cold. Her beauty was too refined, too deep. But the set features of her face right then and there, the unyielding tenacity in her eyes, told Joe all he needed to know. She was with him.

Looking at him, unflinching, she nodded.

She was with him until the end, as such things were meant to be.

★   ★   ★

The shaggy-bearded swap-meet vendor was in the same spot he had been last time, lounging in his chair under the tarp-shaded stall displaying his wares. He tipped the bill of his ball cap to Joe and Clara, as Joe pointed to what they needed and they began to gather it all up.

Pitons, clasps, rope and a large canvas rucksack to carry it all in. Sledgehammer and ball peens and the looped tool belt Joe already had at home from his last visit, along with a hand axe from the garden shed and various knives from the kitchen, even now laid out in the living room waiting for him. However, among the lounging vendor's tables and boxes Joe saw something else he wanted, propped up against a rear tire of the man's pickup truck as if forgotten. A little paper price tag was tied with string around the haft, and Joe knelt, inspected it, picked it up.

The machete was long and shiny and wicked-looking in the bright light of day.

"Going on safari or something?" the lounge man asked, waving Rusty over. He scratched the dog behind the ears.

"Something like that," Joe said with a smile. He turned the machete over, tested the blade with a thumb, and added it to his purchases.

With everything boxed and loaded into the rear of the Explorer, they drove to a dog-friendly sandwich shop with a dining patio. Under the shadow of their table's umbrella the day was comfortably warm. To Joe, as pleasant as it was eating out with his wife on a sunny day, it felt like the last meal before an execution. Rusty didn't seem to mind, though, and patiently awaited scraps from his place under the table.

"I need a gun," Joe said.

He hadn't been too keen on broaching this topic. Raised by a lawman, Clara had a healthy respect for firearms and had always opposed having one in their home. There was no reason for it, she said. Their neighborhood was completely safe, and too many guns in too many untrained hands was trouble waiting to happen.

Joe had never pressed the issue. He'd never really wanted a gun anyways. It was more of a macho thing with his wife and kid in the house, that he felt he had to be prepared for all things. And even if *his* hands were untrained, hers weren't. Clara had learned her way around guns at an early age. *She* could teach *him*.

But he'd dropped the matter. Until now.

Surprisingly, seated across the table from him, Clara merely nodded. She finished her sandwich, washed it down with her soda, and dabbed her lips daintily with a napkin.

"I've got that covered," she said.

Clara swung her purse onto the table, reached into it and pulled out a revolver.

Apparently, in the past, as a mother with a child to look out for, a gun in the house had been a bad idea. Now, as a woman whose child had been murdered and dumped in a ditch, a gun in the purse seemed a very *good* idea. Maybe the best idea ever.

They drove to a shooting range downtown after lunch. Leaving the dog in the Explorer with the windows halfway down, Joe turned at the front door to give Rusty a little wave. Trees in the parking lot provided ample shade for the Labrador, yet he couldn't help but feel a little twinge of guilt leaving the mutt behind, if even for a short time. Clara, opening the door to the shooting range, looked back also, saw the exchange between Joe and the dog.

She leaned close to his ear.

"Seeing you like that with him," she whispered, "would make Evan happy."

He forced himself to face her. Smiled a tight smile. Went past her and inside.

The front of the building was a gun store, with rifles and shotguns on racks along the walls, stacked boxes of ammunition under tables and at the ends of aisles, and pistols and revolvers under glass cases providing the perfect stockpile to hold off any army of marauders during Armageddon. There were half a dozen lanes at the back of the place making up the shooting range, separated from the rest of the store by a wall and viewing area with a large bulletproof glass window. A burly clerk sat on a stool with hourly prices and gun rentals on a magnet board above him. Joe was surprised again when the big man greeted his wife by name and an amiable, full-toothed grin.

"I think you're becoming one of our best customers, Clara," the man said with a bumblebee rumble of a voice.

He brought a box of ammo up from under the counter he sat behind and plunked it down on the glass for her. Clara already had her wallet out and passed over her VISA card. Joe stood by and watched this little routine, for some reason all too aware of how much he'd missed in the last year, how much had changed. He felt guilty about it too.

"Oh, don't play coy with me, Bob," she replied. "I know your ploy here. Reeling in vulnerable young women with all you strapping, handsome men. Get them to buying guns with your sweet talk about muggers and serial rapists on the loose."

Bob — thick as an oak and probably as heavy — blushed like a schoolboy with a crush. Joe half expected an 'Aw shucks' from the large man and an embarrassed, dismissive wave.

"Give me one of those, too," Clara added, pointing to a poster-sized body target behind Bob. Hanging from the wall there, instead of the common black body outline with its zones and circles, the target depicted Osama Bin Laden, caricatured with great bushy Middle Eastern beard and desert robes. "Feel like being patriotic today."

She winked at Bob as he grabbed a copy of the target, making him blush more deeply. Then she waved Joe over to the door that led to the range, opened it, followed him inside, and closed the door behind them.

Talking about owning a gun and actually holding one were two very different things. As Clara pressed the button that brought the target board reeling toward them on its electric track from the far end of the lane, Joe held the revolver, unloaded, in his right hand, turned it over, passed it to the other hand, testing the feel of it. It was heavier than he expected, the weight of it solidifying the purpose of such a device in his mind.

You pull the trigger. Someone dies.

Knowing he had no intention of shooting another human being, knowing the only things he'd be shooting at were hellish creatures from…well, *Hell*…Joe still felt a flutter of sickness tumbling in his stomach. He set the gun down on the counter of the booth they were in, stepped back, waited for Clara.

When she finished attaching the former leader of Al Qaeda to the target frame, Clara sent the desert madman halfway down the shooting range with another button press. Little buffets of wind picked up by the track's passing made the target dance and sway. When she was done,

Clara stepped up to the counter and picked up the revolver. In the small booth together, they were shoulder to shoulder and Joe could smell the soapy fresh scent of his wife.

"This is a Smith & Wesson 38 Special," Clara said, lifting the gun for his inspection, yet keeping the muzzle aimed downrange. Joe tried to focus on what she was saying, but his eyes kept drifting elsewhere. "One of the mainstays of home defense. An old favorite for law enforcement."

Joe nodded when she looked at him to see if he was paying attention. He was paying attention all right, but to something else other than the revolver.

"Most of this is common sense," she said as she released the revolver's cylinder, opened the box of ammunition on the counter, loaded the gun. "But you'd be surprised how many stupid gun owners shoot themselves or family members or friends, because they don't have a healthy respect – and fear – of the weapon in their hands."

Joe watched her fingers deftly sliding the brass rounds home. Each slight spin of the cylinder as she loaded the six bullets was hypnotic. Done, she nodded toward the earphones hanging on the walls of the booth and Joe handed one pair over to her, put the other over his own head. He lifted one foam earpiece when he saw she was still speaking.

"This is a double-action revolver. You can just squeeze the trigger as is, which gives you some resistance. Or you can cock the hammer first..." she showed him, pulling back the hammer with her right thumb, "... and then pull the trigger, which now is much more sensitive, requires less of a squeeze."

She took a strong shooter's stance: right arm out, left a little lower and tucked, left hand cupping the butt of the revolver, both elbows locked, legs set a bit apart, back straight. She motioned to Joe to stand back a bit. He did, covering both ears again with the earphones.

Clara squeezed the trigger six times. Six loud roars rebounded off the stone walls of the firing range, startling Joe even with the earphones on. Half a dozen new orifices appeared on Osama Bin Laden's caricatured likeness; five in the face, one in the throat. The spent casings made a metallic tinkling as they hit the floor and bounced about.

Clara set the revolver down, lifted her earphones off. Joe did the same, realizing he'd taken a couple more steps back from his wife as she'd fired away.

"That's lesson number one," she said, pointing at the target down range, the terrorist's ravaged face. "Never point a gun at something unless you intend to shoot it."

Joe superimposed the cartoon face on the target poster with a real human countenance. Saw the splattered blood and shattered bone quite clearly.

"I am *really* sorry for the way I've treated you."

Clara smiled and patted him on the cheek. She stepped aside, motioned for him to take her place. When Joe was standing where she'd been, the gun and box of ammunition before him, she stepped up behind him, brushing up against him as she looked over his shoulder, gave him instructions.

He thumbed the cylinder open and loaded six rounds in the chambers, far less smoothly than Clara had, nearly dropping a few of the bullets. He imagined the brass shells striking the ground, going off, hitting him in the foot or groin or something. Some rift freedom fighter he'd be then – footless or dickless – hospitalized for a month.

The revolver loaded, Joe closed the cylinder and did his best impression of his wife's shooter's stance. Clara leaned closer, reached slowly around, helped him make some adjustments. Showed him where to look down the barrel of the gun to aim.

The tips of her breasts poked him in the back as she steadied his arms, adjusted his grip on the gun. Brief brushes of her stomach and pelvis against his hips and thighs brought pleasant tremors up and down Joe's body. Earphones hanging askew, he heard his wife's voice quite clearly as she leaned in closer, breathing into his ear.

"Focus," she said, puffing the word playfully into his ear. "You're not going to kill any rift-monsters with the gun in your pants."

She put his earphones in place, rubbed up against him.

Laughing, Joe elbowed her away, focused on the target down range and took aim. Pulled the trigger. Being the one pulling the trigger this time, he thought the roars seemed even louder. He felt each shot reverberate throughout the entirety of his body.

Two found the target, one hitting the edge of the target poster outside all the scored zones, one punching a hole in the desert sheik's shoulder. The other four went wide, missing entirely.

"Shit," Joe muttered, pulling the earphones down too roughly around his neck.

The fun was over. The frightening thrill of the power of the gun was gone. In his mind was only his son, now, on a black, charred landscape, being dragged away by rift-monsters, and Joe firing harmlessly in all directions, missing the freaks, failing his boy. Again.

Clara sensed the change in his mood. She stepped up close again, not in seductive flirtation this time, though, but in tenderness. Set a hand on his shoulder.

"We'll try again."

And they did.

Four of six shots hit the target on Joe's next try. On his third attempt, he stared down the barrel of the revolver, commanding every inch and fiber of himself to be still, *pulling* the target toward himself in his mind's eye. All six shots hit the target.

The shots were scattered. His accuracy could be better.

But they all hit what he intended to hit. That was something.

I'm coming for you, son. I'm coming.

3.

Back home, Joe and Clara eyed the supplies laid out on the table before them. Knives, hammers, hatchet, machete, rope, pitons, clasps, rucksack, and gun. An impressive array for any survivalist camp out in the woods or mountains. For the rift it all still seemed inadequate.

Clara picked up the coil of rope, eyed it, her head tilted a bit in thought. Set it back down again.

"That's not going to get you very far."

The rope had been measured at fifty meters by the lounge-chair guy at the swap meet, and Joe had thought the very same thing then. The impracticality of his plan had hit home, but he hadn't shared his concerns with Clara at the time. There was no saying how deep into the land of the rift he'd have to go to find Evan. The boy could be close to the entrance of the rift *over there*, on that side, or miles away. Having Clara serve as his anchor, keeping the chain of contact that would tie Joe to *this* world and inhibit the exchange of things when he went through, splaying out miles of rope, was unrealistic.

"Tonight is just an experiment," he said. "Think of it as a control test. We need to see if I can get over there, and come back."

Clara moved to the living room sofa, sat down before the television where a couple nights ago Joe had watched a rift-video depicting the silhouette of a child, calling out for him. Her attention wasn't on the television, though, but on the book on the armrest next to her. He hadn't noticed the leather-bound volume until just then, but he knew Clara must have pulled it out earlier.

She brought her legs up onto the cushions, turned so she could see Joe over the backrest. She picked up the Bible and set it in her lap. With a thumb she flipped idly through the gold-edged pages, producing a brushy whisper from the book.

When she spoke she didn't look at him. Her gaze drilled the cover of the Good Book, as her fingers riffled through the pages.

"Do you believe in God, Joseph?"

There it was, his full name.

"Clara, is that really a discussion we need to have right now?"

He tried to keep his tone patient and even. Irritation, frustration, and anger would do nothing but send them both into a twisting, uncontrollable freefall. They'd crash and burn, and the last couple days, during which Joe sensed there'd been something like a reconciliation between them, would be dashed and lost.

"You used to," his wife said. Her tone was soft and vaguely sad. The exhausted sadness of an old, familiar pain. "You were never a holy roller or a Bible thumper," she continued drumming the Bible now with the pads of both thumbs, "and I loved that about you. That your beliefs were just part and parcel of who you were. That you didn't have to shout them from the pulpit, didn't have to shove them in people's faces."

Joe tried ignoring her. He hoped that if he didn't respond she'd drop the issue, move on to something else. He eyed the equipment on the dining table again. That trip to the other side of the rift was looking pretty good just about now.

"Because if you do – still believe in a god, that is – then you have to think about what all of this means." She looked at him then, and though Joe saw her in his periphery, he kept his gaze firmly on the gear and weapons splayed out before him. "God knows I want it to be true. I want our son back. But I can't help thinking maybe this isn't the way. That to do what we're thinking of doing is against the natural order of things. Against *His* order…."

Here she trailed off and pointed upward toward the ceiling, beyond the ceiling, the vast eternity above and in all directions. Joe saw this too from the corner of his eye. Still he didn't answer her; he stared raptly at the things on the table. Something was building up in him and it was of utmost importance that he didn't let it out.

"What if it was meant to be?" she said, her voice cracking. "What if – however hard it is for us to accept – things happened the way they did for a reason? Evan dying—"

Joe slammed a fist down on the table. The hammers and knives and machete and revolver rattled with the blow in a discordant percussion.

Clara gasped.

Leaning on the table, palms pressed against it for support, Joe turned slowly to look at his wife. He struggled to see her for the woman she was, the woman he loved, and not the stranger taking potshots at his heart and soul that he felt she was now and had been a year ago.

"Evan didn't die, Clara. He was murdered. Thrown into a ditch. I saw the pictures. Would you like me to describe them for you?"

He advanced on her. Strode around the table, around the living room sofa so he stood before her. Towered over her.

"He was facedown in the dirt."

"Joe…."

She held a hand out to him, pleading. The thing in him coming out didn't care. It had been there, deep down, for over a year. Eating at him. Devouring him. Waiting, watching, biding its time. Now here it was, and Joe felt like the observer now, waiting, watching, unable to stop the course of events. He felt as if he'd stepped through the rift and something like him, but not quite him, had come out.

"His right arm was snapped like a twig, Clara. Like a fucking stick, broken. Parts of his head were caved in. Goddamn...*stuff* was coming out one ear. I think it was brains. His *brains* were smashed right out his fucking ear."

He leaned over her. Spit the words at her.

She cried, shrinking away. She tried to scuttle away, but the contours of the sofa gave her no escape route. She had nowhere to go.

"Joe, please...."

"Joe, please..." he mocked in a wicked singsong voice, like a petulant child reciting a schoolyard rhyme. "How about you please shut the fuck up?"

He pointed at her much as she'd pointed at the ceiling. But where her pointing had been inquisitive, asking him his thoughts on a matter, his finger jabbed like a sword, stabbing.

"Do you have any idea what I've been through in the past year?" he said. "Evan left me, and then you left me. I was here all alone."

He waved his arms about to take in all the house around them. The walls, the photos on the walls, the family in the photos. The empty spaces where people and the things they did – laughter, smiles, the *presence* of them – had once been.

"All alone, Clara. And no one gave a shit. No one. I spent every day, every week, every month, for a whole fucking year, wondering what I'd done wrong. What did I do to deserve having my son taken from me? And then everyone leaving me to fucking rot?"

The tears racked her as the sobs had in the backyard, when she'd kneeled before the area where the rift had been. When she'd faced him and begged, asking where her son was. It felt good to Joe, passing on the pain he'd felt for so long to someone else.

He jabbed his finger at her once more. "We're doing this." His hand and pointing finger jerked with the words, as if he'd squeezed off a round from the revolver at the firing range. "I'm going through, and you'll stay here to anchor me. Whatever has my son over there...I'll find it, kill it, and bring Evan back. And if that's not part of the *natural order of things* or *His plan*, well He can take His order and plans and shove them up His holy ass."

Something in his wife changed shortly thereafter, too. Just as Joe had released the knotted pain in the pit of his stomach, Clara, having listened to his tirade, released something also. Her trembling subsided. The fear dissipated. She watched him all the while, as he watched the clock and the minutes and the hours pass, but not with dread or worry. Oh no, Joe thought, as he spied glances at her, saw the change in her, it wasn't fear of him anymore on her face. The downcast aim of her eyes. The way she only looked at him askance, and fleetingly, as if she didn't care for what she saw. The firm, stern set of her mouth.

It was pity that Joe saw in his wife's face.

She pitied him, and if Joe hadn't needed her to hold him to this world so that he and his son could get back, he would have told her to leave, screamed at her all the way to the front door. Slammed it in her face as he corralled her out onto the porch, and good riddance.

There was none of that, however, and they watched each other from across the rooms as one keeping an eye on a rabid dog. Keeping their distance.

And they waited for the rift.

4.

The nylon climbing rope was cinched around the loops of the tool belt encircling his waist. The ball peens were in their holsters again at his hips. The rucksack slung over his shoulders carried the loaded revolver, a spare box of ammunition, the hatchet, a couple kitchen knives, the pitons and clasps, a few sandwiches he'd slapped together, and two bottles of water. The machete was slid scabbard-like into a pair of vertical loops on one side of the backpack, and the haft stuck out over his right shoulder.

Clara and Rusty stood at the threshold of the rear sliding glass door, looking out at Joe on the patio. His wife wore an expression of empathy bordering on vague distaste. The dog showed a deep stoic sadness only the canine breed could muster. Those round eyes seemed to be telling Joe this wasn't the way things had to be.

Joe hung his head for a moment. Took a long breath. When next he looked up he faced Clara.

"I'm sorry," he said, feeling like a broken record repeating the same old tune over and over again. "I know it probably doesn't mean anything anymore, but I am. I'm sorry. But I can't do anything else. This is the way it has to be."

He gave the knotted rope at his middle another cinching squeeze, testing it for the hundredth time. He saw how it led from him to a coiled bundle at her feet, and then from there to a small length in her strong, delicate hands. He to her, she to him. Even on this, possibly the last day of their marriage.

"I'll bring our son back. You'll see."

Clara tried a smile. It looked cheerless and not at all like a smile was supposed to. In her eyes there seemed an emptiness that was somehow the worst of all possible things. It reminded Joe of the emptiness of the house in the past months.

Behind him the rift twirled open, a small whirlwind that produced no wind, no motion but its own rotation. Its light, of a shade and luminosity not of this world, vertically slashed like an eye.

Joe approached it slowly but steadily. Each step was a monumental challenge, a marathon dash, an epic climb. Closer, it seemed larger, not an eye anymore but a mouth yawning, stretching, ready to swallow him down into depths unfathomable.

He stepped through it to what lay beyond, and he knew hell, and nothing was ever the same again.

CHAPTER NINE

1.

The ground was hot, as if he trod barefoot across a scorched desert landscape. Even through his boots, Joe felt the heat of it rising up. The surface he stood upon was charcoal – black, burnt bare of all distinguishing features – no dried vegetation, no crisped trees, nothing. Only a dead, cracked plain stretched before him.

The sky was a deep red, almost magenta, like a vast bruising upon creation itself. A moon – not ours – was large in that bloody expanse, so great and bold up there it could have been on a collision course with the ebon volcanic land he walked upon.

Umbilical-like, the rope ran behind him from the waist back into the vertical slash in the air. That spindle-rip, that cold reptilian eye, purveyor of worlds. Joe took up the line in one hand, gave a short, sharp tug to signal his successful crossing as they'd agreed he would. Moments passed and then a tug came in return from the other side.

Turning again to face the breadth of the other realm, the destitution and bleakness, he started out. With every stride the muggy heaviness of the atmosphere, hot and stale, seemed to weigh upon his shoulders. It was like a fist, hard and angry, pressing down on him. Trying to push him into the ground.

Hardly minutes had passed before the weight of the pack on his back added to the discomfort, and Joe felt he carried not a rucksack of supplies but a mountain upon his shoulders. If he could have, he would have cast it off, and was tempted to, but even in the unbearable heat and the stagnant air he remembered his son and kept going. He used the sledgehammer as a walking stick, allowed it with each step to support some of his burden.

He saw the flying creatures first, soaring distantly like specks peppered across the sky. This uncountable flock banked in his direction, though, and came closer, increasing greatly in size. Joe ducked low even as they passed hundreds of feet above.

Their wingspan was meters wide, the wings leathery and thickly veined. Curled claws tipped in dagger points flashed in the strange light of the bulbous moon. Curved beaks protruded from wrinkled countenances with squinty, colorless eyes. Hanging from the serrated beaks were limbs, mostly human. The cries of the alien birds weren't song but the abrasive calls of avian hunters.

Joe set the pack on the ground, unzipped the large compartment, and withdrew the revolver. Pack back over his shoulders, he set out again.

The rope behind him pulled faintly at him as the gravity of the land yanked it down. Trailed out behind him, the weight of it was noticeable. He thought of serpents shedding skin, leaving parts of themselves behind, and Joe looked back again the way he had come, not liking the feel of losing any more of himself than he already had.

Barely half the length of the rope had been fed out from the other side. No more than twenty-five to thirty meters from the rift, he felt as if he'd walked miles. Joe had walked miles before many times, every day for a year. He knew how it felt, the exhaustion in the muscles, the bones, the complete and total weariness.

A ways out, the charred land seemed to separate, fissured, with one part rising and the other falling. Joe approached a canyon or gorge, a place where the land plummeted and then rose a mile away or more. At first glance and from a distance it appeared a flat plane, yet as he got closer he could see the great dipping scar dividing the land. At the rim of the gorge the rope grew taut. A couple feet from the drop of the canyon, even from where he safely stood, Joe could see the scene below.

Spying through the telescope days ago, he'd glimpsed the scuttling things scurrying across the black wasteland. He'd pulled away fast, though, before he could get a clear look at them. Now, a thousand feet or more below him, a legion of the things darted about over white mounds of bone. The colony of shelled, winged, antennae-tipped creatures entered and exited caves and tunnels of skulls and ribs with the chaotic order of ants. The buzz and bustle of their motion scaled the walls of the gorge, echoing and rebounding, filling the space.

Either unaware of his presence or not caring, the bone colony paid him no mind. Not wanting to press his luck, Joe took a step back from the rim of the gorge. Here was the time of resolution, a choice to be made. Perhaps the single most important choice of his life.

The rope was stretched to its length. The crater before him had to be either crossed or circumvented.

Back the way he'd come, the rope to the rift, and to Clara, was his chain of connection, his anchor. Ahead of him lay a realm largely unknown, and the little he did know was lurid and violent. And a boy somewhere out there, maybe, hopefully, lost for a time and waiting.

Joe took up the rope again, looked down the fifty meters back toward the rift. He gave another brief but sturdy tug. A signal, a message, wordless but communicating many things. That he was alive, that he was here, that his resolve was steady and true. A moment later came a return pull, signifying the same from Clara.

The child in him – bent and bruised and battered by life, weary but still there, yet dreaming, hoping, if weakly – for a moment resurfaced as he reached over his shoulder and made a fist about the haft of the machete. Pulling it free, he felt like a knight on a crusade, a stout and noble heart questing for the divine in a world lacking it. Even under the muted light of the alien moon, the steel blade shone.

There in the outer reaches, beyond the farther side of the canyon and its depths with the scurrying bone colony, a great figure rose, standing, man-like but towering over all men who'd ever walked. Even with such a stretch between them, the giant's size was awesome and frightful. It turned its great head and looked Joe's way, fixing him with its gaze, letting Joe know it saw him and marked him.

Then it strode further away toward the black and red horizon.

Joe swung the blade, cutting the tether to the world of the living, and began the long and circuitous route around the gorge to where the man-giant had gone, where he hoped a boy once stolen would also be.

2.

The gorge was wide, but the Grand Canyon he'd hiked as both a child and a man was wider, and the miles he'd walked in remembrance of his son over the past year had prepared him for the journey around the pit that held the buzzing, scuttling bone-bug colony. As he walked, he drank from one of the water bottles he'd stored in the rucksack. Nearly as quickly as he drank, he sweated the fluid out, and lest he run out of water Joe forced himself to do without for long stretches.

When he reached the far side of the gorge, he once again looked back, and saw, like a twinkling gem, the rift still open on the other side. Then his gaze moved to the black earth itself and among the cracks that split the volcanic glassy ground were wide prints of feet far larger than his. Their depth and spacing hinted at the size of the thing walking before him.

After a time, he came upon a rise in the land, a jagged hill not quite a mountain, and along the base a sprawl of makeshift huts and lean-tos. The habitations, weak and fragile, brought to mind primitive jungle villages.

Between this ramshackle village and the gorge behind him, Joe thought of his world, and he considered the quarry where he and his wife had dumped the rift-freak and the cricket mutants. He pondered his home also, and the neighborhoods among the San Bernardino mountains.

A mountain range and a pit, both there and here. In both worlds the same general geographic features, though reversed.

The rift did its dark magic even on a continental scale, it seemed.

The muted light of the large moon on its arc across the red sky lit the primitive dwellings and the wider world weakly, so that shadows stretched in great swaths. Joe considered searching the remnants of this village, but the dark doorways and windows were portals of blackness. Within these black interiors anything could reside, watching him.

Skirting the little village, Joe made for a rocky cleft further along. The giant had been so big that it shouldn't have been lost to Joe, even at a distance. Then he thought of the way the gorge had seemed to appear, the jagged topography of the land hiding it until Joe was nearly upon it.

This small rise before him had been the same, camouflaged against the rest of the land until he'd drawn near.

The striding giant could have taken some sudden turn about such a geological feature. If he scaled the butte, Joe would have a better view of the outlying areas. With a hand before him, he tested the glassy black rock rising skyward.

It was hot and sharp and smooth.

Once more he swung his pack down, unzipped the main compartment, and retrieved the clasps and pitons. He set the climbing tools at his feet, reached back in and found the pair of leather work gloves he'd used the night before to load the beheaded rift-freak into the trash can. He pulled them on and worked his fingers deep so the leather was like a second skin. Then, after putting the pack back over his shoulders and taking up the clasps and pitons, he began to climb.

Even through the gloves' thick layers Joe felt the arid heat of the black rock. He thought of the stones that had returned to him after he'd launched the garden rocks through the rift over a week ago. Of those black arrow-like points that had burnt through the Earth itself. He wondered what poisons he was introducing himself to by just being here in this dark land, breathing the air of the red sky.

He worked the pitons and clasps strategically; the shard-like slabs of the black bluff made purchases and footholds difficult and uncertain. He moved slowly and deliberately, testing each position carefully before pulling or pushing himself further up the obsidian face. Until finally he pulled and pushed and his head and shoulders came over the top. He was at the peak. He pressed himself up and over, rolled, stood.

Joe surveyed what was about him and felt like crying. There was a feeling that something pierced him and he was deflating. Resolve left him; he felt defeated.

A vast caravan of wagons rolled ahead of him some distance away. Immeasurable in number, the vehicles were of a rotted wood framing with fleshy, translucent canvas roofing. The fabric of the canvas resembled the leather-like skin-scrolls that had tumbled out of the rift when he'd sent his initial messages into it.

So sheer were the flesh-tinged canvas covers that he could see the forms of each wagon's load. Arms and legs flailed in an anguish deep and abiding. Hands raked the fleshy canvasing of their rolling prisons in pitiful attempts at escape. The forms were piled atop each other so densely they seemed like a many-tentacled creature floundering in misery.

Joe could hear them too.

The cries and wails were protracted and agonized. A discordant choir of malcontent and suffering. The sobs and shrieks rose in the air and seemed to linger so that even as the caravan continued on its way the weeping of its cargo remained, a permanent fixture of the world as much as the blood-red sky and black land.

Among the twisted mingling of these captives were the shadows of their slave masters, grotesquely slender, tall, and strangely jointed. Whips and pronged staves and clawed rakes and other instruments dangled from their long-fingered hands. With rapid movements these creatures lashed out at the huddled masses in the covered beds of the wagons, and the screams rose higher than Joe would have thought possible.

Driving the wagons, reins in hand, were apish beings, thick and muscled and hairless. Leather-like straps fitted their bodies, attaching them to the wagons like horses fitted to a carriage.

Joe knew the significance in this rolling procession, just as he'd recognized the reverse geography of the gorge and primitive village as mockeries of his home and immediate surroundings. As people in our world commuted for work or recreation, these wagon captives were bused in pain and torment, traveling a dead and desiccated land with no destination and no purpose.

Other than the great and terrible city rising far in the distance ahead of them.

3.

In the history of cities there had never been one like it. Its spires and arches rose to Babel heights, as if poking the Creator with mocking jabs. Roadways veined the sprawl of the place in a web-like network.

But unlike human cities, full of the hustle and bustle of commuters and business and recreation, the rift-city had another purpose altogether.

Industry on a colossal scale pervaded the breadth of the metropolis. Smokestacks rising high against the blood sky sent great black plumes puffing heavenward. Massive cranes and lifts with crisscrossing thick cabling worked new buildings into place or brought down old ones. Steam-powered machines chugged and shook the black earth. Drills the size of redwood trees punctured the land and spit up detritus.

Caravans like the one Joe had watched entered the black city from various directions. The avenues and lanes were choked with the flesh-canvased vehicles, and the human-burdened traffic moved snail-like toward a central location. At this center, where the ape-dragged wagons rolled to, was an immense pit, lit red at the sides and rim by some indeterminable heat from within. Here, as Joe watched horror-stricken, the wagons reversed their course, backed up to the edge of the hole, and upended their cargo. Men and women and children by the dozens, the hundreds, spilled into the pit in a waterfall of flesh.

With each great spill into the pit the smokestacks coughed greater black plumes into the scarlet sky. The powerful machines chugged louder as if receiving fuel with which to increase their work. And the red interior of the pit brightened, stoked by the human misery that fed it.

Joe fell to his knees before the dark grandeur of it all. He trembled at the very thought of going down there among the great black towers and the monstrous machines and the fiery pit that empowered the place.

His son was lost. He was lost.

Before such as this there was nothing he could do.

On the plane of the peak of the bluff a shadow fell over him. Eclipsed by this passing shade, he turned to find its source, but the sinking in his stomach told him he already knew what it was.

The giant stood over him, smiling down, glorious and terrible.

Its appearance spoke of one that had lived for a long time in that harsh world. The giant's flesh was rough and calloused and seemed more like industrial material than living tissue. Its limbs were all different lengths so it stood awkwardly, seeming always about to topple. It wore the hides of men as a sort of loincloth and toga, inexpertly stitched patches that stretched across the torso and groin. Its fists at its sides flexed with an audible sound of tendons working, scarred flesh stretching.

It took a thunderous step forward.

Joe scuttled backward, nearly tripping. He turned, saw the edge of the cliff face falling away toward the black city.

His left hand came up like a visor over his eyes as he looked out again at the vast city, the great factory blooming smoke above it and its streets and charred constructs, the billowing red pit at its center sending tendrils of poison into the fiery sky.

His right hand inched toward the gun tucked in his belt as the crooked giant took another lumbering step. He snatched it and, swiveling fast, leveled the revolver at the behemoth.

Joe fired at the impossible thing before him, so close, like a wall of flesh. He squeezed the trigger until the hammer clicked on the empty cylinder. Each bullet pocked the giant's chest with what seemed like insect bites, tiny and insignificant. He screamed as he fired the gun, and when it was empty, he threw the weapon at the colossus. The giant's great mouth like a hole, almost a rift in itself, yawned open and a throaty wet sound, almost laughter, rumbled out. It smiled.

Joe turned again toward the city. High above it on the peak of the butte, he looked down upon it, and somewhere in that industry of ruination, the factories and machines of desolation, was his son. Eyeing the way down, measuring the gaps from purchase to purchase, outcropping to outcropping, Joe ran and jumped.

And he prayed frenziedly all the way down.

4.

Bruised, battered, and bloodied, Joe walked the streets of the wretched city unmolested by its denizens. Staying to alleys and culverts as much as he could, he nonetheless knew it was impossible that he would go unnoticed by the masses milling around: the wagoners hauling their human refuse, the people themselves staring out from the wagon beds wailing and raking at their confines, the operators of the big machines scattered about building and destroying in equal measure. Why he wasn't rushed and mauled and shackled he had no idea, and though he hoped maybe his injuries and general condition made him seem like one of the destitute despairing at their eternal fate, he thought his insignificance probably played a larger part.

Upon closer inspection, as he walked the streets and saw the industry, the machines and the pit and the construction, Joe noticed the very walls and avenues of the city were made of people. Petrified by some unspeakable process, the cobbles of the streets and bricks of the buildings were biological. Faces contorted in frozen frames of torment were stamped upon the walls and pavement up and down, left and right, in every direction.

As he made his way deeper into the maze of brick and mortar and petrified dead, with the clouds of noxious black rising in putrescent mists, Joe saw others like himself. Huddled in doorways or squirreled in back alleys, the destitute, grime-smeared and trembling looked out with wide raccoon eyes of perpetual fear. Some shied away when they saw him, and others stretched out hands, pleading, which Joe had no choice but to ignore. Faces in yellow-stained windows peered out and ducked away, and crying and wailing and fleeting laughter issued from dark places.

Each face peeking from the alleys and windows and doorways, each face pushing through flaps of the wagon tarps, Joe studied, looking for the boy he'd come to find. Such numbers, so many faces. An impossible task.

And the caravans rolled through it all, a train of captives, a procession of suffering, with the fleshy tarps flapping in the stagnant and heavy air emitted by the machines. Behind the skin-like canvas was a shadow show of agony; the piled dead and dying flopped and flipped in fish-like throes.

His long walk brought Joe inevitably to the wide, deep pit at the center of the dark metropolis. As the wagons rolled up to designated areas where char-black beings like foremen waved their loads forward,

unclasped the wagon-bed gates and let spill their abominable loads, Joe
crept forward from the sidelines. Drawing close, willing himself low
and insignificant, he peered over into the crater, a cavity disease-born
upon the face of the land. A winding railing led down along the sides of
the pit. Spiraling down into a redness throbbing with the stoking of the
deep heat, the railing clanged and shook as the bodies dumped into the
hole invariably struck it on their way down.

Here, too, Joe recognized the pit for what it was, and how it
correlated to some similar yet disparate feature in his world. He thought
of the distance from his home to the quarry and from his home to the
city, and how there'd been the makeshift village and the gorge and the
black city here in the land of the rift. One other feature back there in
the land of the living, ironically the plot in the cemetery where his son
was buried in a hole in the ground, now with its mockery here: a great
pit where innumerable masses were dumped.

Life swallowed by a depthless chasm. A careless snuffing.

Joe stepped out on the stairway and started around and down. Bodies
fell about him, discarded from above like confetti. It seemed the hole
rose up to take him in as much as he strode down into it.

The walls revealed more from below than what he'd seen from
above. In the walkways and avenues of the metropolis the faces of
the tormented were forever encased in the cobbles and stonework. As
he descended, he saw the geologic strata and the rest of the penitent
distributed in the layers: legs and arms and feet and hands and torsos
piled high and scattered throughout. Striations of black earth and the
poured-in dead. A foundation of humanity.

The rattling of the catwalk railing was nerve-racking. The whole
contraption shook as if it was ready to fall apart at any moment. It was
the jangle of metal and the rattle of bones at the same time. He descended
not just a metal framework but a skeletal structure in the earth, the
bones of a colossal beast reanimating, awakening and stretching its limbs
for the first time in ages.

The human fuel fell from above and Joe continued down. Circling the
pit as the railing did with the deep red heat pulsing below like a furnace. Joe

stopped at times and leaned on his sledgehammer and drank from the water in his pack. With his sleeves and the hem of his shirt he wiped sweat from his face; at times it seemed like an endless stream from his pores.

He brought forth Evan in his mind, took the image and set it alive before him. Followed it forward and down before the resolve left him.

Far below – the open top of the pit above like a distant red eye – the railing ended and Joe watched the falling humanity land hard on a system of ramps, funneled into a vat of molten magma. With one last wail or scream, those who survived the free-fall splashed into the liquid fire, died, and fell beneath the slowly churning red-orange waves.

From the railing a tunnel branched off into the side of the pit. Joe turned down the tunnel, the thick odor of charred humanity followed him, and the glow of the vat's lava-like material fed down it for a few yards before giving way to darkness. Again Joe went into his pack and pulled out the Eveready flashlight he and Clara had used at the quarry the previous night. He thumbed the button and the bright beam of light bulleted down the length of the tunnel, revealing the way.

The tunnel branched off into side rooms, little spaces like hovels in a shanty town. Not much more than four walls and a floor and ceiling. When he shined the light into each of these spaces, pale faces came into existence, as if birthed by the darkness itself. Torsos and arms and legs joined the faces as the beam traced them. From each room the heavy and pungent odor of human waste and sweat and fear permeated the air like a tangible thing.

These pale people of darkness didn't react to the disturbance of their isolated, lightless cells. They hardly moved at all. A flicker of an eye. A twitch of a corner of the mouth. The slight bend and fold of a limb repositioned. As if they sat in the dark rooms awaiting something with a resignation born of experience, knowing that what was coming was inevitable, a force of nature.

Room to room Joe moved on down the long tunnel at the bottom of the pit. He saw men and women and children of all shades and varieties. What terror this place was that collected human chattel and penned them in beneath the earth, he didn't know. He thought he at least had some idea lifted from his religion and the religions of the world: a hell where the judged and condemned were sent.

But this didn't fit the things he saw. The ancient scriptures spoke of the innocence of children. How they would avoid accountability. If Evan were here, this couldn't be the place prophets and elders had written about over millennia.

Joe refused to believe it.

Whatever this place was – whatever the nature of the world of the rift – it wasn't the biblical hell of death and judgment. Unless there were other roads to hell than these.

6.

The boy was in a room at the end of the tunnel, almost as if he were the centerpiece of an exhibit. Everything else led to him. Joe shone the light in the room, saw the boy, and froze.

He wanted to speak but couldn't. The words escaped him like wisps in a wind. The thoughts were there, the intention was there, but the strength to say the things in his heart wasn't.

Unlike the dozens or hundreds of others in the rooms Joe had already passed, this boy, naked and holding himself in a corner, stirred at the light of the Eveready. With a slow and deliberate blinking, the round brown eyes fixed on Joe. He could see the discomfort the light caused shining in the boy's face, but if he swung it aside and allowed the darkness to take the boy once more, Joe feared he'd never find him again.

There was a stench of filth in the room, as in the others before it. But this time Joe didn't turn his face away. Here the reek emanated from the maltreatment of this boy, and that was different.

The boy both looked like Joe's son and didn't. A little taller, a bit slimmer, but that wasn't the source of the difference. It was in the eyes and the morose set of the face. The rift and its spawn had done a job on this boy and all the others Joe had seen. The wide, tired, haunted eyes of the boy huddled before him, in the corner of the dark room, had seen things.

"Evan?"

Only the single word croaked out of his throat, slipping between his lips with a momentous effort. The speaking of it left Joe trembling. He wasn't sure if he should move or not, if what was before him in the room was true or an illusion.

Joe entered the room. Walked toward the boy.

He knelt, reached forward. Touched a slender arm. Felt the warmth of life. The boy flinched but didn't run. Joe leaned closer, undisturbed by the boy's nudity, recalling the boy in infancy, the miracle of him pink and fresh and squirming. He took the boy up and held him close.

"I'm here, son," he whispered in the boy's ear. Shockingly thin arms and legs wrapped around him. A tear-streaked face nuzzled his chest, tried to bury itself, attempting to hide. "We're getting out of here."

Joe carried the boy out of the room and down the long, long tunnel. To the red, throbbing glow of the vat and its liquid fire, the bodies still raining down, splashing into it. Up the winding stairs to the pinpoint opening above. The mouth of the pit grew as they climbed toward it. The walls of the pit and the striations, the buried lost, their frozen expressions of pain, stared out at boy and man in accusation. Up and out they went; the wagons still lined up, dumping their loads. They made their way through the dark streets and the black alleys. The gray clouds puffed out by the machines and factories gathered high above the metropolis, spreading far and wide to cover the world. Across the black desert under the blood sky, they passed the lean-tos, the derelict village, and the gorge and the bone colony below. Back to the rift and the severed rope leading from it.

And the crooked giant before it in its human-hide garb, stood sentinel, high and large, smiling with broken and yellowed teeth.

Joe put his boy gently down. He withdrew the machete from its loops at his back, held it tight with both hands.

"Get the fuck out of my way," he said to the great and terrible thing before him.

The huge creature laughed its wet-throated laugh. Joe charged it.

And in the end stepped back through the rift with his son to their world. Or what was left of it.

CHAPTER TEN

1.

It had been night when Joe entered the rift, but it was daylight when he stepped out onto the lawn. The rift winked out behind him and only then did Joe recognize the absence of weight in his arms. The cut cord of rope that had tied him from there to here lay limp like a dead thing on the concrete at his feet.

His son wasn't with him. He'd come back alone.

"Oh God, fuck no."

Dropping the sledgehammer clenched under one arm, he held his hands before his face. Looked about himself in a circle. Clara was gone too, and the dog.

The rear sliding glass door was shattered in a hundred little shining pieces. Joe staggered to the threshold, braced himself against the frame, looked around. His chest and ribs ached with a burning throb. A wetness smeared his lips when he coughed, and every breath hurt.

"Clara…" Joe said. He'd meant to yell it but the effort was beyond him. It came out little more than a moan, and a wave of nausea and dizziness rolled over him.

The dining room was lit by the morning sun shining in the east, and red droplets gleamed in the plush fibers of the beige carpet, leading away across the room. Joe tried reaching across himself to fling off the straps of the backpack. The motion wrenched his back, muscles and tendons stretching, screaming at the abuse. He cried out and rode the wave of pain.

Hanging half off already, the pack slumped to the floor. Joe wanted the knives inside it. Or the machete, gone now behind him, buried in the chest of the giant on the other side of the rift. The blood trail could lead to nothing good and he had to be ready. His every joint and ligament refused, warning him away from the thought with another flash of hot agony. His left arm held flaccidly across his chest as if in an invisible sling, Joe left the backpack where it was and limped inside.

He passed the dining table and saw atop it more scarlet splashes, like paint splattered haphazardly. The two oak chairs on his side of the table were pushed askew as if shoved aside by someone in a hurry. In the kitchen, the drawers on all three sides were pulled open and their contents cast about. Steel blades scattered about the tiled floor flashed messages at Joe he couldn't interpret.

A red handprint was smeared across the refrigerator door.

This time he forced himself to kneel, and picked up one of the knives from the floor. The pain was so intense he thought at first his legs and arms wouldn't respond.

He left the kitchen, returned briefly to the dining room, crossed into the living room. The damnable television screen was now black like an insect's eye. The screen that had shown him and not shown him things in equal measure over the past week, taunting him with both. He went past to the mouth of the long hall, doorways shut or the interiors unseen. The stairs led up to his left. The knife in his right fist pointed with its blade in the general direction of the hallway, and Joe followed its lead and started down it.

His booted feet made soft sounds in the carpet, like tiny cushiony sighs. A quiet chatter preceded him.

The first door on his left opened onto the hallway closet. As he approached it, years of childhood fears of closet monsters hiding in corners and behind boxes came springing at him. His free left hand, the one not holding the knife, trembled as Joe reached out for the doorknob, took it in a clammy, sweat-slick fist, and turned it.

Inside, coats and jackets hung like ghosts. Above these was a high shelf, bare except for a couple boxes holding things long forgotten. Below, on the floor, lay some old shoes, scuffed and with frayed laces.

Joe probed the closet with the knife. He pushed aside the coats, poking, prodding at whatever may have been waiting behind them. Nothing there. He backed out, closed the door again.

He started down the hallway once more.

Thoughts drifted up with each step as if following him. Lurid images of what he might find in the rooms ahead of him blossomed with a flasher's perverted glee.

Clara, dead or dying, strung up, cut open, violated in other unspeakable ways.

The dog, too, rent and destroyed and his furry pieces scattered about.

The first door on his right, halfway down the hall, was a furnished guest room that doubled as storage space. He pushed the door open with the toe of a boot, the sliver of the opening widening much as the rift itself had.

Inside was a bed, a dresser, a nightstand and a desk. The lone window at the far end let the sun in, muted but still bright enough through the drapery to light the room around him. No one lurked in the corners of the room, crouched and ready to spring. Nothing was strewn about, no bloody prints.

At the end of the hall was the bathroom. In there the white tiles and marble were bright white and clean. No streaks of blood. Nothing cast about or pulled off kilter.

But the shower curtain at the far end was pulled shut.

Joe approached it, his leather soles squeaking on the polished floor. These sharp squeaks were like squeals of pain to his ears.

He inserted the tip of the knife between the curtain and the wall and pulled the curtain aside. The metal rings holding it to the shower rod screeched.

There was nothing inside save accumulated dirt and grime. Joe turned away and went back out into the hall.

Becoming used to his pain now – parts in him perhaps were broken, but he still drew breath to keep himself going – Joe took the steps up to the second floor mostly two at a time, breathing hard when he reached the top, his lungs burning.

The upstairs bath was there on his left. Inside, like its twin downstairs, it was stark and white. He caught a glimpse of himself in the clear mirror, bent at the middle, hunched like an old man. Streaked and mussed like the loser of a one-sided fight.

He left the bathroom, continued down the hall.

His office was next and the master bedroom across from it. A choice, the door to each was shut, like on a game show. What was behind door number one? Or should he press his luck and continue to door number two?

Joe doubted bikini-clad models or shiny new cars awaited him behind either. He gently pushed the door of his office open, and went in low and fast with the knife in front of him.

The computer and the desk and leather sofa were just as they'd been when he and Clara had been up here two nights before. Making himself still and quiet, Joe paused in the middle of the room. He looked about the corners and the closet and waited.

Nothing stirred. The stillness was near absolute.

He backed out of the room, crossed the hall to the door of the master bedroom. He opened it onto the things he'd shared with his wife for over a decade. The bed and sheets. The closet where their clothes hung. The master bath that had at times seen as much activity as the bed.

All was as it should be. As if what had occurred downstairs in the dining room and kitchen had been kept there, bound by some force. Up here was another world altogether.

Once more back in the hall. At the end of it, the last room stood before him, the door challenging him.

Evan's room.

2.

Since Evan had never reached the teenage years in which a kid needed a certain degree of privacy, Joe and Clara had never installed a lock on his door. But when Joe reached the end of the hall with the knife held in front of him and tried the knob, he found it wouldn't turn. He tried pushing it open but the door remained shut, wouldn't budge.

Holding the knife awkwardly, Joe took the brass knob in both hands and wrenched harder. He put his shoulder to the pine door, pushed with all his weight.

He heard a scuffle and labored breathing from the other side. A grunt as something pushed back, straining. Joe was stronger and the door pushed inward.

Then all resistance was gone, and Joe fell forward as the door swung inward. The chair that had been on the inside in front of the door toppled over and Joe almost toppled over *it*. Regaining his footing and rising, knife up, he faced the interior of his son's room.

And stared straight into the muzzle of the gun pointed at his face.

Clara was behind the pistol, shaking. A long slash ran diagonally down her right cheek. The dog stood behind her in a corner, taut and low, poised to launch.

"Who the fuck are you?" his wife asked, voice tremulous but firm.

She held the gun in her right hand, that arm trembling, not at all like the strong stance she'd shown him at the firing range. Her left arm was held across her front, holding the torn blouse there.

"What the hell happened here, Clara?"

Joe had his own hands up. He dropped the knife and tried to move forward. His wife thumbed the safety off and took a bold step forward also. Her trembling spoke of fear. Her eyes and the set of her face spoke of rage.

"Take another step and I'll blow your head off," she said.

Another step was out of the question. Joe stood right where he was, liking his head right where it was. But he had to keep talking; *that* he couldn't stop. None of this made sense.

"Clara, I don't know what's wrong, but—"

He didn't get to finish. Clara closed the gap between them, fast and unexpected, and the muzzle of the gun wavered close to Joe's face. Retreating to the doorway, hands up, Joe went silent and waited.

"What's *wrong*?" she asked, not really wanting an answer. Her gun finger was firm on the trigger. Joe didn't like that. With just a squeeze, intentional or not, her promise about blowing his head off would be fulfilled. "What's *wrong*, you son of a bitch?"

The dog came forward now, but slowly, looking at him, testing the air of the room with his snout forward.

"You come out of that fucking thing – that *rift* – and you're smiling, and I think everything's okay. I don't see Evan but you're smiling, so that's something. The rope was cut and I thought something went wrong, but then you came out, smiling."

The rope was cut.

A thought slammed home. Something he should have realized and hadn't. He'd cut his tether, his anchor.

For everything that went into the rift, something came out.

He should have known. Maybe he did, but with the prospect of his son before him, hadn't cared. Or perhaps he cared, but just not enough.

"Clara…" he tried, yet she would have none of it, spoke over him.

The gun pointed at his face like an accusatory finger.

"Smiling at me, and I went to you, hugged you. You hit me," she said and pointed at a redness around her right eye that he hadn't noticed, so prominent was the gash near it. "You hit me and then threw me down. Tore at my clothes…tried to…tried…."

She couldn't complete the thought. The words caught in her throat and came out like rough, wet coughs.

"But Rusty was there," she continued. "And he went after you."

The dog was coming forward again. Still testing the air between them, finding whatever he was looking for and trotting over fast before Clara could stop him.

"Rusty, no!" she yelled too late.

Braving the pointing gun, Joe lowered himself to greet the dog. The movement made his insides cry anew. He moaned and clenched his teeth, and when the dog stood on his hind legs and planted his forepaws on Joe's shoulders, that didn't help and the pain surged higher. But Joe bore the agony and even smiled.

"It's good to see you again," he said between tongue smears.

From his kneeling position on the floor of his son's room, the boxes packed and stacked about him, Joe looked up and over the dog at Clara. There was a dawning on her face. Something fell away and something else replaced it. The pistol lowered in clock-arm ticks of motion as if counting down, acknowledging a passing.

"Joe?"

Just a one-word question, but so much was in it. A tide of thoughts and emotions. Fear and hope and all things in between.

He nodded. Then he rose.

She came forward and embraced him.

Her arms about him, squeezing, brought his pain to higher notes, but Joe moved through it gritting his teeth, feeling his wife against him, welcome and wondrous after all that had come before.

3.

"You're saying someone that looked like me came out of the rift? Did he say anything?"

Joe had his shirt off and sat on the closed toilet seat while Clara moved about him with the gauze, prodding and testing his ribs with her hands before wrapping him mummy-like about the middle. Even through the pain he watched as she bent over him with her work. The way the torn blouse dipped low to reveal what it covered sent a thrilling shiver through him. Then he thought of some other man doing the tearing, groping her, and anger replaced desire.

"Did he hurt you?"

As she poked and prodded and wrapped him, Joe tried doing his own inspection of her. He touched her face gently, tracing the length of the cut there. He held up the frayed top of her blouse when she couldn't, as her own hands were busy playing nurse to his injuries.

"I don't think anything's broken," she said, ignoring his initial question. She sniffed as she clasped the gauze wrapping tight with little metal hooks from the first aid tray, as if binding him together so he wouldn't fall apart. He *felt* like he was falling apart. "I've only done minor doctoring to girls falling on their butts or twisting an ankle, that sort of thing. But I don't see any obvious signs of breakage."

She gave his right side a little pat when she'd finished with the wrapping. He winced and she said sorry and knelt over him and kissed him lightly on the forehead. Then she stepped away, made for the doorway, where the dog sat in the hall watching them.

With a hand on her wrist to stop her, Joe pulled her back. He rose from his seat and turned her to face him.

"Did he…do anything else?"

Even realizing his earlier question was extraordinarily stupid, he couldn't let it go. Of course whatever had come out of the rift had hurt her. The cut on her face and bruising under her eye were evidence of that. But there was hurt…and then there was *hurt*.

"No," she said, meeting his gaze, looking up at him kindly. "He tried, but I didn't let him. The dog didn't let him."

Joe said nothing, wanting her to say more.

"Rusty attacked him when he threw me down, got on top of me," Clara said. "I got a good kick in while Rusty kept him busy. I got up, ran inside, went for the kitchen. He was right behind me. I got to the knives but so did he. I stabbed him in the shoulder, but he got me here."

She pointed absently at her face like a woman pointing out her new hairdo. Joe again touched the area softly. It was red and raw, but only bled lightly. When he tested the wound with finger and thumb, it didn't separate, and he didn't think stitches were necessary.

"Rusty was on his heels, snapping at his legs," she continued. "He turned to the dog and I got him again low in the back. Then I snatched Rusty by the collar and ran up here to Evan's room."

Joe saw it all in his mind's eye. Every horrible moment of it.

"How long were you in there?"

"All night," she said.

Despite what he himself had experienced on the other side of the rift, Joe found himself shaking his head, thinking about what his wife had gone through. Barring the door to the bedroom, unable to sleep. A constant terror, waiting for someone to barge through.

He stepped away from his wife, out of the bathroom and into the hall. Picking up his shirt on the way and slipping it back on, Joe went downstairs and Clara followed him.

In the dining room they both paused to right the furniture, then moved to the kitchen and picked up the scattered utensils on the floor.

Joe thought aloud as they worked. "Every time I sent something through the rift, something came back. Except when it was anchored here by a chain of connection."

"The fishing rod and the box," Clara said.

"Right. So when I cut the rope over there, I made an exchange. Myself for...something else. This other me. But I didn't have to wait for seven tonight to get back through the rift. It was open over there already, waiting for me."

Putting everything back into the drawers, Clara then went to work with a cloth and liquid soap on the bloody print on the fridge. Joe parked himself at the table, thinking. Rusty sat near him and put his head in his lap. When he stroked the dog, things became clearer, and a calm slowly settled.

"Remember me saying I thought the rift exchanged things?" Joe said. "It wasn't just corrupting the things I sent through. It was giving me something *like* them from its side. Or like me, something was over *there*, passing stuff back through like I was over *here*."

"Like, what? A trade?"

Finished with the fridge, dumping the stained rag and the bottle of dish soap in the sink, Clara joined him at the table. She sat down heavily as if a weight pulled her down.

"Exactly. I think I can go in and out at any time. Because I'm not just an object. I'm...a trader. I'm the one calling the shots on this side of the rift."

"That doesn't make any sense, Joe. How can you open such a thing as that?"

She gave a vague wave of her hand in the direction of the backyard. The shattered sliding glass door framed the space the rift had occupied.

"I don't know, Clara. I don't know. But you should have seen the things I saw over there. Maybe it was Evan. Maybe he found a way...."

Her hands were on his arm again. Gripping him claw-like as she had on the patio last night when the rift had opened before them.

"He was there, Joe? Evan was there?"

So much in those few words. An entire story, a history. Volumes of loss and desperation and a weak, pitiful hope.

Joe nodded. Put a hand over hers.

"Yes. He was there. But I couldn't bring him back. I tried, Clara. I had him right here, in my arms." He pantomimed the act, lifting his arms in a little cradle, even as Clara gripped him. "But I couldn't. I couldn't bring my son back."

Gently, he pried her fingers from his arm, then held her hands. Gave them a squeeze, and let go. Joe held his own hands up, empty, before him.

Readying himself for the verbal tirade coming his way – about how he'd lost their son a second time, maybe something about what kind of a father would let that happen – Joe looked down at the tabletop before him. But there was only silence for a time.

"You asked if he said anything," Clara finally said.

Caught off guard, Joe blinked and shook his head. "What?"

"You asked if the...other you said anything. He did. He said what you did just before you went through. He said, *'I'm bringing back my son'*."

"What the hell does that mean?" Joe said.

And then the answer came to him. He remembered the mirrored geography of the land of the rift. A gorge there, the quarry here; the ramshackle village there, their neighborhood here; the industrial metropolis there, puffing out its poisons, fueled by the bodies of men and women, the city here much the same. And the pit, the glowing red molten core of it, and his son buried beneath it in the network of tunnels in a small earthen cell.

Here, his son was also buried.

Joe had gone for his son over there. It only made sense that the rift version of him would go for his son over here.

4.

The still and quiet Sunday made the green expanse of the cemetery seem like a photo, a snapshot in time as seen on a postcard or calendar. Scattered mourners passed among the marble monuments. Wreaths upon cold stone marked their visits.

Where their son's plot should have been was a hole in the ground.

Cemetery employees and a deputy were already gathered around it, looking in and trying not to. Worried mutterings. Papers were passed and shuffled and signed.

When Joe and Clara walked up to the small gathering, the deputy and a short man in a suit turned to take them in. Something in Joe and Clara's posture and approach revealed who they were, and heads lowered in embarrassment and pity. The little man in the suit seemed apprehensive, like a kid caught stealing. Joe pinned him as the manager of the cemetery.

The deputy took a position in between the two camps – family and cemetery personnel – and tried to make it seem casual. The open grave where their son should have been was now strategically behind the officer, along with the manager and his employees. His hands on his thick leather belt would have made the deputy an imposing figure once upon a time, before crawling sticks, giant mutated crickets, and a world that fueled itself by melting people. As it was, sore and tired, Joe merely stopped before him and nodded to indicate the grave.

"What happened here?"

An unnecessary question. He knew what had happened, even if those before him didn't. He knew the gist of it if not the details.

A father had come for his son.

"Are you family of the deceased?" the deputy asked in a matter-of-fact tone. His hard face tried a calculated measure of sympathy, but it was an alien thing; he knew this, and stopped the effort.

Once upon a time Joe would have been angry. The hole before him was a violation of all things decent. The weaselly suited man rubbed his hands nervously on his slacks, probably seeing the signs of a lawsuit on the horizon. The other employees gathered about as if at a show. Today, however, the fight was out of him. Joe *was* angry, but it was a tired thing, directionless.

"Yes," he said. Joe heard the same matter-of-factness in his own tone. As if nothing out of the ordinary had occurred. This bothered him but he squashed it down. He didn't have the time for it. "We're the parents."

"Uh-huh. Well, unfortunately, it seems there's been some vandalism. The full extent of it we're still investigating...."

Clara beside him had no such problem with her anger. She let it out as if freeing a caged animal. The deputy blinked and flinched.

"The full extent as I see it is our son's body was dug up. What kind of fucking place do you run here?"

The question was directed at the suited weasel, and his sweaty hands clenched and wiped at his pant legs with greater vigor, as if scrubbing a stain he couldn't remove.

Joe put a hand on his wife's arm, but it was unnecessary. Rather than react, the officer blinked again, looked them each up and down, seemed to take in their general condition for the first time. The cut across Clara's right cheek. Joe's stiff and awkward posture.

"Are you two okay?" he asked. He pointed at Clara's wound. "You should have that looked at."

Unable to answer his question, neither of them tried. What would they tell him? There was a rip in the air in their backyard? Through it was a vast and abiding hell? Instead, Joe took a step forward, pointed at the open grave. He asked what they knew, and the deputy and the manager both pulled out their papers again and read from them, made notations, and asked Joe and Clara for signatures. They both did this without reservation and the deputy said he'd be in touch, and the short, suited cemetery manager seemed pleased with the signing away of certain legal rights. Only then did the gathered depart, leaving Joe and Clara to gaze into the hole before them.

The dimensions of the hole were just so, to hold the box that had carried their son. Now both were gone and it was just a rectangle of emptiness.

The walk back to the car together seemed very long, a trek across a wasteland despite the greenery about and the blue above. But they held hands as they walked, and each found a strength they lacked by themselves.

5.

Joe felt like they were in an escape pod as the cemetery fell out of view behind them. Ejected in the nick of time before some cataclysmic disaster left them adrift in the great black reaches of space. Rusty, in the backseat behind them, leaned forward between the seats, and Joe, behind the wheel, and Clara in the passenger's seat, alternately reached over to pet him and gently push him back.

"The…other me," Joe said. "I think he wants to get back through the rift." Joe didn't know how he knew this. But it rang true to his ears. Apparently to Clara's also, because she voiced no argument.

"With Evan's…body," she said instead. The last word was little more than a weak choking sound that hung in the air.

"Yeah." Joe stared long and hard at the road before him, rolling out ahead, determining his course. "But if he ran off last night and didn't return, then I think he can't get through until seven o'clock tonight."

"You were able to come through before then. What if he can too?"

Joe kept his eyes on the road. "He can't."

He had no explanation for this either. The only other option, though, was that the…other…him was already gone – through the rift with their dead son – and if that had happened Joe wasn't sure about anything.

Clara didn't bother arguing about this either. He thought she knew the desperation inside him. She felt it like he did.

"Then we have to stop him. Tonight," she said.

Joe looked at her. He saw the determination there, and the strength. Born of pain and sorrow. "We'll kill that son of a bitch. Bury…what should be buried." Eyes back on the road, he nodded. The mountains were coming up quick and sure. Their home was up there, as if above it all. *No one's above it all*, Joe thought. *No one.*

"And then we're going through," Clara continued, and Joe looked at her once more, hands gripping the wheel. She was staring out at the road now as he had been. Dead ahead, as if at something she didn't want to lose sight of. "We're going through together and we'll turn that hell upside down until we find our son."

CHAPTER ELEVEN

1.

When Joe was thirteen, he came home from school one autumn Monday to the news that his father had been in a car accident, but he knew something was wrong before he even entered the house. Everything was where it should be: his bike was in the yard, his mom's van in the driveway, and, inside, the coats and hats hung on the rack in the foyer. His mother's purse was on the dining table with the list of her day's errands nearby. The old sofa and the television sat across from each other as if conversing. Yet it all seemed untouched, as if a spell had stilled everything. He was reminded of the frozen scenes in the dioramas his class had made in American History.

His mom then stepped almost shyly from the kitchen, the phone in her hand held to her ear. When she saw him, she said a quick goodbye to whoever she'd been talking to and set the receiver down. She motioned him forward, gathered him up, and told him what needed to be told.

That same feeling of wrongness – of something behind the facade of normalcy – came upon Joe when he and Clara pulled up in front of their home in the foothills. He put the Explorer in park but left the engine idling, looking past his wife out the passenger-side window.

The ranch house looked the same as it always had, as familiar to Joe as his own body. But staring at it from the sidewalk across the yard, he thought it seemed…off kilter. Unbalanced. He thought of the Leaning Tower of Pisa. This wasn't nearly as extreme, but nonetheless it was the impression Joe had of the house before him.

Unbalanced.

He squinted, cocked his head one way and then the other.

"What is it?" Clara asked, following his gaze.

She looked around the driveway, the yard, the fencing, trying to identify what it was that had his attention. Then her eyes fell on the house itself, and she likewise tilted her head, like a museum patron considering an exhibit.

"Something's wrong," she said, and Joe nodded.

Digging into the purse in her lap, Clara withdrew the pistol. It looked as sinister to Joe as it had earlier, when it had been pointed at his face. The black hole like a black eye staring with a depthless gaze.

"Lucky I still have this."

"How many of those do you have?" Joe asked.

"Enough."

Her hands caressed it as if it were an old, reliable friend. Jealous, Joe wished he instilled as much confidence in her as the gun.

"Enough for what? Armageddon?"

"If need be," she said. She looked at him, winked. "Don't worry, I'll have room for you in the fallout shelter."

Opening the door, Clara started to get out. Joe sighed and got out too. Moving fast, Rusty was out the door before Joe could shut it. The three of them gathered on the sidewalk together, looking at the house again. Trying to pinpoint what it was that was wrong.

"It looks...crooked," Joe said.

He made vague gestures at the walls, corners, roofing, indicating everything and nothing at the same time. Tentatively, he took a step onto the yard. He felt and heard a papery dry crunch beneath his feet. Kneeling, he looked closer.

"What is it?" Clara asked, coming down to his level.

With the toe of his boot, he nudged the grass. Most of it was crisp and green as it had always been. Interspersed with the green, however, were charred blades of grass that flaked apart with the slightest touch. These ashy pieces scattered to the ground and were gone.

Joe stood, backed up a step, took in the whole of the front yard.

Leaning first one way, then the other, he saw tufts of the black grass throughout the lawn. A checkerboard pattern of life and death.

Still kneeling, Clara reached out to touch a patch of the black grass. Joe moved fast, stopped her abruptly with a hand on her shoulder. She looked up at him, then back at Rusty, who needed no warning to stay off the lawn.

"We'll take the walkway," he said. Clara nodded and got to her feet.

Circumventing the lawn, the three of them made their way to the front door slowly, still looking at the house. Carefully staying on the cement walkway turning up toward the front door, Joe and Clara looked around, taking in the perimeter flower beds, the windows of the garage, the walls and paneling.

On the porch, Joe eyed the brass doorknob carefully, squatting so it was eye level, before reaching out to grab and turn it. The dull light off it and the tiny, distorted reflections reminded him of the muted, mangled world of the rift. It was only a brass knob as far as he could tell, though, and he stood up straight again and opened the door.

Single file, they entered.

In the foyer, Clara saw the veins first.

Thin and light-colored, Joe initially thought they were merely imperfections in the painted walls. Hairline cracks, perhaps, or old paint flaking away, leaving behind jigsaw puzzle lines. Then, leaning closer at Clara's beckoning, he saw the three-dimensionality of the web pattern, and, yes, just maybe, the telltale motion of something passing *within* them. A slight wiggling like a hose with the water turned on.

Clara traced the routes of the crisscrossing veins with a finger. Not touching them, but following along their courses like over the lines of a map. Joe saw the veiny striations everywhere along the walls, similar to the black grass outside amid the healthy lawn. And they were spreading, like an infection.

"What the hell's going on?" Clara asked. She spoke in a near whisper, as if afraid of being overheard. Maybe the house itself was listening.

Joe considered the black stones that sunk into the backyard on those first two nights. And the skin-scroll and the crawling, undulating stick. The rift crickets, filling the walls and the floor and ceiling, doing whatever abominable things *inside* the walls before coming out. He remembered thinking of it as an infestation, but that wasn't entirely accurate, he realized.

It wasn't simply the things of the rift invading.

The rift *itself* was the infestation.

Side by side – human, dog, human – they moved further into what had once been their home.

2.

Upon realizing what the rift-Joe had planned and breaking numerous traffic laws to arrive at the cemetery in record time, neither Joe nor Clara had bothered with covering the empty hole left by the shattered glass door. So when they followed the pumping veins in the walls across the living room and into the dining room, they were met with what was in the backyard in full view.

Squatters pitching a tent out there came to mind first for Joe, as absurd as that seemed. But that was no more preposterous than a rip in the sky zippering open in his backyard. He stepped carefully out onto the patio, avoiding the shards of glass still sticking out of the door's metal frame, and approached the canvas-like structure.

The sides of it billowed with every slight wind. The sunlight revealed the framework of it beneath the surface, like an X-ray. Broad at the base and tapering at the top, it formed a badly measured dome. There were panels on it, three of them, two small and the third large, with stitching where they could be unlaced open or tied shut. Currently shut, the stitched flaps gave the tarp-like tent a slapdash, haphazard look, as if a cobbler had done what little he could for a worn-out shoe. And with the whole of the structure continuing to billow up and down, in and out, Joe saw that it wasn't just the wind blowing the thing, but the skeletal frame of it *flexed* and *stretched*.

As Joe moved closer – Clara and Rusty remaining behind at the threshold of the glass door – he realized he'd seen this material before. The skin-like canvas. The flexing framework beneath. Once he recognized this, he saw what he should have seen straight away.

The flesh-tent sat atop where the two holes in the earth had been burned through by the black stones the rift had spat out days ago. Drawing closer still, creeping, he could see through the thin fabric of the thing the vague forms of the holes there at the center of the floor of the tent. Two dim circles and from them a network of web-like lines, and he thought, *Roots, these are the roots of the rift.*

Turning from the flesh-tent, billowing, breathing before him, Joe faced Clara there in the doorway, holding on to the frame as if she might fall.

"He's making his own house here," Joe said to himself as much as to her. "When he said he's bringing his son back, he didn't just mean back through the rift. He meant here, to our home."

Joe looked back at the fleshy tent structure again.

"Only it won't be *our* home here anymore."

★   ★   ★

After a time, Clara came out to circle the flesh-tent also, and being the guardian he was, Rusty moved from one to the other, man and woman, taking stock of his charges. After seeing the flesh-tent from every angle, Clara returned to the patio, where she and Joe watched it together, silent in the strange presence of the thing.

"We can't stay here," she said.

"We have to. We can't let him go through the rift."

She slumped against the nearest wall. Then, remembering the veins pulsing in them, she pushed off and stepped away.

"If he takes…the body through…" she began.

"What'll come out?" Joe finished for her.

Clara found one of the patio chairs. She inspected it for veins or other anomalies and, finding none, fell into it. She put her face in her hands. Too tired to cry, she just breathed into them.

"But *we're* still going in."

She looked up when he spoke. Confusion made her face a map of pain and exasperation.

"We're going in, Clara," Joe said. "We just can't let anything else get out."

Her hands parted in a helpless gesture. *How* is what she wordlessly asked, and this Joe had an answer for. He smiled.

"We'll trap the fuckers."

3.

How was Clara's question, and Joe had to admit it was a good one. *How* were they to trap whatever came out when the three of them went through? Because Joe had no doubt about it: when his wife and the dog went through, something would take their place on this side. Just as when the other him had come out of the rift when he'd cut the rope. The other Joe they now had to kill.

He tried not to picture what these things would be. What horrific mirror images of the woman and dog the rift would provide.

Briefly, Joe wondered, as he had when first deciding to tell Clara about the rift, if his wife and dog should even be involved. What sane man would even consider taking others into the dark world he'd seen on the other side?

But the answer was as obvious as it was perhaps irrational. The dog had saved him when Joe hadn't had the strength to save himself. His wife, likewise, had been the first of them to have the resilience to move on after Evan's death, and fight for something resembling a life. The woman and dog were both stronger than he was. Joe needed them.

He needed his family.

This settled, his eyes fell on the aluminum storage shed in the corner of the yard. Keeping wide of the billowing, rippling flesh-tent, checking the backyard lawn for those black patches that had invaded the front and seeing none, Joe strode over to the storage shed. He

THE RIFT • 147

opened it and stepped inside. He looked around, stepped back out, and waved Clara over.

Ten feet by twenty with a peaked roof, the storage shed looked large enough to contain the strange tent in the yard, and the rift when it appeared, with room to spare. They could bind the door from the outside somehow, locking in whatever came through on the inside. Right there on a shelf was a padlock and chain that Joe remembered Evan had used for his bike long ago. The length and width of the chain looked about right to loop through the handles of the shed door.

Joe relayed all of this to Clara. Standing beside him, poking her head into the storage shed, she took it all in, seemed to measure and weigh things in her mind. When he was done explaining, she stood back, looked from the shed to the flesh-tent.

"It might work," she said.

"Yeah, it might."

"That's a good bit of labor," she added, nodding again to the shed. "Taking it apart, putting it back together over that...thing...."

"Yeah. But we've tackled bigger things together."

Joe offered her a smile. She flashed one back.

"Remember our first date?" she asked, catching him off guard with the change of subject. Though she still faced the shed Clara seemed to be looking past it at something far away. "I wanted to go dancing. You talked me into bowling."

The shifty-sly glance she gave him made Joe look briefly away, embarrassed.

"I told you I wasn't a dancer," he offered weakly in his defense.

"Bowling, Joe. *Bowling.*"

He laughed, his body aching anew. But her smile brightened, making the pain worth it.

"If we do this thing – kill the other you, trap whatever comes out of the rift in the shed, and find our son over there – we're going dancing."

"It's a deal," Joe said.

★ ★ ★

From the garage and the shed they gathered hammers and wedges and screwdrivers and ladders. The roof of the storage shed came down first. Joe and Clara hefted it from their perches atop opposing ladders and carried it down with measured steps. The walls followed, leaving the floor of the shed alone in the grass. They shared an uncertain look. They stared at the larger house behind them, as if they could see into a future where everything was gone from them, broken down, taken apart.

In the warmth of the late morning, Joe wiped at perspiration running down his face and saw his wife do the same. She rolled up her blouse sleeves and undid a few buttons down the front. Her skin was pale and glimmering and slick. Noticing him watching, she smiled and undid another button, all casual-like, as if she'd meant to do that anyway. As they moved walls and roof over to and about the swelling, flapping flesh-tent, Joe found reasons to move by her, close, brushing against her in brief, light touches. He needed that tool there, or the screws here, and *sorry, didn't mean to get in your way, let me squeeze on by.*

Until the shed rose and hid the tent within it, and the roof was over the top and the doors re-hinged. Shoulder to shoulder, husband and wife peered in, like guards before a cell. Inside, the flesh-tent pushed outward, its skeletal framework flexing and stretching slowly, nearly touching the sides of the shed. The front of the shed faced the patio and the back sliding door, and within the shed, the stitched-shut flaps of the tent's own entrance. The length of chain coiled like a snake on the ground in front of it all, the padlock atop it.

"Now we wait," Clara said, part question, part statement of fact. All exhausted resignation. She breathed heavily, hands on hips, her blouse open and spread down to the middle. Dewy beads of sweat glistened in the sunlight.

Joe pulled his gaze with effort up to her eyes. "I have a better idea," he said. He took her hand, led her inside.

If there was one thing they could do to stake their claim on the house, against all intrusion from this world or any other, he knew what it was, and — just in case it was their last time — he meant to do it long and well.

4.

Standing in the corner adjacent to the shattered glass door in the dark, Joe waited and watched and listened. Across the length of the dining room, past the center dividing wall into the living room, he could just make out Clara's form at the long picture window, a ghost of herself, a shade, and the sofa there next to her, and the dog beside her. She peered out the window and back at him every few seconds. He nodded to her, and she gave a little wave, a fluid motion of inky blackness in the dark.

A short while ago, when they'd turned off all the lights as evening settled, each had spoken softly to the other in the darkness. Though they stood in the home that they'd spent a decade in together, with the veins in the walls and the flesh-tent outside, it was a different place, alien and unfamiliar. In soft voices they'd comforted each other in the gray-black gloom, telling the other that it was okay, everything would be all right.

Clara had the gun with her, which made Joe feel a little better. Not much, but a little. Reminding himself of the holes punched in the target at the firing range, he told himself she was good with it.

He had the sledgehammer again gripped in both hands, balanced on his shoulder. It had sat propped in the very corner where he now stood since he'd come back from the rift, like an old friend waiting for him.

When the rift appeared, it glowed from beneath the wrappings of the flesh-tent like a candle in a paper lantern. Its lazy, wavy undulations were hypnotic and taunting.

Joe turned away, looked to his wife across the room to see if she'd seen it. She had, and was staring back at him. Then behind her, through the thin drapes of the windows and through the windows themselves, out there in the muted shapes and forms of the front yard and the street beyond: movement.

A low figure, hunched, coming across the lawn. Squat and thick and shuffling.

"Clara..." Joe whispered, pointed, hoping she could see the gesture in the dark.

She did, and turned. She pulled aside a corner of the drapes to look out.

Then she backed away, nearly tripping over Rusty. The curtain fluttered back into place as if to shut out what was beyond. It shimmied a bit and then was still.

Clara half turned to Joe. It seemed to him she didn't want the thing out there completely out of her sight, but didn't want to look at it either. Stuck between the two motions.

"It's carrying something...." She hissed the words out quietly.

Joe moved away from his corner and glanced at the flesh-tent behind him. The glowing center of the rift inside it. He understood his wife's terrified indecision perfectly, not wanting to let the breathing thing behind him out of his sight, but needing to move to her at the same time.

Choosing her, he strode across the dining room and met her halfway at the dividing wall. As he leaned against the pillar there, he looked past her and saw the thing through the window. Coming in its shuffling gait through the yard. Then it found the walkway, and the slapping of its footfalls against the hard concrete were clear in the otherwise silence about them.

And, yes, through the sheer fabric of the curtains, through the slight tinted windows, Joe could see something clearly bundled in its arms. Small limbs dangling from a cradled position. A lolling motion of a limp head rolling on a wilted neck.

Clara raised the pistol in one shaky hand.

Joe brought the sledgehammer off his shoulder, at the ready. He could barely hold it aloft, it felt so heavy.

Rusty at their feet made a noise somewhere between a whine and a growl.

The thing out there moved out of view as it turned toward the door.

The doorknob rattled. The doorframe creaked and groaned with pressure put upon it.

Joe moved sideways, past Clara, bringing the foyer and front door into view. Tiled floor and an overhead bulb in that little niche — white in the greater gloom — gave a vague glow to the space, like an afterimage. Enough for him to see the doorknob turning.

With the door in sight, it seemed Joe could hear better too. The click of the knob as the lock stopped it from turning.

And the heavy breath of the thing out there on the porch. An urgent sound. An eager sound.

Joe no longer wanted the other…*him*…here. Whatever plans he'd had — of killing it, of going through the rift again, of finding his son — no longer mattered. All that mattered was that thing *out there* should not get *in here*.

It wasn't something he wanted to see.

It wasn't something he was *meant* to see.

He knew that now. This was the result of the past week. Of experimenting with the rift. Of wanting to know about it. What it could do.

Sometimes not knowing was better.

"Go away," he said to the doorknob, and the thing on the other side of the door, breathing out there in the night. "Go away."

The doorknob stopped moving when he spoke. But the breathing continued — inhalations long and slow, exhalations quick and fast. With the rattle of the knob gone, the breathing seemed louder, closer.

Then there was laughter.

Unlike any Joe had ever heard. There was no humor in it. No mirth. It was a wicked sound. It was the noise a demented child would make when kicking a small animal.

It was harsh and abrasive. It was a sharp sound, like glass shards crunching.

Inhuman.

Then it spoke. Its voice was like that of the backward, head-inverted rift-freak he and Clara had sent tumbling aflame down the quarry, stuffed in a trash can. An arid desert wind blowing across a barren landscape.

"We're home...."

It whispered the words with a singsong lilt. Though it stood just outside the door, those slapping sounds of its footfalls came again, as if maybe the thing danced a little jig there on the front porch.

Clara sidestepped until she was next to Joe again. So intent on the door had he been that he forgot she was there, and her motion startled him. He realized he held the sledgehammer high and at the ready.

"Open the door," she said, a phantom there beside him. The vague shape of the gun raised in her right hand pointed in the general direction of the front door. "Let me kill it."

The doorknob started rattling again. The frame shook harder as the thing on the porch pushed more insistently.

Joe wanted nothing more than to do what his wife had just asked. He wanted the thing to go away, either on its own, or if need be, by one or both of them destroying it. By hammer or gun, it didn't matter. It just needed to *go*.

The doorknob fell silent again.

Clara took a step toward the door. Joe stopped her with a hand on her arm. He shook his head when she looked at him. He pointed to his ear. Then he leaned forward, listening.

Neither the breathing nor the slapping of the feet could be heard. All was quiet beyond the door.

Joe nodded to Clara.

He took a position near the door, one hand outstretched ready to flip the locks and turn the knob. When he swung the door open, whatever was out there would be met by his wife with her back against the wall of the foyer, gun blasting away at the porch. She nodded, ready.

Joe flipped the locks, grabbed the knob, turned it, threw the door open.

Rather than shooting, Clara screamed.

Joe turned to better see what was out there. He saw the dead boy in his little black suit and tie curled on the porch. The gray and mottled flesh. The shape of the skull beneath. The eye sockets black and empty.

He screamed, too, so long and loud it hurt, and didn't know if he could ever stop.

CHAPTER TWELVE

1.

The wailing of the sirens drawing nearer could have been echoes of Joe's own cries. Joe looked down at the thing on the porch – the tight, drawn skin, the sunken features, the missing eyes – and nothing made sense. Nothing mattered. Not the world around him, nothing inside him either. All thoughts fizzled out as quick as they formed, like the last embers of a dying fire.

"What the hell is going on over there?"

A loud and angry voice from somewhere along the street. The distant flicker of a light on a front porch winking on. Another a couple houses down. Bathrobed figures slipping out to watch.

So *now* they heard, and *now* they saw. Only when it had come to this, the grim delivery on his porch. Joe could have laughed.

He did laugh. He laughed and cried.

He leaned against the doorframe, holding himself in his laughter. Then he punched the door. He looked at the thing on the porch. Looked away.

Clara behind him had backed away, a hand to her mouth, then to her eyes, as if to shield herself against what she saw. She drew near again, perhaps to make sure she'd seen what she had. Seeing it again, she made little mewling sounds like an animal dying.

The sirens, oh so close now. High and shrill and calling out, announcing their arrival.

Rusty was there at Joe's feet. Poking his head out the door. Sniffing. Smelling the grotesque package left on the doorstep.

And then a hint of movement at the corner of the house. Moving around the corner toward the fence there out of sight. There was a shuffle and a bump and a dragging sound as something went over the fence and landed on the other side.

Joe stepped out onto the porch.

He knelt and took up the dead boy in his arms.

It was so light it was startling. Held in his arms, it was like a husk of something. A shell and not the remnants of a life. Not a person at all but some doll or mannequin.

He knew what he had to do. Looking into those empty sockets set in the skeletal face, tufts of brown hair hanging like weeds, he knew he had to see it through to the end. He'd had it backward the whole time.

It wasn't his son *over there* he had to find and bring back. It was the thing in his arms *here* that he had to relinquish and let go to where it belonged.

The living were the living, and the dead were the dead.

There was a veil – a rift – between them for a reason.

Turning around, stepping back into the house, he was met by his wife standing there, mute and dumb with horror at what she beheld. The burden in his arms. The wasted thing that they'd once known.

The sirens were very close now. He'd have to move fast.

"We're taking him through," Joe said.

"Oh God, Joe."

A trembling hand reached out to touch the corpse. Pulled away just short, as if shocked. She turned away, leaned against a wall, bumped off it, making progress across the room in little fits.

Joe followed her.

The dog trailed them.

At the shattered glass door they gathered together and looked out at what awaited them. The flesh-tent swelled at the seams, pressing against the confines of the shed around it. The stitched flaps now unstitched and hanging open. Windows and a door like their home behind them. Through that and in the dark center the rift alight and whirling, stretching tall, taller than ever, and wide, wide enough to admit them all.

And standing before it all – rift and tent and shed – the other father, wearing what Joe himself wore, a button-up shirt with the sleeves rolled up and jeans and boots. But its face was like a mask, badly fitted, hanging on the skull beneath it like a rag. A hand held out as if in welcome, pointing them to the rift.

Joe led the way for his family. All of them, dog and human, living and dead.

Behind him, Clara took up the chain and padlock, fed the links through the handles of the Duramax shed. She pulled the doors shut, clicked the lock through the chain, and pocketed the key. With the chain between the doors, they didn't close all the way; a gap about a half-inch thick let in the moonlight.

But Joe no longer cared. It would have to do for whatever came through.

Into the rift for one last exchange.

2.

He felt himself go through this time. On his first trip through the rift, anchored by the rope to his wife and their world, Joe had felt nothing at all. Almost as if the rift wasn't there and he'd merely stepped through the empty space of an open door. This time, though, there was a tingle, almost a slight burning that traveled the length of his body, head to toe. It was like the pins and needles of limbs fallen asleep, but more intense.

As he passed through, the world went white, the bright yellow-white of staring dead on at the sun on a clear day. This whiteness and the pins and needles burning were the same thing. Joe wasn't sure how he knew this, but he did. It was the rift enveloping him, washing over him as if he'd stepped under a rushing waterfall. He heard it, too, like waves and surf rolling in.

In this electric humming whiteness he felt Clara beside him but didn't see her. He felt the weight of the burden in his arms. Rusty, too, on his other side. And then something moved by them, around them, as if they passed through a crowd, jostling and being jostled. Something *leaving* the rift as they *entered*.

Out onto the bleak landscape the three of them emerged. The four of them, if the little body in Joe's arms counted. And it did. It counted most of all.

The black stretched in all directions, and the red sky unraveled above.

The behemoth – the man-creature standing taller than all men, wearing the skins of men – no longer lay dead where it had fallen, with the machete plunged deep into its chest. Joe thought initially it had been carried away, maybe. He looked around for pieces of it. Perhaps scavengers of the rift had dragged it away. What *these* looked like, Joe didn't want to know.

But then he saw that the rope he'd cut – freeing himself of Clara, his anchor, as he'd pursued his son – wasn't on the ground before them, either. Though he couldn't be sure, looking around again at the rift-world, he thought the geometry was a bit different. Glassy black all about, to most eyes all the expanse would probably look the same. However, whereas during his first trip through Joe had the impression of the land being relatively smooth – the far features like the gorge and the butte camouflaged by distance and illusion – this time he could actually make out geological configurations not so far out.

No, he wasn't in the same spot as before. This time, now that Joe was unanchored to their world, the arrival in the rift-world had apparently been less targeted, more random.

"Cover him."

Joe flinched at the sound of Clara's voice. Staring out over it all – the desolation, the great emptiness, the burden in his arms – he'd felt alone. Even hearing his wife's voice, he felt alone still. He looked from the wasted thing in his arms, cradled to his chest, to the woman beside him. "What?"

"Cover him. Please."

Arguing the point was useless. He didn't have it in him. It no longer mattered. Nothing mattered but completing the task before him.

Joe knelt, set the body down. He found himself adjusting a lock of the hair hanging from the leathery skull. Leathery like the scrolls deposited from the rift.

At this thought he pulled his hands away. He stood up, removed his shirt and motioned Clara over. Hesitant, crying again, she nonetheless came forward. This was a job for the both of them.

Joe spread his shirt wide on the ground like a blanket. Clara took it by the shoulders, he by the hem, pulling it taut to its full length and width. Joe lifted the body again, set it down on top of the shirt. Clara took over from there. As if swaddling a baby, she made a bundle of their dead son.

The legs and arms dangled out. But she made sure to cover the face. She tucked the head down beneath the neck hole and collar of the shirt.

So when they stood, Joe in front, she in back, they carried the body between them. Joe leading the way, they started out. Rusty trotted along beside them like a guard to the procession.

The black earth and the red horizon led to nowhere and everywhere and to all spaces between.

3.

In this charred black land of the blood-red sky and bulbous, cancer-yellow moon, the heat bore down upon the travelers and their burden. Even with no sun in the sky, the heat seemed to permeate the very air, thick and heavy like a noxious gas from some hidden vent. It was as if they trudged through a mire, pushing through an invisible barrier.

Joe didn't consciously choose their route. He just found a point somewhere on the horizon and walked toward it. Shirtless, he sweated a river; it ran down in trickles and dripped off to sizzle on the glassy black ground.

Walking his invisible line to the horizon, Joe watched as the sky changed color. From the blood-red it had been since he'd first glimpsed it through the telescope, it dimmed to a darker hue, a magenta almost purple, and then to purple itself and deeper yet to black. Once black, the sky and the dark earth seemed a void in all directions, an absence of everything. They walked in an oblivion without dimensions and the piss-yellow moon above was like an eye watching their procession.

The ground beneath his feet told him it was still there, so Joe kept walking, the boy's body held behind him, and Clara, also bearing it, following. In time he became aware of sounds in the blackness. Though the muted light of the cancer moon revealed nothing other than itself, there was the noise of things out there navigating the black space. Dragging sounds and the flaps of wings and long breaths drawn in and exhaled and a chittering like laughter and other sounds. Things moved in the dark, following them unseen.

At some point in their travels the sky lit again, black to purple to red, and the obsidian earth reappeared like a thing sketched into being. Before them lay a scattered gathering of lean-tos and clapboard shacks, a destitute village like the one he'd seen before at the foot of the butte. Maybe this was the very same one, as a rocky face behind it rose to the sky, with contours and features Joe thought familiar.

Whether it was the same village or not, Joe moved through it this time rather than around. The burden lugged behind him pushed away all other concerns. Through the village was the straightest course to his point on the horizon, so that's where he went.

This time the occupants stood waiting, watching.

These wretched creatures could have been human once upon a time. In some distant age long ago before the wickedness and cruelty of this land had assailed them. Their bodies were twisted by unspeakable tortures and torments, wasted thin by hunger and thirst. Bent low and hunched from decades of arduous labor in poor conditions, they moved in shifty jerks and slow shuffles.

Subhuman eyes watched Joe and Clara and Rusty and the bundle between them from within sunken and shriveled faces with features both familiar and wholly alien. Noses and mouths and jowls and such should have been identifiable but all ran together in a shapeless melding.

There was a space like a path running through the approximate center of these creatures' village. This gathering of hovels. Along the sides of this dirt lane they lined up and waited like an honor guard, standing to attention, attending some ceremony.

Joe led Clara and Rusty and the wrapped dead child down this central road. The dirt lane led between parallel stony risings, towering stalagmites like monoliths. Faces could be seen in the rocky features if looked at from certain angles. Whether these were intentional or natural, Joe led the way between them, feeling eyes on him, a gaze more powerful than the furtive ones of the twisted subhumans.

Out of this place with its strange inhabitants, the road continued for a ways and then faded back into the black crags of the land. Once they left the village, the sky again went from red to purple to black, until once again they walked in impenetrable blackness.

And the sounds of the things in the dark followed them again.

At one point, Clara tripped and cried out. The sound of her fall and her cry seemed a response to the noises about them: the wing flaps and the shuffling and the chittering and the laughter. These in turn seemed to respond to her. When she fell the shirt-wrapped bundle went down with her, wrenched from Joe's grip, and the body tumbled.

For the first time since they started this procession, Joe was overcome by fear. His son's body was somewhere near him, rolling and tumbling in lifeless acrobatics. The sound of the dog whining his concern could have just as easily been some creature – some *thing* – slithering and coming toward them.

Coming to take his son and to leave the task incomplete.

"Clara! Are you okay?" He whispered these words frantically. He felt that should the things out there hear him, they would come circling in like vultures and descend upon them.

He reached out, felt around. The dog came first, furry and breathing loud, and Joe almost struck him in fear. Then Rusty's tongue found him with wet slaps to the face and he hugged the dog briefly then pushed him away.

"Clara!"

The laughter was out there around them. Mocking. Contemptuous. The movement of things circling, coming around, sniffing at them, drawing near.

Joe's hand fell on another. He squeezed it. He started to draw near its owner before he registered its texture and temperature. Dry and cool. Following the length of the angular arm, he found the bony shoulder beneath the suit jacket. Further up he felt the tight skin of the face. His fingers lingered at the edges of the holes where the eyes had once nestled. Joe almost snatched his hand back in revulsion, but fought back that impulse and kept it there. He stroked the cheek, traced the hanging brown locks.

"Joe? Did you find him?" Clara. Whispering as he had been. The shuffling scrapes of her coming closer. And then she was there beside him, pressing against him.

"Did you find him, Joe?"

He nodded, then, realizing she couldn't see him, spoke. "Yes."

"Do you hear them out there, Joe?"

"Yes."

"Moving out there. Just waiting. Watching us."

"Yes."

They sat in the darkness for a time with the body before them and listened – to the things out there and to each other. The sound of the other's breathing. The beating of their own hearts. Finally, they found the tied ends of the bundle, took up their burden and started out again.

After a time, the sky came alive again, shifting from black to red, a kaleidoscopic heaven, and before them stretched out a great dark ocean. Waves rolled in along an obsidian glass beach, and with the unveiling of the lit sky the sound of the black waters arose, as if on cue with the crash of waves and the foam and the surf. A small wooden dock stood in the midst of it at the shoreline; a modest rowboat was tied to the dock.

They searched around for its owner. Finding none, they loaded the body in it, and climbed in after. Rusty leaped in too. They took up the two oars at their feet and pushed out into the dark waters. As they rowed out into the lapping ripples, Joe realized this was similar to how they'd first met. He looked back over his shoulder at his wife. Her eyes met his and he saw clear as day she was thinking the same thing.

But that was what the rift did. It reflected things, joining them one to the other. Forcing a reconciliation of opposites. A resolution to things that sought separation but could never be separated.

As they'd begun their life together rowing on a lake, so too would the rift seek to end them, voyagers now upon an ocean of death.

4.

Not too far out from the black glass shore, upon the dark waters, a gray fog rolled in and over them. So thick was the mist that once it settled they had a hard time even seeing each other; Clara at the bow, Joe at the stern. The dog between them sat near the body at the center. He leaned out cautiously over the starboard side and looked out into the fog. He sniffed and twitched his muzzle at the smells and then lowered his head and lay down.

The boat made a quiet sloshing sound through the water and the oars pulled them onward. Out in the dim grayness were other sloshes and splashes and the sounds of things breaking the surface or dropped into the ocean. Through brief lapses in the fog Joe saw other boats drifting by in all directions, and he pointed them out to Clara, and she to him. Rowboats like theirs, canoes, and larger vessels with vast sails crackling in the wind.

There were passengers and crews working the oars in these other vessels or dark helmsmen at the wheel. Seen through the veil of the fog, they were but silhouettes. Shadows pulling, shadows pointing, shadows staring out into the great sea. Without buoys or lighthouses or compasses or other bearings, Joe wondered how these others knew where to navigate. Then realizing that hadn't stopped him, he guessed it wouldn't have stopped them either.

Especially if they had cargo such as his.

After a time the fog lifted and they were alone on the surface of the lolling deep. No other vessels and no other crews for as far as they could see in all directions. Directly ahead, though, an island loomed, black and craggy and sharp as the land they'd come from. Absent a fire-pluming peak, it could have been a volcano erupted from the earth. Along the shoreline they approached, another small wooden dock stood with moorings and rope for them to tie off and anchor their boat. Which they did. Joe then lifted their cargo up and out onto the planks of the dock, boosted Clara and Rusty up also, and finally pushed himself up.

A dirt path like the one through the village of wretched creatures stretched away from the dock and up in curves around the black mountain. Joe nodded at it, took up the front of their bundled load again, and his wife in place taking up her end, they set out once more.

The extent of the island seemed only the thin shoreline, the dock, and the high, wide mountain before them. As they scaled the path leading up, Joe and Clara looked out over what lay below. The black waters stretched outward far into the distance behind them. But here above, the path and the mountain dominated.

They continued to climb.

At some indeterminable height the path ended and led into a cave. It was dark at the entrance, but deeper in Joe could see a flickering light.

"Are we going in there?" Clara asked. Her tone held neither reluctance nor determination. It was beyond resignation. She seemed merely a machine speaking programmed words.

"There's nowhere else to go."

They knelt to clear the low-hanging entrance and walked into the dark cave.

The chamber they entered was roughly circular. Stalactites like stony tears hung from the ceiling. Light flickering from around a bend in the tunnel cast strange forms along the rocky walls, like a shadow puppet show. When the light hit the walls in certain ways Joe could see things drawn there. Drawings and scribblings of things reaching. Things grabbing. Things standing upright and stalking. Harsh, fast markings as if the artist had slashed with his paints in a frenzy.

It was the language of the rift. The same markings as those on the scrolls he'd translated days ago. The hieroglyphs like Egyptian writing.

"Do you know what they say?" Clara asked from behind him.

Joe wished he did. He thought it imperative he knew what was written on the walls. That understanding the markings there would bring a greater understanding of other things.

But he couldn't read them. The knowledge of the walls was out of his reach.

"No," he said. "I have no idea."

And he started walking again, pulling Clara with him on her end of the funereal procession. After crossing the large central chamber, he led them to the branching tunnel through which the light flickered, beckoning, the source unseen.

This path was smaller, tighter. Though they and their burden and dog trailing them all fit, the walls were close and the ceiling low. Joe felt the tunnel was constricting around them. Swallowing them like a throat.

He remembered thinking this about the rift itself, when it spat the burning black stones out on those first nights. He wondered if that's what had finally happened, if the rift had consumed him.

A chamber lay at the end of the tunnel, smaller than the one with the writing on the walls. A fire in the center of it, orange-red. A boy sat on the far side of the flame, staring out over it at the new arrivals. It was the boy he'd carried from the pit in the center of the smoking metropolis.

The boy that had vanished from his arms.

5.

The boy motioned for Joe and Clara to remain where they were with a palm-out gesture. They set the mummy-wrapped cadaver down to one side and stood, waiting, as the boy instructed. The dog settled down nearby, watching the whole interplay with a stoicism befitting his kind.

The boy, as naked as he'd been when Joe carried him out of the pit, stood also, and walked over to the bundled body. Stooping, he rolled the collar of Joe's shirt down, revealing the face and head of the dead boy beneath the makeshift shroud. He looked at it for a time, crouched in that way like a tracker looking for signs of something that had passed. Then the naked boy stood again and returned to his place on the other side of the fire.

"Give it to me," the boy said.

His voice had a flat, echoing quality, like a recording of something played back on a large sound stage.

"What?" Clara said, and took a step forward.

Joe, however, knew something like this had been coming. He'd known the purpose of this crossing since they'd stepped through the rift. He grabbed her arm, pulled her back.

"Was my son ever really here?" Joe asked, taking a step forward himself.

The naked boy sat behind the blaze, said nothing, but stared into the fire. The flames licking up before him seemed to caress his face like fingers.

"Because you're not him," Joe said. He pointed at the boy through the fire. As the fire snapped and licked, features of the boy seemed to ripple, blur, come in and out of focus. "Whatever you are, you're not my son."

The boy met Joe's eyes directly for the first time with orbs of black, depthless and penetrating. Without his shirt Joe felt exposed, not half naked but fully so. Those dark eyes saw everything. He took a step back until he was beside his wife again.

"You called *me."*

It wasn't a boy's voice it spoke with. Not now that the charade was over. Now that it was known for what it was, it spoke with its true voice. Like crunching glass or an infernal machine engine coughing to life, its words shook the walls of the cave. Dust fell in little clouds as if the world were coming apart.

"I never—" Joe began then stopped, having to sidestep a fist-sized piece of the rock roof of the cave coming down. He was confused and afraid. He'd called nothing. Least of all anything like the boy-thing on the other side of the fire. He didn't even know what that meant, or how to call something such as it.

"In your misery you called me. And I answered."

Joe tried to process all that was happening. All that had happened before. He tried to piece things together like a frustrated child assembling a difficult puzzle. Whenever two pieces seemed to come together, though, others didn't fit.

"Give it to me."

The face across the fire rippled and shifted again. The boy-thing raised an arm and pointed at the bundled corpse. And then Joe understood.

As with every other thing cast into the rift, the trade had to be freely made. The offer extended and the counteroffer accepted. First with the stones, and then the notes, he'd cast things in not fully knowing, but expecting *something* to come back. Even with the crickets, intending to send them through still anchored to his world, the intent had been to see if something there could come back. To *test* the rift. To *learn* from it.

Every time he'd sent something in, he'd wanted something back.

Here, too, with the dug-up cadaver of his son, the trade had to be done willfully.

The other father – the other *him* – with its draped-on face a mockery of Joe's, had left the body on the porch, knowing that Joe would take it through when he saw it. The temptation would be too great. For mankind it always was.

Joe stepped forward again. He knelt and took up the dead boy in his arms. He stared one last time into the sunken, lifeless face, framed by the collar of his shirt like a child sheet-wrapped, sleeping. A dead child.

His son was dead and gone.

That was the way of things. He felt a weight lifted from him. In content resignation he breathed in deep, let it out. Even in the stale air of the cave, such a breath, such a release, was good.

Joe stepped forward with the body.

The false-child behind the fire, face rippling, a face *behind* the face peeking through, rose, smiled, held its hands out to receive the offering. The parted lips of the smile showed yellowed teeth. Black gums. A wormy tongue.

"Fuck you," Joe said. He turned away from the thing and dropped his son's body into the flames at the center of the cave.

The shirt caught fire quickly. The flames spread across the entirety of it. The dry husk of the corpse was a fine kindling. The fire leapt higher with a whoosh.

The false-boy cast aside its disguise, like garments shucked off. Its true form emerged from within, pushing out from the thin frame and flesh. Bursting into being with ripping and tearing sounds, it came for them.

A cold terror filled Joe, slipped into every limb and made coherent thought impossible. He wanted to run but couldn't. He wanted to scream but couldn't. Backing up a step, he collided with Clara and they fell together, entangled. She clawed at him in her terror, attempting a scrambling retreat.

It rose before them in all its terrible glory, all eyes and mouth. So it could see, and seeing, devour. Stretching open before them. A black tunnel where the hints of things swelling, pulsing, led down to a further blackness.

This was the rift, Joe knew. Not the tantalizing light that had tempted him with mystery and false promises. This was the real rift. A blackness more absolute than any night, deeper than any stretch of space. And he *had* called it forth. He knew that now. By rejecting everything else after the death of his son – friends, family, work, *life* – he'd welcomed this thing because it was all that remained when those others were gone.

It descended to scoop him up. To take him into itself.

Then Rusty was there.

Standing before the living darkness. Such a small thing before something so vast and dreadful. But the dog stood his ground, growling, hackles rising, poised and ready to launch. To give himself before the darkness could take his family, his human charges, his very reason for living.

The yawning darkness roared. A terrible sound like a whirlwind. With blind rage and hatred at the light of things, the light of life, it roared mightily. A sound for nightmares. A cry to shake all of creation.

Then it retreated.

Mere inches, nearly imperceptible. Then further, a foot or more, and the dog advanced, jaws clacking, further still.

The fire in the center of the cave flashed once with a great ignition. Then the flames died down to a steady flicker, and Joe saw the body of his son was gone. No bones, no pieces, all of it gone.

The darkness retreated within a fissure at the rear of the chamber, drawn back and into the wall as if by some great suction. There was a loud wail of rage and frustration as it departed.

The dog trotted back to them.

Joe stood again, helped Clara to her feet, and they turned back the way they'd come. Down the black mountain, across the black water, through the gray fog, into the obsidian wasteland, back to the rift.

They stepped through it, back to their world, to the remnants of what had once been their home, and the new family that had claimed it.

CHAPTER THIRTEEN

1.

The house seemed like a desolate shack in the middle of a ghost town. An empty dwelling where people had once lived before some catastrophe or other had hollowed it out. The glass of the sliding door was still lying on the ground, shattered and twinkling in the morning sun. But the doorway was covered by a translucent plastic tarp, and yellow police tape crisscrossed it.

Leading up to the covered doorway, splinters of the tool shed lay scattered about the yard and patio. Parts of it floated in the pool.

The flesh-tent was gone. The holes in the yard where the stones had melted through were gone. The rift itself started to close behind them and Joe and Clara and Rusty turned together to watch.

This time around it wasn't a simple winking out of existence, like parted curtains being drawn back together. Or the zippering up of the sky in a fluid motion. Rather than the deliberate closing the rift had previously done, this time it seemed to twist and buck and jerk. Then it folded in on itself like origami, corner to corner, side to side, and reshaped itself, smaller, smaller still, until it seemed to collapse. Like the swirling of water down a drain, the rift was *sucked* by something, and then it was gone.

Clara moved first for the rear entrance where the tarp hung and the yellow tape crisscrossed like a ward against them. She reached for one corner of the tape, crinkled it in a fist and tore it down. The sound of the tape ripping free of the doorframe was loud in the silence of the morning.

She entered. Joe and the dog followed.

The dining room and kitchen were as they had left them. Nothing was out of place, as it had been before, when the other Joe had stormed through the rooms in pursuit of Clara. The table and the chairs, the hutch, the appliances on the countertops, the dishes in the rack at the sink; all were in their places, as if Joe and Clara had merely stepped out for the evening and come back.

What had become of the other Joe, the other father? Joe's twisted twin that had waved them through the rift that last time as if in invitation? Though Joe's mind had been occupied by other things – like the boy's body occupying his cradled arms – he'd been sure the doppelganger would have savaged the house again during his and Clara's absence. Or torn it down altogether to be replaced by the budding flesh-tent.

But, when he took in the dining room, kitchen, and living room, nothing seemed amiss.

Joe moved past Clara for a closer look. He touched things as he passed them. The solidity of the furniture reminded him of what was and always would be. In the kitchen, he saw the closed drawers, the cabinets, and then at the sink he looked out.

Across the street someone looked back. The officer leaning against his black-and-white cruiser immediately put a hand to his radio, lowered his head to speak into it, and started across the street in a jog. One hand rested not so casually on the butt of his service pistol.

"Shit," Joe said.

Clara came to the window and saw it too. The officer on the sidewalk, now on the grass, kept one eye on them as he strode toward the front door.

Joe turned from the kitchen window and saw the butt of the pistol poking out from Clara's waistband, where she'd had it tucked the entire trek through the rift. Her purse was on the counter.

"Shit, Clara, the gun! Put it in your purse!"

For a moment she only looked at him with mild confusion. Then the doorknob rattled and the door creaked open. Terrible understanding dawned on her face. She hurried over to her purse, slipped the gun from her jeans, and tucked it down deep.

Together they walked slowly and with their hands out and high and visible around the corner into the living room to meet the officer. Young and fresh-faced, eager and worried, he stopped at the far end of the room, hand still on the butt of his own gun, and looked them up and down.

"Stop right there," he said.

They already had. Rusty, too, stood patiently at Joe's side. He gave a swish of his tail as if he thought it was all some game, the rules of which he'd soon be let in on.

"Are you the owners of this residence?"

The officer's tone was almost reluctant, as if he hoped they weren't so he could draw his weapon. Like he wanted a story he could share with the other guys at the station.

Joe nodded and went slowly for his wallet and his driver's license. Then he remembered he'd left them on the dining table before he and Clara had gone into the rift. He hadn't seen them there when they'd returned so he figured the police must have taken them. Shirtless, scuffed and dirty from his travels through the rift, and now without identification, Joe didn't think he was inspiring confidence in the officer.

"My wife has her ID in her purse," Joe said, nodding toward the kitchen. When he thought about what else was in her purse, a sick feeling rolled in his stomach.

"Go ahead," the officer said. "Get it."

Clara turned slowly and moved toward the kitchen. Each step she took seemed to tick away time like a metronome. Joe prayed for her to be quick, not to raise the officer's suspicion, so the young man wouldn't follow her, decide to find the identification himself, rummage through her purse and find the gun.

Then Clara was back, holding out her hand, and she and the officer met in the middle of the room. The officer looked at the plastic card. Looked at Clara. Glanced at Joe half-dressed and here the man's face drew into a strange frown as if he'd bit into something sour.

He passed the card back to Clara. He took his hand off the

butt of the gun. The tension visibly went out of his body and his shoulders relaxed.

"There was some sort of disturbance here last night, Mr. and Mrs. Jimenez," he began. "I'm afraid we're going to have to ask for some of your time to answer some questions. Excuse me a moment."

Joe and Clara nodded and the officer stepped out of the house, his head lowering again, to speak into the radio. As his voice faded, Joe turned to his wife.

"We thought we heard sounds of an intruder last night. More than one. So we ran. I felt foolish for running, so we didn't immediately report it. Then we came back home and found it like this. No more, no less. It's not a perfect story, but the simpler we keep it, the better."

She nodded.

The cop came back and told them his captain and a detective were on their way. He gave Joe leave to get dressed. He asked for the dog to be put outside.

When the others arrived – a captain and a plainclothes detective – Joe and Clara told their story, kept it short, kept it simple. Looks were exchanged. Impassive faces stared at them, belying nothing. The detective asked if they knew about the vandalism to their son's gravesite. Joe said yes. The detective asked how that made him feel. Joe said it pissed him off but there was really no one to blame but the perpetrators.

Other questions were asked. Lies and half-truths told. But Joe thought they did pretty well. Keeping a mental checklist, he was pretty sure neither of them had given any conflicting details.

The officer and his captain soon left. The detective was last and on the porch he turned back to them and said he'd be in touch. With a tired frown that said he didn't believe them, didn't believe much of anything, he walked to his unmarked car and drove away.

Joe thought that was a pretty good philosophy, one he could have benefited from over a week ago. Don't believe anything, and the world can't touch you. And without pain, loss, or disappointment, without expectation, life would slowly roll on by and then it would be over.

2.

After walking through the house room by room, upstairs and down, Joe and Clara showered. Clara took the downstairs bath, Joe the master bath in the bedroom they'd once shared. He briefly thought of inviting her in with him, but he was tired, and seeing the slump of her shoulders and the lines of her face, she looked more so, and they parted at the stairs. Rusty parked himself on the mid-landing of the stairwell, as if unable to choose between them.

In the bathroom Joe cranked the shower knobs on. While he was waiting for the water to get warm, he backed out, took off his clothes. Naked, he turned to face himself in the mirror. The glass was beginning to steam up, so he bent forward to run a hand through the condensation.

A space cleared, but it seemed his reflection was delayed. There was a brief moment when it seemed to rush into place to mirror his movements. It was so fast, Joe wasn't even sure he'd seen it.

He leaned over closer to the mirror. Looked long and hard at the tired image of himself staring back. He lifted a hand, moved it side to side in a broad wave.

The mirror Joe traced the motion with synchronized perfection.

He stepped away and gingerly climbed into the shower, under the hot spray of the water. Soaping himself into a thick lather, he tried to scrub away the memories of the past week along with the dirt and grime of the prior night. The filth swirled away with the water down the drain, but the memories remained.

When he exited the shower, Joe looked at the mirror again. It had steamed over once more, so he wiped it clear again with the bath towel. He watched it periodically as he toweled himself dry.

His reflection moved as it was supposed to.

Once dressed again, he headed back downstairs. The dog met him at the halfway point and they strode to the kitchen together. Clara, in a loosely belted blue robe, was over the stove, frying eggs and sausage. Toast and glasses of juice already sat on the dining table.

"Looks good," Joe said.

She turned to him. Her short, wet curls shone with droplets and her skin was still flushed red from her own shower. Now that she was fresh and clean, the exhaustion had left her to a degree and she smiled. Her smile lit her up.

"So do you," he added.

"It's over, isn't it?" she asked, as she turned back to the sizzling pan to flip the eggs and roll the sausage links. "The rift? It's gone, right?"

Joe nodded, sat down at the place set for him at the table. Elbows on the edge of the table, he put his head in his hands. He rubbed his temples, trying to release some of the pressure that had been there for a long time now. He closed his eyes and focused on breathing, trying to relax himself.

"I think so," he said. "It's gone."

"Because you...dropped Evan's body into the fire. You... released him."

"Yeah. I think so."

He opened his eyes to look at his wife.

There in the kitchen, before the stove, were two of her, one superimposed upon the other like an afterimage. One Clara stood over the pan, frying breakfast. The other Clara was over some sort of fire pit, a hole in the ground like at a campsite, with a spit over it and on the spit something roasting. Something black and charred and roasting and still *alive*. This other Clara wore no robe, was completely nude, and like the other Joe that had dug up his son's corpse and delivered it on the porch, this Clara's face seemed draped loosely over the skull beneath it. As if with but a slight tug it would come off and drift to the floor. The rest of its skin was likewise loose and seemed to droop like baggy clothes.

Joe stood up fast, knocking the plate of toast and sloshing the orange juice. Even with this horror before him, by second nature he reached for the tall glass to steady it. Once it was righted, he turned back to the two Claras.

But the other Clara — roasting whatever living thing had been skewered over the fire pit — was gone. Only his wife was there, red-faced and wet and robed, looking back at him.

"What? What's wrong?"

She held up a spatula in one hand like a sword. Her frantic look took in him and her surroundings at the same time, trying to find where an attack might come from.

Joe looked around too. The living room. The dining room. The empty threshold where the sliding rear door into the backyard had been.

Everything was as it should be.

He faced Clara again. He shook his head and held a hand to his temple. "Nothing, I'm just tired."

"What, Joe? What did you see?"

Joe knew she was wired by fear. The tension in her was like a spring, needing release. He wondered if she would ever be the same again after seeing the things she had. Knowing *he* never would, he thought he probably had the answer to that question already.

"Nothing," he repeated. He pointed at the food in the pan. "That really looks good."

She served them. Rusty, under the table, awaited his obligatory scraps. They ate in silence. There was the sense of something missing that once found would put things right. But neither knew what that was and so they pretended it wasn't there to be missed in the first place.

Once the meal was done, Joe helped with the dishes and then went online. They hadn't called a glazier yet to replace the sliding door and Joe thought the sooner things in the house were back to the way they had been, the sooner they could be back to the people they once were. Or at least a semblance of them.

Joe found a shop that wasn't that far away, jotted down the number, then went to the phone. He dialed the number and waited.

The phone rang three times before the line went dead. Joe hung up and listened for the dial tone. Then he dialed again.

The phone rang three times on the other end and went dead once more.

"Something's wrong with the phone..." he said.

He reached to put the receiver back in the cradle. He could try one of their cell phones to call the glass shop. But before he could lay the receiver down, he heard a noise from the earpiece. It was distant, like a bad signal from a radio station. He raised the phone back to his ear to hear it better.

There were clicks and beeps from the phone line. Pressing the receiver tighter to his face, Joe listened. Clara, at the kitchen sink, stopped her washing and stared at him, waiting. From the phone line came the hiss and fizz of a bad connection.

"Hello?" Joe said in a hushed voice into the receiver. "Is someone there?"

There were voices coming up through the clicks and the beeps and the hiss. More than one, speaking over each other and in unison. Joe could almost understand them but not quite.

"You're going to have to call back," he said. "We've got a bad connection."

He knew that didn't make sense even as he spoke the words. *He'd* made the call. No one had called *him*.

Before he could pull the receiver away from his ear to return it to the cradle, the voices fell, faded, until there was only one. Through the clicks and pops and fizz of the static, its words were vague but unmistakable.

"Get out of our house."

Joe slammed the phone down and backed away.

3.

For an hour Clara tried to get him to tell her what had happened, what he'd heard. Joe refused, unsure if he'd heard anything. What he'd thought he'd heard – and seen – couldn't be so. He had to have imagined it.

They'd won. He'd closed the rift.

His son's body in the fire had sealed the deal. Completed the transaction.

He tried walking away from her to other rooms. Wherever he went, though, Clara followed, first pleading with him to tell her, and then yelling at him to do so. Until it was so bad, he had to get out. He scooped up his keys, went out to the Explorer with Rusty trailing, and drove away. In the rearview mirror he saw that Clara stood in the yard watching his departure. Despite everything they'd been through in the past days, though he was sure they were together again for good, Joe couldn't help but feel he was fucking things up.

His plan was to swing by the glazier's shop in person. He'd taken the measurements of the rear doorway a couple times before, when fitting curtains or replacing the glass when Evan, in his early years, decided to try to run through the squeaky-clean glass, thinking the door was open. Joe knew the dimensions from memory.

The world continued on around him as if the rift had never been. His fellow drivers made U-turns and lane changes, pulled in and out of parking lots, honked horns and flipped the bird. Oblivious to the fact that some rip between worlds had opened and sent demons and monstrosities through. That behind the normalcy and the mundane, things were plotting.

Joe didn't think he could ever forget those things. Though he and Clara had come out of it okay, he knew he'd go to sleep every night for the rest of his life staring out the windows, wondering when and where another rift would open, and what would come out.

Coming up to the plaza the glass shop was in, Joe slowed at a red light, flipped on his signal for the right turn into the parking lot. He glanced in the rearview mirror at the traffic behind him.

He saw not a yellow Labrador in the backseat, but some wet, glistening thing. It was tall and wide and round and within the folds of its wet flesh many mouths opened and closed. Thick strands of a mucus-like substance stretched across the mouths, some of which were snapping, others with tendrils drooping and swinging.

Joe screamed and wrenched the wheel.

The Explorer went up fast and hard over the curb into the parking lot. Wrenching his attention back to what was ahead of him, he pulled hard on the steering wheel just in time to avoid a lamppost.

He hit the brakes and the car squealed to an abrupt stop in the middle of the lot. Caught off guard, he heard Rusty tumble to the floor space behind him.

At least he hoped it was Rusty.

Joe turned, leaned over between the seats. The dog was scrambling to his feet, trying to climb back onto the seat he'd been dumped from. Pushing at the dog's rump with both hands, Joe boosted Rusty back up.

"Sorry," he said, looking at the backseat area as he spoke. Nothing there but the dog.

Facing forward again, Joe clenched the steering wheel with both hands. He stared down into his lap. Counted to ten. Told himself it was okay to look into the mirror. He hadn't seen what he thought he'd seen.

His nerves were frayed. That was understandable. He'd seen things no one should ever see. Done things no one should ever have to do. But it was over now. He'd bested the rift.

It was over.

Raising his head, he looked up again into the rearview mirror. The dog's reflection looked back at him, chagrined from his fall.

Nothing else.

No blobby thing with fat folds and many mouths. Only the dog and the seat and rear window and beyond that the street. Another driver had pulled to the curb and was calling to Joe and waving in concern. Joe leaned out the window, said he was fine, waved the man away.

"What the hell's wrong with me?"

He had no answer, and neither did the dog behind him.

When he went in to order the replacement glass door, he took Rusty with him, and when the proprietor told him Rusty would have to wait outside, Joe told the burly man what he wanted, how much he thought it would cost, and was waved in, dog and all.

*　　*　　*

The detective was there again when Joe returned home. Waiting on the porch, talking to Clara. The older man stood in a way that said he was comfortable in all situations, and he was comfortable because he knew things that you didn't. He kept his hands in his pockets nonchalantly, as if he fiddled with spare change or keys. Because he was oh so damn comfortable and he wanted you to know it.

Joe shook the man's hand when he reached the porch. The detective's grip was firm and brief, then his hand returned to his pocket. Rusty trotted through the open door without greeting the man, and the detective looked after the dog with an interested expression as if it carried with it some clue he hadn't yet perceived.

Joe took up a position beside Clara.

"Good to see you again, detective."

"I'm not so sure about that, Mr. Jimenez," the older man said with a sad little shake of his head. The lines of his face were drawn down just enough to show his concern, and then reverted back to stony flatness. "Milton Cooper has gone missing."

Joe didn't have to feign surprise. That was the last name he'd expected to hear. Not that he'd forgotten his friend, but after all that had occurred, what had happened to Milton had become something like a footnote. Collateral damage. Joe had succeeded in pushing it from the front of his thoughts for later consideration. There would always be time to mourn that loss after all other accounts had been settled.

Cold, maybe. Callous, perhaps. But it was how he was dealing with things. One at a time in piecemeal fashion. His son first, and everything else after.

Joe didn't say anything. Just stared at the detective.

"He was a colleague of yours, right? At the high school?"

Joe nodded, still didn't speak.

"According to some of the other faculty, the two of you were friends? He's been missing for over three days, now, Mr. Jimenez."

The way the other man's gaze remained on him, Joe thought a response was expected this time. Probably also the right thing to do at a time like this.

"Any idea what happened?" Joe asked. His mouth was dry and his lips smacked. Reaching out blindly, he found his wife's hand and squeezed it. She squeezed back.

"No," the detective said. "That's why I'm here. I was hoping you might know something. Maybe Mr. Cooper called you. Gave you some indication of his thoughts or whereabouts."

"Yeah, he called me. A few days ago. We just talked about work. He wanted to know if I was coming back. We talked all the time."

There. His first mistake. He knew it even as he said it. Joe hadn't spoken to Milton for the better part of a year. Until the rift had appeared. When he'd needed his friend's help. Then his friend had died or — considering what Joe knew about the rift — worse.

"And he said nothing that caused you concern? Nothing that would make you worry about his wellbeing? His emotional state? Anything different about his demeanor at all could help."

Joe was thinking of his friend coming around the side of the house that night. Seeing himself and Clara in front of the rift, arguing. Milton running up, trying to calm things. Milton tripping in the confusion, stumbling, falling into the rift. *Sucked* into the rift.

All because Joe had enlisted his help. He hadn't murdered his friend, hadn't lifted any weapon against him. But Joe was still culpable in his death. He knew that now as certainly as he knew anything.

"Are you okay, Mr. Jimenez?"

Joe realized he'd looked away from the detective. He looked back to the man's implacable face and tried to mirror what he saw.

"You just told me my best friend went missing. Of course I'm not okay."

The detective took one hand from his coat pocket. He held it palm out in a gesture of peace and took a step down off the porch.

"I meant no offense," he said. "I left my card with your wife. If you think of anything, please get in touch."

Halfway down the walkway, the detective turned back.

"Sometimes, Mr. Jimenez, we're not aware of things we know. And that's okay, because we're all human and we can't see everything all the time. But sometimes we do know things, and we're aware of these things, and we keep them to ourselves for selfish reasons. That's *not* okay. You get what I'm saying?"

Joe knew very well what the detective was saying. He'd said the very same thing to himself, or nearly so. More than once in recent days. He nodded.

The detective gave a dip of his head in return. He pointed their way in a one-finger, thumb-up gun salute, then turned it into a wave and walked away. But even in his car as he drove off, the man stared out the window, watching them.

Pushing Clara gently ahead of him, Joe went inside and closed the door.

4.

The noises from Evan's room started that afternoon.

Joe and Clara sat on the sofa watching a movie, something they hadn't done together for a long time. Rusty was curled at their feet, alternately snoring and kicking out his legs in the throes of canine dreams. Shoulder to shoulder on the sofa, being so near each other should have been a comfort for Joe and Clara. But they sat woodenly, backs stiff, unmoving, saying nothing.

Joe tried not to make too much of it. This was the first day after the death of the rift. Things would take time. It wouldn't always be this way between them.

Or so he tried to tell himself.

On screen a hero fought off a thug. Then he made love to a slim, sultry woman. There were explosions of a different sort after the lovemaking and then the star was fighting off another thug.

The movie made things seem so simple. The sequence of events, one to the other, dictated by a script. There was a beginning and an end. The credits rolling away let you know that the end of the story had come and all things were right with that cinematic world.

Joe yearned for that simplicity. For things to be laid out for him, his lines and his scenes. So he could know what to do and how to do it.

There was a muted but audible thud from upstairs.

Both Joe and Clara jerked in surprise. Rusty stirred awake and lifted his head.

The sound came again. A bump and a scraping, like something was being dragged.

"Get the gun," Joe said, on his feet now and staring up at the ceiling.

Clara left quickly and came back with the weapon in her right hand. She flicked off the safety as they moved to the stairs, side by side.

She looked at him with a wide-eyed fear.

"What the hell *is* that, Joe?"

The dragging sound came again from the second story. It was fast and harsh and abrupt, as if careless movers lugged furniture to and fro without regard for the objects they handled. Hard knocks against walls. Heavy weight dropped to the floor.

At the top of the stairs, Joe and Clara stared down the hallway. The door at the end led to their son's room. His belongings inside, boxed and bagged and ready for whatever organization they chose to give them to.

And with that thought, Joe knew what was happening.

He darted down the hall. Reached out for the knob to the bedroom, grasped it, turned it, flung the door open. Clara's footfalls pounded close behind him.

The boxes they'd packed together were open again.

The room was fully furnished once more.

And the suited cadaver he'd cast into the fire in the land of the rift sat atop the bed cross-legged, an action figure in one hand, a Hot Wheels car in the other. The corpse boy moved the toys across the blankets in little circles, making spittle sound effects of collisions and explosions and gunfire.

It looked up at Joe and Clara.

Without eyes it stared at them. From the lids of the empty sockets frayed stitches hung and batted slightly like lashes. It tried a smile and the stitches in the mouth snapped, revealing a dark, rank cavern where rotted teeth protruded like stumps.

"Mommy. Daddy. Play with me."

Joe thought it spoke to him. To Clara. His heart froze at the mere thought of being so near the horror on the bed. Much less actually sitting with it to play. Then movement in the far corner caught his attention and he saw what it was the dead child had actually spoken to. The other father and the other mother, who'd roasted the skewered thing in the kitchen, sat there in the corner, now rising. The father held a toy rocket. The mother carried a stuffed bear. Their faces were draped over their skulls like tablecloths, and shimmied a bit when they stood.

They joined their child on the bed.

The dead boy pointed at Joe and Clara in the doorway.

"Let's play with them!"

CHAPTER FOURTEEN

1.

The house *swelled*, as if it breathed in distress. Just as Joe had seen his wife and the other woman – she of the draped face and runny flesh – in the kitchen at the same time, one over the other like signal interference on a television, so too did he see the old familiar walls around him and... something else. A membranous substance like thin translucent flesh bulged outward from the walls, quivering slightly, straining.

Inside his son's room, the other family sat atop the bed, lightly bobbing while the house swelled and shifted about them. As if they were in a boat on stormy waters. The other father handed the dead boy the toy rocket. The other mother gave him the stuffed bear. The dead boy sat the bear atop the rocket and flew it around himself, making laser sounds and explosions with his dried, cracked lips. Aiming the rocket and its pilot toward Joe and Clara, the dead boy let it sail through the air, where it dipped and whirled before diving and skidding along the ground to a stop near their feet.

"Play with me," the dead boy repeated.

Something under the bed stirred. The hem of the covers billowed out as a long limb flopped and repositioned beneath it. The mattress and frame rose and tipped as what was beneath them pushed and slid out.

The bulbous, gelatinous mass Joe had glimpsed in the rearview mirror in the back seat of the car. The thing with the mouths between its fat folds.

From one of these mouths now came a sound like a wet cough. Then it was repeated from another of the mouths, and another, until a chorus of wet phlegmy barks resounded. An appendage at one end of it wagged awkwardly.

The other family pushed to the edge of the bed. They slid off and to their feet in near unison and started across the room side by side.

Just like days ago, when Joe had fallen before the infestation of the rift-insects spilling through the holes in the house; or when the towering, whirling vortex of mouth and teeth in the cave of the rift descended upon them, Rusty charged, heedless of his own safety. The Labrador leapt at the dead boy first as if offended by the mockery of his former master. He collided with the black-suited, stitch-eyed cadaver, and the two fell backward in a tangle. Jaws snapping, nails scrabbling, dry fibers of old suit and dead flesh were tossed into the air and rained down like feathers.

The other three members of the rift-family turned their attentions to the dog. The other father and mother reached down, each grabbing a leg. The blobby mass reached primate-like with its appendage tail and wrapped a grip around Rusty's hindquarters. The dog was lifted in the air up and down like a jumper on a trampoline, higher and higher with each swing. Finally at the pinnacle the dog was released, and he flew across the room in a head-over-tail arc.

Joe tried to intercept the dog's path. He dashed, reaching out with his arms to catch him or cushion the landing, but he was too slow. The dog's arc ended in a hard crash against the near wall. There was a yelp and then silence as the limp form tumbled to the ground and was still.

Behind him he heard his wife cry out. Joe knelt over the dog, felt for breathing, for a pulse. He turned and tried to watch his wife at the same time.

She leveled the pistol at the other family, all four now facing her. The mother and father with their hanging faces. The dead boy with his stitched eyelids. The dog-blob and its glistening, swishing tail. She fired.

New holes punched into each of the horrors in turn. Each staggered back but remained standing. Some of the shots missed and struck the walls beyond.

The swelling flesh-walls. The translucent bubbles of the house, breathing.

The swelling there burst. Black fluid, dribbling like an oil leak, spilled forth, making little pattering sounds. Like the blood of the backward-headed rift-freak they'd cast into the quarry days ago, where this dark fluid landed it burned and tendrils of smoke wafted up.

Clara's pistol clicked on an empty magazine. She tried pulling the trigger a few more times as if willing it to fire again. When it didn't, she threw it, and it bounced off the head of her wicked twin. The other mother and her family started across the room toward Clara once more.

Joe scooped up the dog and ran across the bedroom. Along the way, he chop-blocked his own double, sending the thing careening and colliding with the rest of them. They spilled one atop the other and Joe leapt over the tangle and to the doorway, where Clara stood.

"Let's go!" he said.

Down the hall, down the stairs. While all around them that double-exposure effect, of floor atop floor, walls within walls. A house within a house. The swelling flesh expanding, breathing. From behind them came hurried movement. Things in pursuit. At the bottom of the stairs they made a hard turn and there was the front door. Closed. With Rusty in his arms, unable to turn the knob with his burden, Joe moved aside to let Clara do it.

He turned to face the stairs. Saw what was coming down.

The other family descending. Step by step, unhurried now. Smiling wicked smiles. Shedding their guises.

"Open the door, Clara!"

It rattled as she tried. Joe stood against the adjacent wall now, looking up at what was coming and able to see his wife at the same time. She frantically tried the knob but it wasn't turning; the door was still shut.

"Open the fucking door, Clara!"

"I can't!"

The other family was halfway down the stairs. Gathering on the landing. The draped faces of the rift-parents were cast aside. From the stitch-draped sockets of the dead boy new eyes shone a dark light.

Things moved beneath the semblance of the human forms, pushing out against their fleshy trappings.

Joe pushed the unmoving dog into his wife's arms. He shoved her aside and tried the door. It wasn't the same door anymore. No longer wood now, it was rusted steel with a crossbar, heavy and thick. Caked and flaky brown streaks crisscrossed it in the rough smeared shapes of hands. Hands grasping, hands beating, hands pleading. Wanting out.

Realizing he gripped empty air where the knob had once been, Joe moved to the crossbar. He bent at the knees and pushed up with all his strength, but it didn't budge. It sat stubbornly nestled in its rusted hooks.

"Joe! Open the fucking door!"

He tried again. Failing, panicked, he turned to look at the stairs.

The things there – tentacled and clawed with wide mouths yawning – stood at the bottom of the stairs, only yards away. Coming closer. The human husks shed and fallen like garments disrobed and piled on the floor.

Back to the door. Joe punched it. Kicked it. He yelled at it. Cursed it. Cried and screamed. Nothing.

"This is still my house!"

The old door – *his* door – flickered back into being in that double-exposure effect. He shouted again, told the door this was his house, his home, and though it still wasn't solid, the old door *came forward*, and the steel dungeon door *slipped back*. Like occupants in a line switching places.

Joe grasped the knob. Turned it.

The door opened.

Joe and Clara spilled through the doorway together onto the porch. The stale breath of dead things wafted close behind them. Something snagged Joe's shirt. It stretched and tore and then he was free.

Pounding down the walkway, into the driveway, to the doors of the Explorer, Joe fished in his pockets until he found the keys. He hit the button on the foam rubber fob. The doors unlatched.

Clara opened her door even with the dog in her arms. Joe opened the driver's-side door, climbed inside, punched the fob again to lock the doors behind them. Flipping through the keys on the ring, he found the right one and jammed it home in the ignition. He turned it and the car roared to life.

He switched gears to reverse. Hit the gas. Swung the SUV in a wide arc backward into the street. The front of the house and the porch swung into view.

The other family was gathered at the threshold of the house. That horde with the limbs and eyes and mouths. Bunched up in the doorway and spilling forth onto the porch.

Joe switched to drive but kept his foot off the gas.

He sat there, staring past his wife, at their house and the intruders wiggling, bulging, stretching on the porch.

"What the hell are you doing, Joe? Let's get out of here!" Clara yelled.

The dog cradled in her lap stirred weakly. Rusty's left eye opened a sliver and closed again. Joe saw the unnatural bend of the dog's back. A trickle of dark blood leaked from one nostril.

Through his fear, he felt something else. Like the double-exposure effect that even now showed both their house and another structure, something like a large dome stretching high and wide, Joe experienced something similar inside. He was terrified, astounded they'd gotten out of the house. He trembled and wasn't ashamed of his fear. But sitting there in the car, staring out at the other things standing on the porch of his home, he was also angry. And with every passing moment the anger grew.

Until it was a rage.

"Is the gas can still in the trunk?"

Clara stared at him, uncomprehending.

"Is the gas can still in the trunk, Clara?"

She blinked. Glanced quickly at the things on the porch. Then she turned back to him and nodded. "Yes."

"And the matches?"

"Yes."

"Get out," he said. "Go across the street."

She did as he said. Standing there with their dog in her arms, she looked like a refugee. Or a pallbearer in a grim procession.

Joe put the car in reverse again. He swung the wheel until the nose of the Explorer pointed at the house. At the porch and the other family.

He floored the gas pedal and the car leapt over the lawn, and the things on the porch seemed to leap forward to meet him. Then there was the crunching of metal and the shatter of glass and everything went black.

2.

If bones hadn't been broken on Joe's first trip through the rift, when the behemoth had barred his way from coming back and swatted him like an insect, they were broken now. Every slight move delivered jabs of hot pain at the part that had dared move, and these sent aftershocks throughout the rest of him. There was a pressure on his chest like a great weight atop him.

Joe tried opening his eyes, but a stickiness coating his lids and lashes made that simple motion a torture. When they finally fluttered open, he saw through a film of red. He was in the car but it seemed smaller. It *was* smaller. The front fender and hood were crushed inward, like a soda can squeezed in a fist. The windshield was webbed with cracks and little holes where pieces had fallen out gave him glimpses of the world outside.

The living room of the house was caved in as if it had been bombarded with mortar fire. The Explorer had plowed through the sofa and end table and entertainment center, sending them every which way into other furniture or the walls or both. The SUV had finished its course by colliding with the dividing wall, buckling the support pillars there, and a large section of the ceiling had given way and fallen, leaving the interior beams and wiring and other innards of the house laid bare.

Distantly, he heard shouting. The screaming voice sounded female. It could have been Clara, or a neighbor, or someone else altogether.

Then, he heard his name called out. Clara. He tried calling back, but his chest hurt and his lungs burned.

Joe tried to feel with his left hand for the driver's-side door latch. Again the pain shot out along the length of the arm, but he had expected that and resolved to fight through it. Yet his arm still wouldn't move.

Then, looking down, he saw the steering column had come forward a foot or so, was pressed against him. His left arm was held across his middle as if to stop the steering wheel. He wiggled that arm, saw a bulge in the forearm move in a disconcerting way, and another flash of pain accompanied it and he stopped. Instead, he tried his right arm and found it responded. He reached awkwardly across the steering column, found the door latch, pulled it, and gave the door a push.

When it swung open, bits of detritus fell like a small avalanche. Eyeing the way to freedom, Joe wanted out of the tight confines of the crumpled car, and steeling himself, he tried to move the left arm again from beneath the steering wheel. This time he heard the grinding sound of bone on bone, and the strange bulge in his forearm moved again. He gasped, closed his eyes against the hot agony.

When next he opened his eyes, he saw movement through the crisscrossed fissures of the windshield. Pinned between the accordion-condensed fender of the car and the ruins of the dividing wall, odd limbs reached up and floundered about. Reaching this way, stretching that way, testing the space about them.

A thudding sound came from underneath the carriage of the Explorer. The drum sound of metal dimpled in and out with exploratory probing.

Joe moved his feet. His legs. The right knee throbbed but moved when he willed it to. Pressing his feet against the floor, he pushed back against the cushioned seat. His body moved a fraction of an inch away from the steering wheel. His left arm slid free.

Joe scooted out slowly and tried to stand. Both legs buckled and a wave of nausea hit him and he fell to his knees. The right leg went from a throb to a scream, and the nausea jumped a few notches higher. He vomited and his throat burned with the acid.

Behind him something flopped out whip-like from under the car and slapped at Joe's legs. He crawled away, his right hand smearing through his own regurgitation. The whip smacked against his legs again, higher up on his thighs, and he kicked out, pushed forward.

At the wall adjacent to the foyer, he used his good arm to push and pull himself up. Shattered remnants of picture frames crunched on the floor beneath his feet. Others hanging askew on the walls were slapped and sent swinging as he grasped for purchase. The frozen, glossy faces of his wife and son and dog looked back at him from the pictures with expectation, seeming to call to him wordlessly. Telling him things, things about failure and responsibility.

Up on his feet, he turned around, setting his back to the wall so he wouldn't fall again. He couldn't fall again. Not now, not ever. He'd fallen so far already.

What had been the other family – the dark family, the mockeries from the rift – were pinned by the Explorer. But they jerked and pushed and pulled, and the whole of the vehicle bucked and lurched from their flailing.

Joe moved for the trunk. He felt for his keys, then realized they were still in the car. He looked in the Ford toward the front seat. The whipping tentacles there on the ground were slapping about, searching. And now a head, inhuman, slid out from underneath the car, looking, scanning the ruined house, and then, seeing Joe, fixed on him. The mouth opened wide, wider, revealing rows of teeth like saw blades.

Joe couldn't go that way. No fucking chance.

Grasping the trunk latch, he pulled hard. He willed it open. Commanded it to open. Locked, it remained shut.

Joe stepped away from it, faced the still-open driver's-side door again. The long limbs there were flailing. The head inched forward on a neck stretching as if made of putty and not flesh and bone, the mouth open and the teeth grinding.

Skirting the rear of the car in a stumble-walk, Joe looked at the passenger side. There was motion from beneath as things there bucked and flexed and arched. The car rocked from side to side.

But no tentacles lashed out. No malformed head with rows of dagger teeth.

Joe shuffled for the passenger door, grasped the handle with his good right hand and wrenched it open. He dove inside, landing badly on the left arm, and he hissed in pain. Reaching across the seats, he fumbled for the keys in the ignition. His fingers flailed and knocked them jingling and the head there across from him rose on its serpent neck, peering in at him from the driver's-side door.

Joe grabbed the keys, wrenched them free. The head darted forward, snapping. Kicking backward in a crab-walk, Joe fell out in a tumble, hitting the floor with his head and shoulders. He pushed up with his good arm just in time to see the wicked-toothed head darting forward again, eyes filled with a staunch hatred.

Joe shouldered the passenger door, slamming it on the serpentine neck. The head, poking out, shrieked and pulled back into the car. Joe kicked the door shut.

He dashed back to the trunk. Tried inserting the key into the lock but the Explorer bounced and rocked anew as the dark family beneath it raged. He scratched and dinged the car several times before the key found the lock and slid home. Joe turned it, threw the trunk hatch up and open.

The interior of the trunk was a mess. Bent and warped parts of the car's frame poked through the paneling. The gas canister was knocked over. Punctures in the container leaked amber liquid. The fumes hit Joe and he grimaced. Yelling a stream of fucks and shits, he reached for the plastic can, righted it, saw the silhouette of the liquid against the translucent sides, heard the slosh of it, prayed it was enough.

Then he reached back in for the matches. He saw the box open and the matches scattered about. Many were drenched and worthless. Leaning in, he rummaged through them, searching for those with dry heads. Something on the ground beneath the car brushed his ankle and Joe screamed, did a little hop, fell halfway into the trunk, and scattered the matchsticks further.

Joe stretched deeper into the trunk, reaching for the matches that had spilled beneath the rear seats. His fingers clawed, danced spider-like, persuaded a few of the small sticks closer. He snatched them up, pocketed them in his shirt, and squirmed out of the trunk.

Something encircled his calf. Began to squeeze.

Standing now, Joe looked down. Something like a snake or an eel, scaled and fuzzy with coarse hair, wound about his left leg, and started climbing.

Screaming, Joe grasped the gas can to his chest, then with his right leg he stood on the bumper of the Ford, pulled, and tried to free himself. The snake-eel thing pulled back, so Joe pushed harder, jumped from the bumper, wrenched and twisted as he leapt away from the car.

He landed hard on his left arm. Something in there popped and he cried out. His eyes blurred with tears and he saw through scarlet redness and a wet sheen. The world seemed bloody.

But his leg was free. He looked back toward the car. The thing there was reaching out for him but falling short. Beneath the bumper he saw other things moving in the shadows. Moving and rolling with a wicked chittering. Laughter and hissing.

A flash of several eyes, white and black-pupiled, watching him.

Joe got up again and unscrewed the gas can's cap awkwardly, with his injured arm and hands. He stepped forward, close enough to slosh the gasoline out in arcs and splashes on the car and ground around it, but far enough from the reach of the things beneath it. When the can was empty, he dropped it and felt for the matches in his breast pocket.

He struck the first one with his thumbnail. It hissed but didn't light. He dropped it and tried the next but it was damp and did nothing.

The Explorer bucked, jumped, and then started to *rise*.

The things under it stirred and lifted and inched forward.

The third match hissed afire and Joe flicked it toward the car. The ground lit, the carpet catching fast, and then the tires. The flames reached, stretching, tickled the trunk of the car, and then that too whooshed alive and the flames climbed higher still.

Joe turned and ran.

The house's front window was caved in and inaccessible. The front door where he'd steered the car through was like the entrance to a mineshaft blown shut. He saw holes and glimpses of light, but no way through.

With a hot wave the Explorer's gas tank caught and exploded and Joe fell as if pushed. His head hit the remnants of the wall where the door used to be and everything went dark.

3.

The blackness faded and came again in fits and starts, like a cover put over his eyes and taken away and put over them again. He was moving and saw light and shadow in turn as something pulled at him and he slid across an uneven ground.

They have me, he thought. *They have me and they're pulling me down, down into the pit and they'll eat me.*

It was hot too. He could hear the crackling of fire and feel the licks of it reaching out to him. Blinking rapidly, trying to see, he couldn't and his panic quickened. If these were the fires of hell, no doubt he deserved to be burned by them, but he wasn't ready.

"Please...."

His voice was weak and pathetic even to his own ears but there was no room for shame. He wanted only to live. For the longest time he'd wanted his life to end, but hadn't the courage to end it himself. Had disengaged himself from everything else – family, friends, work – so he'd just waste away. If he couldn't kill himself, he didn't have to sustain himself either.

Things were different now, though.

"Please...not ready...my wife...want to live...."

He heard grunts and moans from above him. A shape began to blearily form in his vision. The hands that pulled him gripped him by the ankles and they clasped tight like shackles. His head thumped as he went over the edge of something and then the heat of the flames suddenly lessened. The air was cool.

The silver moon high above in the black stretch of night seemed an eye, and when Joe blinked, it seemed to blink back at him. A blink or a wink, as if sharing some small secret.

The shape pulled him a little further. Stopped, dropped his legs, knelt over him.

It was inky and thick in his teary blurred vision and Joe tried to turn away from it.

It grasped him by the sides of the face and forced him to look at it. He closed his eyes, crying, didn't want to see it.

It said things to him but his ears rung from the explosion and the collision of his head against the wall. The sound of the thing's voice was thick and muffled.

He cried a bit longer and then, exhausted, could cry no more. With his eyes closed, he turned to at least face his assailant even if he couldn't stomach looking at it.

"Make it quick then...you ugly fuck...."

It spoke to him again and this time the words found their way through the fog and he heard them as if from across a large chasm.

"Maybe I shouldn't move back in, if that's how you feel."

He opened his eyes. Blurry still, it was like looking through a wet window now, the image warped but recognizable. Clara knelt over him and looked down on him with a frown.

"In almost twelve years of marriage, through thick and thin, you never called me ugly," she said. "I'm hurt."

Joe rolled his head to one side. He saw, across the street and across the yard, his house burning. And the garage door rolled up where Clara had opened it, before dragging him through the foyer and out the garage.

He turned back to her, pushed himself up despite all the aches and agonies from what seemed every inch of his body, and sat upright on the sidewalk. He used his good right arm to pull her close. Then he fell back and pulled her atop him. She laughed and he tried to but coughed hard instead.

"You came back for me," he said when he could find his breath.

"Of course," she said.

Her face was above him and beyond that the moon and the great vast expanse, star-peppered and rolling out forever in every direction. He pulled her closer and kissed her hard.

The dog crawled to them. Each inch was a labor, but Rusty scooted in close beside Joe and Clara. Joe turned, stared deep into the Labrador's eyes, saw the pain there but also a quiet contentment. Craning his neck, leaning his head close, Joe kissed the dog too.

"Hang in there, bud. If I'm going to live then you have to also."

The dog closed its eyes, trembled, and went still.

4.

After she called nine-one-one from her cell phone, Joe insisted that Clara take her car and get Rusty to the nearest emergency veterinarian hospital. She wanted to stay with him, didn't think it was safe even now, with the house burning and falling in on itself and the creatures from the rift trapped inside.

By this time the neighbors were there. A few of them stood around Joe or knelt over him, asking how he was feeling. He struggled halfway to his feet, lifted the dog, dumped the unmoving body into his wife's arms and gave her a push toward her car. Two men cajoled him back down to a lying position on his back, and once Clara was in the car with the dog, starting the engine and pulling away, Joe acquiesced.

He closed his eyes and though he didn't lose consciousness he wasn't fully awake either. Events seemed to pass for a while as if in a dream, not strictly chronologically but haphazardly, like a poorly edited film.

Red and blue lights flashed about him. A high wailing permeated the night. He was lifted, seemed to float for a time. In a small white space people in blue worked over him, touching him here and there, one holding something to his face. There was a sense of motion and the red and blue lights and the wailing followed him.

Everything went black for a time and when next he opened his eyes he was in a larger white room and masked men and women stood about him, poking and prodding and saying things behind their masks he couldn't understand. Another mask descended into view, covered his mouth and nose, and he finally slept.

At some point, he awoke again and had the presence of mind to look around. Things were fuzzy and moved in and out of focus. His whole body and mind seemed numb and *cushioned*, as if cotton was packed snugly around him. Clara was in a chair beside his bed. When he stirred, she leaned forward, smiling.

He tried to ask about Rusty, but Clara shushed him, told him to rest. Yet he saw it in her eyes and though he thought he hadn't the energy for tears anymore, they soon came and he cried and tried to hide his tears in the flat hospital pillow. But she wouldn't have it, and she turned him to face her so he saw her crying also, and they shared the sorrow together.

★   ★   ★

On the first day of his release from the hospital, Joe and Clara stopped by the veterinarian's office to claim Rusty's ashes. Each of the staff hugged them and told them they were so sorry, they'd all tried so hard. Joe nodded and accepted the simple clay urn slowly and with a certain reverence, as if he held a great treasure.

Next they drove in Clara's car to her apartment. From the storage room she rented they carried out two kayaks, loaded them atop her car in the rack, strapped them down. Back in the car they drove in silence for a time, the clay urn on the seat between them.

Joe hadn't been out this way for a long time. The landscape passed from brown mountains to white desert to green forest in a patchwork fashion.

The lake seemed as it had when last he'd seen it. But the blue was startling in the midst of the dense forest and no memory could do it justice. He breathed in and out slowly as the waters revealed itself.

They unloaded the slim vessels at the loading dock. The plastic hulls splashed lightly in the water and sent ripples in all directions.

Joe carried the urn but he and Clara paddled side by side. With his left arm in a cast, it was hard, painful work, but he pulled each stroke through the water without complaint. When they reached the center of the lake, she asked to hold the urn for a time and he passed the clay vessel carefully across to her. She held it in her lap. She lifted it before her face and held it aloft before the sun.

When she passed it back, Joe twisted the cap off and, leaning over, spilled the contents in a little ashy stream into the water. There it mixed and stirred and after a time sunk in the crystal-blue depths. He set the urn and its top into the water, where they bobbed and dipped for a spell and then took in water and sunk as well.

In his mind Joe had thought they'd do this deed and then quickly leave. However, sitting in the kayak in the middle of the lake, he had another idea. He turned to Clara, floating beside him.

"Think you can make it around the whole lake?" he asked.

"You think *you* can?"

Her small smile was coy and daring and held many things in it. Promises and maybes. Things he'd have to find out about.

He looked around, taking in the length and width of the lake. So far it stretched. A mirror of the sky and the woods and the world. He squinted under the sun as if to see things from a better, clearer angle.

"I think so."

It sure beat walking.

★ ★ ★

In time she showed him many things. About the world and how to survive in it, despite the injustices and failures and the fallen nature of it all. She taught him how to smile and how to laugh and how to see the miraculous in small things. The whisper of a light wind. The rhythm of rainfall on gray days. The music of the motion of things in their courses and traversing.

She showed him how to dance, and how to *live*.

ACKNOWLEDGMENTS

Thanks to Dean Koontz, for feedback and insight into an early version of *The Rift*. Thank you also to editors Don D'Auria and Mike Valsted, for helping to further refine the story and smoothing away the rough edges. And a second serving of thanks to Don D'Auria, for believing in the story for the better part of a decade. Finally, thanks to Mom and Dad, who never have to worry about demonic rift-doubles, because each of you are one of a kind.

FLAME TREE PRESS
FICTION WITHOUT FRONTIERS
Award-Winning Authors & Original Voices

Flame Tree Press is the trade fiction imprint of Flame Tree
Publishing, focusing on excellent writing in horror and the
supernatural, crime and mystery, science fiction and fantasy.
Our aim is to explore beyond the boundaries of the everyday,
with tales from both award-winning authors and original voices.

•

You may also enjoy:
Thirteen Days by Sunset Beach by Ramsey Campbell
Think Yourself Lucky by Ramsey Campbell
The Hungry Moon by Ramsey Campbell
The Influence by Ramsey Campbell
The Wise Friend by Ramsey Campbell
Somebody's Voice by Ramsey Campbell
Fellstones by Ramsey Campbell
The Lonely Lands by Ramsey Campbell
The Haunting of Henderson Close by Catherine Cavendish
The Garden of Bewitchment by Catherine Cavendish
In Darkness, Shadows Breathe by Catherine Cavendish
Dark Observation by Catherine Cavendish
The After-Death of Caroline Rand by Catherine Cavendish
Dead Ends by Marc E. Fitch
The Toy Thief by D.W. Gillespie
One By One by D.W. Gillespie
Black Wings by Megan Hart
Silent Key by Laurel Hightower
The Playing Card Killer by Russell James
Demon Dagger by Russell James
Will Haunt You by Brian Kirk
We Are Monsters by Brian Kirk
Those Who Came Before by J.H. Moncrieff
They Stalk the Night by Brian Moreland
Stoker's Wilde by Steven Hopstaken & Melissa Prusi
Stoker's Wilde West by Steven Hopstaken & Melissa Prusi
Land of the Dead by Steven Hopstaken & Melissa Prusi
Whisperwood by Alex Woodroe

•

Join our mailing list for free short stories, new release details,
news about our authors and special promotions:

flametreepress.com